THE TEN
OF TH

Norman Lewis was born in London. He has written thirteen novels and ten non-fiction works. *A Dragon Apparent* and *Golden Earth* are considered classics of travel, and *Naples '44* has been described as one of the ten outstanding books about the Second World War. He relaxes by his travels to off-beat parts of the world, which he prefers to be as remote as possible; otherwise he lives with his family in introspective, almost monastic, calm in the depths of Essex.

Norman Lewis

THE TENTH YEAR OF THE SHIP

V

VINTAGE

VINTAGE
20 Vauxhall Bridge Road, London SW1V 2SA

London Melbourne Sydney Auckland Johannesburg
and agencies throughout the world

First published by Collins, London, 1962
Vintage edition 1992

1 3 5 7 9 10 8 6 4 2

Printed and bound in Great Britain by
Cox & Wyman Ltd, Reading

ISBN 0 09 970330 0

TUR

THE first Tur, a restless and intro-
spective merchant of Catalonia who had seen the French
Revolution and had moved about in France both before
and after that cataclysm, produced a maxim based on his
experiences. Don Nemesio Tur had set out to provide the
mechanism for his descendants' elevation to the Spanish
ruling class, and this maxim summed up the counsel he left
them along with his fortune. 'To the common man,' he
said, ' progress is the half of a half-truth. To the aristocrat,
it is merely a lie.'

Don Nemesio elaborated this view in a number of letters
to his son, who stayed at home managing the family pig-
farms near the Pyrenean town of Vich. He had observed,
he said, that for the privileged classes progress meant a
steady process of dilution of the joys of life. Less and less
were the nobility everywhere able to command the
acquiescent labour of men and the willing embraces of
women, while at a more refined level of consideration they
were increasingly stripped of their function as encouragers
of the arts. It was more than doubtful too, Don Nemesio
thought, that the lower orders got anything out of progress
either. In France he had seen them take their newly

acquired liberty like medicine, with long faces. The Spanish peasantry, untouched in their comfortable servility, remained economically depressed, but cheerful. The first Tur's huge, scandalous fortune had come from the supply of provender to the Napoleonic invaders of his country. But Don Nemesio had gone further than merely founding the family's fortune. Obsessed by his opinions, he had set himself to work out a method by which his successors could at least stall off the changes that might diminish their enjoyment of their inheritance.

Tur the First had spent several years towards the end of his life looking round for a small remote kingdom, inaccessible from Madrid, although not so barbarously cut off from civilisation as the South American colonies, where the people lived in primitive style and bureaucracy selected from the lowest grade, would be too bored and indifferent to pay any attention to small abuses of power by feudal landowners. He found what he was looking for in Vedra, a small island in the Canaries group. Most of Vedra he was able to buy up at low prices in the slump conditions that followed the war. Here Don Nemesio succeeded in organising what seen from above was a kind of stagnant Utopia, in which he and his descendants did their best to enjoy a *douceur de la vie* supposed to have disappeared elsewhere.

When Don Flavio, the seventh Tur, took over from his father just after the First World War, he found his ancestor's system still working fairly smoothly. Besides owning all the land worth having, the Turs controlled the island trade by their ownership of the shipping. Their fleet consisted of a half-dozen sailing vessels, small, archaic and beautiful. These ships, their dependance on the wind only fitfully relieved by unreliable auxiliary engines, carried the island's exports of bananas and vegetables, plus a few miserably accommodated passengers, and such imports as Tur personally approved of. In this way the outside world was kept out. The Turs' isolation policy had always been favoured by the fact that high winds flailed the seas round Vedra throughout the spring, autumn and winter, and that the old harbour was too shallow to shelter ships larger than the Turs' schooners. Every attempt over fifty years to deepen the harbour had been blocked by the family's opposition and their readiness to spend large sums in the right places. Only in the middle thirties, with the coming of the Republic, and with it the slackening of Don Flavio's contacts in the capital, it seemed certain at last that dredging operations would begin.

The situation was saved by the outbreak of the Civil War. The revolt had started in Tenerife, and Don Flavio having been thus given an opportunity of studying the revolutionary movement at close quarters and of deciding what it stood for, instantly went over to His Excellency's side. The few Republicans of Vedra—always distrusted by Tur—were instantly put out of circulation. Tur had contributed generously to the insurrectionists' war-chest. He had looked for no recompense after His Excellency's victory, but it had been noted, all the same, that work on the harbour had never been recommenced. For ten years things had gone on quietly, as before. Then, out of the blue (it was shortly after the year of his daughter's marriage), a private company had arrived in Vedra to undertake the work of dredging, and in spite of all Tur's appeals and bribes, his friends in the capital could find no excuse to intervene on his behalf. A year's work, and the harbour was ready, and after that the steamship began its weekly service, and its regular discharge on the quayside of Vedra of those explosive components of modernity that Tur knew would, in the end, blow his world to pieces.

In weekly instalments the ship's derricks picked the twentieth century out of its holds and presented it to the people of Vedra. After a few years of this process, Tur was quite sure that a Vedran returning from a long stay overseas would hardly have recognised the island. There had been some unseemly rebuilding, but the change was more a spiritual than physical one. Morally the island had been turned upside down. The ship had brought visitors by the thousand, and they had spent their money and left their mark. Vedran women were beginning to go in for sea-bathing, and to appear in public in sleeveless dresses, and at home they expected to sit down at meal-times with the menfolk. The birthrate was falling fast. Crimes of violence were on the decrease, but it was no longer possible to leave one's wallet on a café table and hope to find it still lying there untouched a few hours later when one discovered the loss. Ancient island ceremonies had become folk-lore, but were performed these days only for the benefit of tourists. Peasants had ceased to employ the form of address ' your grace ' to any man owning roughly a thousand acres of land.

Nine years passed, and despite a worsening situation Tur would have said he was still fairly well in control, manipulating the local authorities, holding up a development scheme here, refusing his sanction there. But it was in the tenth year of the ship that the schemers, the land-speculators, and the industrialists came on the scene. And in the tenth year of the ship Tur realised at last that he was fighting with his back to the wall.

CHAPTER 1

Half the island was there to wait and watch for the ship's arrival: the island aristocracy, concealed like forest animals among their club's potted palms, eyes hardly showing; the established English fruit merchants and their families; the shopkeepers; the maids on the rooftops; the rich hospital patients wheeled out in litters; the mad, crouched behind barred windows; the roving sellers of sandwiches, horoscopes, panpipes, lottery tickets and plastic spaceships; above all, the peasants, who had made the usual excuses to take a day off from their fields, recessed in the crevices of the island's tortured landscape, and had come bicycling down to the town.

' But why do they always play the same tune? ' Laura, the blonde English girl, asked.

The town band had come into sight, its trombones sawing out the gay, skipping bullfight air that suddenly flagged and fell away so disconsolately to its minor key ending.

Beckett's answer was lost in the maw of excited crowd sounds. The mobilisation of the band meant that the ship's approach had been signalled down by a lookout, posted with his flag on a housetop. The *Almirante Cervera*—The Ship—had been coming for ten years, but the Vedrans had

never got over the shock and excitement of its first appearance. A decade before, when the ship had loomed up out
of the sea for the first time, siren booming and funnels
feathering the sky with black smoke, a majority of the
peasants gathered along the sea-front had fallen to their
knees and crossed themselves—just to be on the safe side.
Even in these days, only a part of this reverence had
evaporated.

'And now the Guard of Honour,' Beckett said.

Urban policemen were rushing about like frantic scene-
shifters, pushing and pulling at peasants who had wandered
into the path of the advancing column. The too-soon-
discouraged music of the town band weakened before its
total obliteration by the army's tambours and shrilling
trumpets. Then the soldiers, stocky automata, eyes narrowed
by the sun, trudged by, their arms flailing in a kind of furious
somnambulism.

'Who's expected today?' Laura asked.

'The new Civil Governor.'

'The *new* one . . . What happened to the old one?'

'They sacked him. Surely you knew?'

'No,' she said, 'I didn't know. And actually it only
seems a few weeks since we were sitting here, at the same
table, watching the band and all the V.I.P.s going down to
meet him off the ship.'

'For all that, it's nearly a year ago,' Beckett said.

'Why did they get rid of him?'

'Because he wasn't any good, I suppose. Or because
they needed a victim. That trouble in the port last year,
when the fishing boats from Las Palmas got smashed up.
He had to carry the can back, I expect.'

'What happened? I don't remember,' she said.

'It was the result of a fiddle,' Beckett said. 'Someone
took a bribe to let the trawlers from Las Palmas take over the
local fishing grounds. Naturally there was trouble. The

same thing's going to happen again this year as soon as the fishing season starts.'

'How exciting,' Laura said. 'You always seem to know about these things.'

'I have a cleaning woman,' Beckett said, 'whose husband's a police corporal.'

'That's useful.'

'At times even more than you'd imagine.' He smiled one of those tight, rather malicious smiles that invited further questioning.

'Go on,' she said. 'What have you found out now? I know you're dying to tell me.'

He looked round with pretended caution. The Mirasol bar was the stronghold, on such occasions as the coming and the going of the ship, of the remarkable, hispanified English of Vedra. They were in the main holders of residence papers, whose families had for generations controlled the local fruit trade. They walked slowly, dressed darkly, took siestas, prided themselves on the purity of their Castilian accent, avoided the midday sun and peasant hats, and yet now were infiltrated—hatefully to Beckett, a recent convert to sobriety and purpose—by an advance guard of bearded fakers of the sort that appeared spontaneously, in these days, in any warm climate by the sea where liquor was plentiful.

'Can you keep something under your hat?'

'I should think so.'

'There's going to be one hell of a clean-up.'

'What do you mean by that?'

'They're going all out to get shot of the beats,' Beckett said. 'It always happens when there's a new governor. My woman says her husband's seen the list.'

'That's interesting,' Laura said. 'I wonder who's on it.'

The opportunity had come, but as Beckett fumbled to take it, he was interrupted by the arrival of the canary man, balancing his cage on its pole.

'Tell him to go away,' Laura said. 'I had a destiny from him last week, and I didn't like it a scrap.'

Beckett held up a ten-peseta note to the man and shook his head when he felt in his pocket for change. Destinies were two pesetas, but seven years of this environment had brought Beckett close to the native point of view that even canaries could be bribed, and fate coaxed.

The man raised the little wire gate in the cage and the canary hopped down, shuffled with its beak among the pile of folded destinies and picked one out. Before Beckett had time to take the paper, the canary let it drop on the pavement. Beckett winced and tried to shut out of his mind the possibility of this being a bad omen. He picked up the paper, unfolded it, read it, and made a face.

'I told you so,' Laura said.

Beckett got back to his subject.

'With all its shortcomings, I imagine you'd agree that this is an agreeable place to live in.'

'I suppose so. Yes. Why?'

'As well as being ridiculously cheap.'

'If you like stockfish.'

'Or even if you don't. I mean to say the climate's out of this world. Everybody treats you like a human being. There's no winter worth speaking of—I haven't had a cold for seven years. What I mean is there's nowhere in the Med that I know of that starts to compare—would you agree?'

'Excuse me,' she said, 'what's all this rigmarole leading up to? Is it anything to do with the famous list?'

'In a way.'

'You mean I might be on it. Is that it?'

'I don't know. I think you *could* be. Perhaps.' He smiled again, uncomfortably. It was a guarded, compressed smile, meant to conceal discoloured and badly shaped teeth, and it suggested a strain of austerity, which by a chance actually lurked in the recesses of his character.

' And have you any objection to letting me know just why? ' Laura asked.

' Really, it all boils down to When in Rome et cetera. I think it's the one important thing to remember in a place like this, and if I'm to be perfectly frank, I think that it's a thing you're sometimes inclined to forget.'

' You couldn't be a little more specific, I suppose? '

' Well, for example, you strike me as refusing to make any concessions to local prejudices. Also, the races don't mix well.'

' And what am I supposed to read into that remark? '

' There's been a certain rumour going the rounds.'

' You associate with such unpleasant types. Go on.'

' I prefer not to.'

' I insist.'

' Well, for what it's worth you're supposed to have received a beating-up the other day. At the hands of some jealous wife.'

' Oh,' she said. Laura felt the blood rise, over-flooding in her cheeks; coursing into her temples and neck. She wanted more than anything to cover her face. She felt in her bag, found a pair of sun-glasses, turned away to polish them, and put them on.

Beckett passed judgment on her silence. ' I gather there's something in the story then.'

' You can gather what you like. To be accurate, I was insulted by a ghastly female. Not beaten up.'

' You're angry now.'

' No, I'm not.'

' You wanted me to be frank, and I've been frank. All I'm doing is trying to help. The point is these things are noted. Every time a foreigner gets into some sort of public squabble a black mark goes down against his or her name.'

'Shall we drop the subject?'

'By all means,' Beckett said, thinking that he had taken on a thankless task, and was almost certainly wasting his time. The palace, he thought. That was at the root of the trouble. Living in a palace—even a ruined one nobody else would live in—had turned her head. Only three years ago she'd been a little schoolmistress staying over the Christmas holidays with relatives in Tenerife, and she'd heard about the palace for rent at a few pounds a year. She had come over to Vedra and installed herself in this enormous semi-ruin, given up her work and lived on sporadic journalism and an allowance from her father of three pounds a week. Being called Doña Laura had gone to her head. The feudal atmosphere had been too much for her. A collection of native hangers-on had camped in the courtyard and the lower rooms, and ran to open doors and bow and scrape whenever she put in an appearance. She saw herself as a châtelaine these days—someone a bit above the run of ordinary opinion. A beautiful girl for all that, Beckett thought sadly. He was half in love with her most of the time, too. That was the trouble . . . Had he said enough to make her understand what they were all thinking about her?

'You're an English girl on your own. It's only natural that people should feel concern for you. And not only for your reputation but your safety.'

'How absurd! I can perfectly well look after myself.'

'You can't—and I can quote a perfectly good instance to prove you can't.'

'I thought we'd changed the subject. Look, there are the funnels at last. It's only an hour late today. They must be out to impress the new governor.'

Beckett, who suffered from eyestrain, peered through narrowed lids, seeing at first only the clockwork rocking of small boats in the humps of water at the harbour's mouth,

under a hot, white, wind-marbled sky. Then he saw the
ship's funnels, purple and yellow, sliding raked behind the
breakwater. Seagulls were dancing like gnats in the ship's
wake. As the white, wave-smashing bows came into sight,
he felt a kind of shiver of excitement travel through the
peasant crowd.

' I'm thinking now of the time when you were seen in
tow with one of the locals, who in this case happened to
have a police record.'

She couldn't make up her mind whether to show her fury,
or to pretend to be amused.

' And where did you dig that story up? '

' If you mean the part about the police record, from the
police.'

' I don't believe you.'

' If you'd like to know exactly what happened, Cartwright
and I went to the police together.'

' Cartwright and you! '

' We were worried. You'd been seen more than once with
this chap. We happened to know he'd done time. So that
was that.'

' You mean to say you actually went to the police about
me? You really dared? '

' We saw the major himself. Naturally he wouldn't tell
us much beyond confirming what we already knew—that
the man was an old lag. What we were going to do was to
ask the police to take your residence permit away, but
luckily enough you seemed to drop him at about that time,
so we didn't have to go to extremes.'

Laura got up and began to walk away, a delayed-action
rage burning inside her. She hated to think how she must
have been spied upon. The police major—that aged,
dried-up, corseted libertine, Don Arturo—how he must have
smacked his lips over her.

Beckett was trying to take her arm.

' But surely you can see—I had no alternative? '

Laura pushed forward into the excited, thickening crowd of peasants, trying at first, without success, to shake Beckett off, and then giving in. She slowed down and allowed herself to be carried by the crowd's currents towards the ship, her face averted from Beckett at her side.

The ship had turned into the harbour, dribbling a little sunshine over the water in its wake, and the crowd at the quayside was dense now. Retired shopkeepers who sat all day fishing in wicker armchairs were shifting their positions as the ship bore down on their lines. The band had come to the end of its brassy romp and started the same sad, jaunty tune again, in homage to the captain's dashing manoeuvres as, starchily uniformed, and white-gloved hand rising and falling he brought his vessel swinging in to the quayside. The ship's bows divided a raft of half-melons floating like red full moons over the spot where the town's refuse was tipped into the sea. A gush of grey waste, suddenly released from the ship's iron bowels, brought the gulls screaming from its mast tops. The passengers pressed along the rail saw the town eagerly through rigging and pennants, and a little drifting funnel smoke. They saw the tiered necklaces of the town's streets, the seagulls dancing like feathered puppets under a crenellated skyline, and the wide-eyed, mute assemblage of peasants waiting on the quayside as if for a dependable miracle. The engines went into reverse and the ship shook itself like a dog. The anchor chain rattled out, and small fish darted in to suck at the encrustation on the metal plates.

The police and customs had made a little square enclosure with ropes round the spot where the gangplank would go down. Here the stage was set for the enactment of a delicate comedy by a reception committee of the island notables.

There were four men of great importance, a fifth who was of no consequence at all, plus a little anonymous flock of village alcaldes—outright peasants who stank sharply of sweat-rotted rope-soled sandals—who in due course would be lined up to bow as they muttered their names, then be dismissed.

Ironically, it was the fifth man—the person of no consequence—the Alcalde of the city, still occasionally called the voice of the people, who would step forward as the Governor came ashore, and be the first to shake his hand, before introducing the others. This man stood apart, wearing his scarlet sash of office over the jacket of his stiff black suit, while the men that mattered gossiped together with sporadic amiability. They represented the Church, the Army, the Civil Guard, and the rich landowners; and behind a front of indestructible politeness and the exchange of mild, cynical banter, they were engaged in finely balanced wrangling, in the creation of shifting combinations among themselves, and temporary aggressive and defensive alliances to further their special interests. Don Firmín, the old Bishop's secretary, out of reluctant courtesy to the Church, would be the first to be presented; followed either by Don Arturo O'Neill of the Civil Guard, or the acting Garrison Commander Perez, according to whichever was victorious in their last-minute struggle for precedence. Tur would come last, although until recently he had owned everything worth owning on the island and was still thought by most people to be the most influential of them all. Tur had no official status—only wealth.

The four sharers of power watched the gap narrow between ship and shore. The Governor, in theory, would arrive clothed in paramount authority, but each man, in his way, was determined to bend him to his will. Don Firmín, silent, aloof, ambitious, a scourge of heretics, wanted to get himself appointed extraordinary film censor, and proposed to harness the zeal expected of a newcomer to the tasks of putting an end to the immorality of the foreigners, and of suppressing an outbreak of spiritualism on the island. Temporary Major Perez's instructions were to insist that the enormous garrison be relieved of its purely useful occupation on public works, and be returned to such character-building employment as the Colonel's pet project of whitewashing the whole of the rocky hillside on which the barracks were built. Don Arturo's aspirations were negative. He was a student of numerology, a believer in Fate, and in letting things work themselves out. All he hoped to do was to keep the new governor from meddling—as the old one had regrettably done—in things which did not concern him. In Don Arturo's view the function of the police was, ideally, precautionary and decorative, rather than repressive. He half listened, smiling noncommittally, occasionally caressing through his uniform various parts of the left side of his body which had recently been affected by a stroke, while Don Firmín fixed him with his small, burnished eyes, and tried to explain his intended reforms.

Tur, dressed in a dark pin-striped suit made in Cambridge, had drawn apart from the others. He was in a depressed frame of mind. He detested crowds, and in particular crowds that came to gape at the ship, which in itself had proved the evil genius of Tur's existence. The antipathy provoked in him by the ship was so great that the mere act of coming as close to it as this provoked an unpleasant, tickling irritation in his nasal membranes. He had been depressed that morning, also, to observe that despite all his objections, his manoeuvrings and his wire-pulling, work on the new fish-canning factory had gone ahead, and that the hideous building was nearing completion. Tur's instinct warned him that as soon as the fish-canning factory went into production severe trouble could be expected with the fishing population. He foresaw bloodshed—it had happened before—the whole island in an uproar. The new Governor's arrival had been too long delayed for Tur to be able to bring pressure to bear on him to stop the project. Had he arrived a month sooner, it would have been different, but by now the thing had gone too far. He would have to content himself by inducing the Governor to discover and implement the new measures that were so urgently required to keep the peasants on the land, and of course, by obliging him to enforce the restrictions on wages that had so deplorably been allowed to lapse.

Laura had wriggled her way through the crowd to escape Beckett. She reached the ropes protecting the reception committee just as the gangway went down and the band began to race through the familiar paso-doble once again. A man now appeared at the top of the gangway amid a small, stunted forest of raised hats, looked down anxiously, dabbed quickly at his forehead, and jogged unsteadily down the incline to come ashore. The double line of soldiers sloped, then presented arms. Laura could hardly believe that this putty-faced, badly dressed, undistinguished man could be the Governor. He stood at the bottom of the gangway looking round as if for a way of escape while the Alcalde, walking as if across furrowed earth and followed by the four other dignitaries, advanced on him.

The Governor removed a panama hat that was too large for him and had previously rested on his ears, and held out a cautious hand. The Alcalde bowed over it, buried it in his brown paw, then presented the others. The Governor grimaced at each in turn, and moved his lips inaudibly.

A rope was now unfastened, and a lane opened through the crowd by the police. The Governor seemed to hold back, as if reluctant to go first, and then, urged on politely by Tur, who had now gained his side, trotted away, followed by the other members of the welcoming committee. Carried along by the crowd's whirling movements, Laura was in

time to see the party reach an amazing old car, the
gubernatorial Hispano-Suiza; the first and last car Tur had
allowed to be brought to the island in one of his schooners,
and which was largely shaped like an upturned boat, with
body-work of costly woods. At this point the Alcalde was
left behind, and the five men crowded into the car. The
chauffeur squeezed a bulb at the tail-end of an undulant
metal python; the snake's gold-plated head, thrust fiercely
forward, jaws wide, beyond the headlamps, honked once
mournfully, and the car shuffled away.

With the Governor's departure the crowd released Laura,
and she was making for the Mirasol again, when reluctantly
she heard Beckett's voice close behind her through the
shouted greetings and the whinnyings of pulleys and
winches.

He came up with her. ' Fantastic crowd. Thought I'd
never find you again. Did you manage to get a look at the
new man? '

' I did,' she said.

' What did you think of him? '

' He was rather sweet in a way. He looked like a bird.
A robin redbreast.'

' He's supposed to be a tough nut, for all that.'

' You wouldn't have said so to look at him.'

They walked on a few paces. Beckett tried again. ' To
get back to what I was saying——' "

' Do you mind if we don't? ' she said. ' Please not now.
I simply couldn't be bothered.'

' All right then. Just as you like.'

Laura's anger had calmed. She had been distracted by
the excitement, and the climate's warm tides of lassitude
had begun, as ever, their work of pacification. She tried to
close the incident on a note of brightness. ' Look at all the
girls,' she said. ' They're out in full force today.'

The first stage of the weekly ceremony of the ship's

arrival was over, and now the second part of the programme had begun with a marriage mart. An area spontaneously cleared along the sea front had been taken over by mothers parading their nubile daughters; the old peasant women, faces brimful of rapacity and harsh, earthy quality; the girls on their arms looking about them with the vacant sanctity of madonnas.

'Some of them can be terribly attractive,' Beckett said.

'Of course they can,' Laura said, and then was angry again. The audacity of his stupid remark about the races not mixing, when everyone knew he was doing his best to seduce Tur's daughter. Beckett, the pious fraud, had once boasted in his cups of seducing one in three of all the women he painted.

But that too, in all probability, was no more than another attempt to bolster his self-importance. And most likely his story that he and Cartwright had been to the police was all part of the same thing. *And* the story of the rumour going round about her. (Yet how could he have made *that* up? How could he have known?) She would wait quietly for a day or two, and then find some way of discovering the truth.

The tables outside the Mirasol were crowded now. The café aristocracy of Vedra came late. One Mexican hat alone showed among all the staid clothing. It belonged to a rare out-of-season migrant, a girl, one of a pair of transients, who had been left stranded by her lover, and was now on the lookout for someone to pay for her ticket back to Gibraltar. Laura felt strengthened by a sensation of comparative stability.

Then she saw the Murrays.

The Murrays were the slowest moving of the slow-moving, established members of the colony. They were second-generation residents, in a big way in the fruit business, who lived surrounded by a cohort of silently moving servants, in the perpetual twilight of a Sevillian-style house.

Grudgingly, and assuming herself to be the victim of social mass-suggestion, Laura had allowed herself to be impressed by the almost oriental reserve and aloofness of the Murrays. Now—with a sensation of panic—she saw that they were sitting with the Cartwrights, who were also in the fruit business, but relative newcomers, and therefore—like Laura —only of late admitted to the Murrays' intimacy.

Eve Murray who, thirty years before—had she been in circulation then—would never have been separated from a lorgnette, looked up and saw her. Laura, moistening her lips, started to smile. She raised a hand cautiously, but the noble repose of Eve's face remained unchanged. Laura found herself looking into the marble eyes of a statue.

Then an extraordinary thing happened. Eve Murray laid her hand on her husband's arm. He looked up quickly, stared straight at Laura, then bent over to say something to the Cartwrights. Both Murrays then stood up and went off in the other direction. The Cartwrights, too, had half risen, and in sitting down again, seemed to have shifted their position so that their backs were now turned to Laura.

She felt Beckett take her arm and tug at her. ' Come on, there's a table over there.'

She shook herself free. ' Do you mind going away? ' she said.

CHAPTER 2

LAURA wandered away in the direction of the fishing port, hating herself, and hating Vedra.

At that moment it seemed to her that all the things that had attracted her to the island were a sham. She had shared the complacent illusions of the tourist, based on a perverted affection for the poverty and the backwardness of others. The charm of the place was a sham, and the charm of the people was a sham too. Their celebrated good manners were no more than a parade of the empty clichés of courtesy behind which the poor hid their broken spirit and the rich their arrogance. If there was anything spurious in a person's character Vedra could be relied upon to bring it out. One had only to remember the annual quota of fake suicides among the members of the foreign colony—the overdoses of barbiturates and the wrist-slashing, which were the histrionics of bored, hemmed-in, and also demoralized people. They were emotional cannibals who fed on each others' tensions, and she had certainly provided a juicy bone for them to pick over this time.

Laura wondered whether she would ever quite get over the humiliation of what had happened to her—or whether this was one of those experiences that left a permanent scar. She had been quite disarmed by the girl's manner. When

she had come up to her, calm-faced, showing not the slightest
trace of hostility, Laura had stopped expecting to be asked
the time. Suddenly the girl had craned her neck forward
and shot a mouthful of spittle into Laura's lips, and Laura's
imagination had compelled her then and since to savour its
rank taste. After that, running away down the street, with
all the women in their doorways, she had been pursued with
cries of ' whore '. This malignant creature had quite obviously been Toniet's woman. She had waited for the agitation and the shock of the encounter to die down, instead of
which the memory of it became uglier and uglier, in the way
a storm cloud blackens as it rolls away towards the horizon.

This experience, by a brutal coincidence, had been
followed by another upset only two days later, when she had
overheard part of a drunken conversation in a bar. ' Poor
old Laura . . . one of those, eh? Well I never.' Until then
Laura had always seen herself as the architect of her own
life, a woman detached from considerations of class, who
chose her lovers where she liked because of a conscious
rejection of artificial taboos. In two lacerating minutes she
learned that she was thought of pityingly; a good-natured
freak, who couldn't do without a man and who went down
to the port because that was the easiest place to get one.

Her illusions had gone, pulling one another down as they
fell. The false stability built up over three years of life in the
pretentious ruin known as the Palace of the Viceroy instantly
collapsed. She was one of the freaks and failures who were
beginning to discover the island. They were all going to
create something of lasting value one day, and this licensed
them in the meanwhile to sponge, booze and cheat. Doña
Laura! She had deluded herself that she was respected for
the uncompromising determination to lead her life by her
own standards, but they had all been laughing at her behind
her back. ' Poor old Laura. Who'd have thought it? '

These were largely the myths of depression. The facts were

that for years she had been engaged in the search for the short cut, the key she knew must exist, the successor to salvation through prayer. Only one life to live, and that slipping away faster and faster. Laura's instinct assured her continually that something more had been designed for her than this makeshift existence with its shadow satisfactions. Once she had even surrendered herself for a few weeks to a breezy western evangelism. She had tried Zen, psycho-analysis, a year of married life, creative work represented by abstract painting, employment in humanitarian projects for the relief of suffering in Africa and the Far East. Her latest phase—the escapist one—had included a repudiation of intellectual artificialities in favour of a frank and innocent paganism, and the forthright fulfilment — wherever possible—of the natural instincts. The drawback of this primeval simplicity had been its enormous complications, and from it she had been brusquely baptised to a new life by the woman's spittle.

Suddenly she saw Mila coming towards her. On this of all days she had to run into him! Mila had seen her too. He had put on one of his persecuted smiles in preparation for accosting her, and had slightly increased the swagger in his walk. Mila had been the biggest of her mistakes since she had lived in Vedra. Some cheerful slummer had picked him up in a bar and brought him along to a party at which Laura had got drunk. She had not prevented his taking a liberty with her, and immediately his normal manner of flashy, rather obsequious gallantry had switched, and he had become sullenly and persistently proprietorial. Laura did not believe Beckett's story that Mila was a gaolbird, but he alarmed her all the same. She had quickly discovered that the impudent smile of the impostor concealed a gloomy and resentful character.

She turned round and walked off as quickly as she could in the opposite direction. Mila shouted after her. Laura saw a taxi nosing its way through the crowd. She ran to

stop it, got in, and on an impulse told the driver to take
her to the shipping office. They had a single second-class
berth left on the *Almirante Cervera* sailing for Tenerife next
morning, and Laura took it. At all costs she had to get away
from this humiliation that was dragging and clutching at her
spirit, to take refuge in a place where she was only remembered as a schoolmistress on holiday. She sent off a cable
from the office to her cousin in Tenerife to ask them if she
could come and stay for two weeks. She would spend a quiet
fortnight in Tenerife and after that take her bearings again,
and if by then she felt no better, she would come back to
Vedra, sell up her things, get someone to take the house off
her hands, and leave for good.

For the moment what she craved was a respite from the
limitless, shapeless void of her own freedom, she wanted to
surrender herself to the gentle domestic tyranny of her
cousin's household. Laura's cousin and her husband lived
miniature, Japanese-tea-ceremony lives, secure in their
neatly carpentered framework of social, class and religious
observance. They carried out the rituals of their existence
with severe devotion. Her cousin had three well-spaced
children and a whirling-spray. They formed their opinions
on the way the world was conducting its affairs through their
air-mailed English newspapers, received only two days late.
Ralph had taken to smoking a pipe—Susan had written—
to avoid the risk of lung cancer, and they had lately worked
out an anti-cholesterol diet. In seventeen years' time Ralph
would retire on a good pension, and they would then start
a chicken farm in Kent. They knew exactly where they
would spend their retirement—at least, to within ten miles.
There were no surprises in their existence. In the past Laura
had felt a certain contempt for them, but now she had
changed her mind.

There remained one unpleasant task to perform before
she caught the boat at seven o'clock in the morning. She

would be obliged to keep a last rendezvous with Toniet, and to break the news to him that she was seeing him for the last time. Mila, she admitted to herself, had been a mistake. She had nothing but loathing for her memory of the Mila episode. Toniet was different. He was a mistake too, but largely from the standpoint of her present self-disgust. Toniet was to be swept into a corner together with all the other debris of her past life, and yet she couldn't help remembering that in slightly different circumstances she would have been happy to marry this fisherman. Laura could not forget that she had once entertained the fantasy of 'taking him in hand', educating him, so that they could have 'civilised interests' in common. At the moment the very idea that she could have contemplated such a thing seemed a piece of silliness only worthy of an adolescent.

The meeting had been arranged for ten o'clock that night in a deserted garden under the ruins of the town wall, and Laura went there with reluctance. She had spent most of the afternoon looking for Toniet in the neighbourhood of the port. Then she had written him a briefly-worded letter and left it at the Bar Micalitus where he went every evening, but when at half-past nine she went back to the bar and found the letter still there, there was nothing for it but to keep the appointment. Impatient to get the thing over with, she arrived a few minutes before the time. She was nervous of her surroundings and angry that she should be nervous. She glanced repeatedly at her watch. Were he to be five minutes late she would feel justified in going off, but at two minutes past the hour she heard Toniet's footsteps coming up the path.

Toniet had been out fishing with Gabriel. Already with the waning of the August moon, the pulse of the sea was livening. The big fish of September: the tunny, the melvas, the bonitos, were already appearing cautiously in twos and threes. It was too early yet to think of netting them, but they were beginning to take the hook. The problem was that these early advance-guards of the great invasion from the deep sea only appeared off headlands that were remote from the port, and barely within reach of the fishermen's small boats. What made it worse was that the big fish were only hungry in the early morning and at sunset. This meant leaving port in the small hours for a long trip in a boat powered by an uncertain engine, or a longer-still pull on the oars. When they reached the fishing ground at seven that morning Toniet and Gabriel had put down their lines for two hours only. After that they had gone ashore and slept most of the day. They had fished again for an hour and a half before sunset, and then started home. Total catch, five fish. They reached port at nine o'clock. Toniet had just time to get home, wash, and change his clothes, before rushing off to his meeting with Laura.

They met always by night, in the same garden, outside the range of eyes and ears of two towns; the town of the fishermen, and the town of those the fishermen called ' the others '. This sub-rosa arrangement was more of Toniet's doing than of Laura's. The young fishermen went with foreign women whenever such rare and splendid opportunities presented themselves, but these meetings were always subject to discretion in matters of time and place. When the *Almirante Cervera* had brought several high-spirited, adventurous and unattached girls with the first batch of its winter season visitors to Vedra, the young males of the population who naturally came into touch with them—the guides, the waiters, the taxi-drivers, and the fishermen who took parties out on fishing trips—began to indulge in fantastic hopes. Later a more realistic appraisal of the situation prevailed. Few of the girls came of rich families, or had serious intentions. A small amount of wild marrying took place. Such a marriage lasted weeks, months, or at the most a year. And then one day, called by the *Almirante Cervera's* siren, the fairy princess from the north inevitably returned like a creature of Celtic legend, to the sea whence she came, sometimes taking a baby with her, and nearly always leaving a weeping husband. Toniet was an optimist purely on a tactical level. He knew that circumstances only provided a small scope for change in his existence.

So far only one fisherman had pursued romance to its logical, and in his case bitter, end. In the ordinary course of events the fishing population was manacled to local standards of rectitude in all such matters. Every man, with the exception of acknowledged misfits such as Mila, was either engaged or married to someone else's sister. It was not love for the women—which in most cases had quietly expired many years before—but an unspoken, iron contract between the men which kept these endless courtships going. The better boats that Tur had been frightened into selling the fishermen on credit after a minor revolution in 1934 had greatly reduced the loss of life at sea, and had meant less widows, more children, more mouths to feed, more poverty. This in turn compelled the fisherfolk to marry later and later. Toniet's future wife, Luisa, was Gabriel's sister. They had been courting for ten years, and in that time Luisa had turned from a lively, boisterous, laughing girl, into a sullen woman who would soon be nothing more than a harridan. The bonds that bound Toniet to this woman were Gabriel's ten years' fight with the sea to get together his sister's meagre dowry; Gabriel's ten years of the night's sleep broken off in the small hours to go out to fish, the ten years of arguing prices with the merchant, the ten drenching winters and scalding summers—and in the same way, and for the same reason that he was under an obligation to Gabriel, Vicente, his sister Rosa's lover, was under moral contract to him. In this way every man felt himself in debt to a father or a brother, and default was unthinkable.

But love for a foreign woman—those approachable and conceding demi-goddesses, those divine harlots of the north—was tolerated so long as it was prudently concealed. Toniet took good care to know nothing of Vicente's single stroke of luck in this direction, and Gabriel was equally blind and deaf where Toniet was concerned. Not only this but Gabriel had severely, although uselessly, reprimanded Luisa for the ugly scene she had made in public over Laura, whose surreptitious meetings with Toniet had been reported to her by the wife of a shopkeeper whose bedroom window overlooked the deserted garden. The men understood and felt for each other. Toniet had no false ideas about his sister Rosa's charms any more than he had of those of Luisa. All their womenfolk had become too withered to be loved in marriage. The springtime of a woman's youth in the fishing community merged quickly without an intervening summer into autumn. Most of the women became tame, acquiescent shadows like Rosa and a few, bitter harpies like Luisa. Their brains seemed to creep into a corner, appalled at the prison-cell monotony of their lives. Their bodies slowed and lost shape, so that by their late twenties they were middle-aged, and by the time they were forty, they were old.

Walking up through the night-emptied streets, the moonlight drawing away from him to the housetops, walking out of the blind-walled, ramshackle silence of the fisherman's town, towards the faint leakage of music and voices from the open windows of those who were not obliged to sleep, this was the ironic thought that came into mind. The fishermen were confronted now with the alternatives of good and bad luck. The trawlers from Las Palmas were about to attack them. If they could find some way of defeating the trawlers, that would be good luck, because from the exceptionally early appearance of the fish, the melva catch promised to be the best for many years. On the other hand, this good luck with its windfall of cash would remove the last excuse for further matrimonial postponements in the case of at least a dozen men. Soon after the fishing was over Gabriel would take him aside, and with formalities dressed in an awkward attempt at nonchalance, would make it clear to him that Luisa's dowry was complete; while the moment would also have come for Vicente, his last fling behind him, to bow his neck to Rosa's yoke.

Sighing, he thought of Laura, the splendid, blonde, arrogant Laura, above all the mysterious Laura. Laura, who would never be cheapened by his comprehension of her. Laura, yielding to his hands, yet never completely and totally possessed. Laura, the woman with the body smooth as a child's and the spirit so much quicker than his, soaring away from him. Laura's delicacy, her sudden boldness, her evasions. Every man in the port who knew of what went on envied him Laura. None envied him Luisa. Luisa the heavy-bodied, Luisa the sullen-eyed. Yet soon the good fortune of the next few weeks' fishing—if good fortune it turned out to be—would lock him away with the sullen-eyed, heavy-bodied Luisa for every night for the rest of his life. He had already been sentenced to Luisa's love. It only remained now for the sentence to be carried out.

The garden was graceless and neglected-looking by daylight, and at night it was sinister. It had once been severely scrupulous in its complex of clipped hedges, copied from an English design of the eighteenth century by the great-aunt of Tur's whose face had once been recognisable in the angel figureheads of the Turs' ships. Since then the hedges had billowed out into gloomy thickets. The garden was the accepted place in Vedra for such clandestine meetings, but it was used, as well, as a latrine into which people stole to relieve themselves at all hours of the day and night. A fragrance of jasmine blossoming somewhere out of sight was

imprinted lightly on a dark, shifty reek. Laura and Toniet
were not the only people who had been driven by necessity
of one kind or another to visit the garden. Almost every
bench was occupied by its dark amalgam of human shapes.
Half the garden was in weak, hallucinatory moonlight, but
as soon as they met, Toniet tried to manoeuvre Laura
towards the skirts of deep shadow spread by the town wall.

Laura wanted nothing of this. She had been here before
with Toniet, but this time she was oppressed by the sordidness
of the surroundings and revolted by the frank assumptions
behind visits to such places.

Toniet—out of a sense of masculine duty, and influenced
by a legend originating with the hotel guides of Vedra that
confidence and direct action were the two ingredients of
success with any foreign girl—was ready to persist. He put
a hand under her blouse and cupped it over a breast.

Laura felt a cool thrill of revulsion. She dashed his hand
away and began to walk more briskly. The path narrowed
between bulging thickets of undergrowth that had once been
herbaceous borders. He caught up with her again. ' I'm
sorry,' she said, ' I can't stay more than a few minutes.'

Toniet was disappointed but not surprised. Foreigners
were as unpredictable as the winds in summer that blew in
from all points of the compass. They were creatures of
magnificent imprecision; impossible to pin down. Being
rich and intelligent, they could afford to indulge caprices
beyond the reach of others. Only the poor and the stupid
were imprisoned in an iron regularity of conduct.

' I have to go home to pack. I'm off to Tenerife in the
morning.'

To Tenerife. Thus they came and went. No woman of
the fishing port had ever left Vedra. A visit to a relation in
a village ten miles away along the coast would have been
planned, discussed, prepared for with the gathering together
of a kind of trousseau of borrowed and altered clothing

months in advance. Of the menfolk, only Mila had been to
Tenerife in the days when he had worked as a deckhand on
the *Almirante Cervera*, before he had been ordered to
remain in Vedra under police supervision. The displacement
of a single human being in this community so tightly knitted
together in the bonds of kinship and obligation produced
currents of swirling excitement. But foreigners in their
godlike irresponsibility simply came and went.

'But when will you come back again?' Toniet asked.
'When shall we see each other again?'

'I don't know. It's impossible to say.' The easy way out
to cut across all possible arguments would be to invent
an urgent domestic reason for her departure. 'It depends
how things are when I get back. I've had some bad news
from home. My mother——'

'Your mother. Then I'm sorry. Of course you must
go immediately.' They were almost out of the garden when
he made another dutiful attempt to corner her in the small
maze of trunks of an ancient dragon tree. The lower part
of her calf touched something soft, which was withdrawn.
She looked down in a spasm of frightened disgust at what
appeared at first glance to be a thick, pale, half-exposed
root which was suddenly covered, and she realised that a pair
of lovers were sprawling at her feet.

She broke away from him. 'Please leave me alone.' She
found it hard to translate her ill-defined sense of irritation
and self-disgust into a language which she spoke only
with cold precision—without any command over evasive
subtleties.

'I'm sorry. I have offended you?'
'No, it's not that. I can't explain.'
'But you are very changed.'
'Am I? Yes, I suppose I am.'
'And it is nothing I have done?'
'No, you haven't done anything.'

' Then please tell me why you are angry.'

' I'm not really angry. Oh, I don't know, I can't explain
what I feel.' She looked round for the right word. The
equivalent of disgust both sounded worse and was more
certain to give offence in Castilian: *asco*—a word made
from the flesh and bones of loathing. All she wanted to do
was to get the thing over. It was astonishing what Eve
Murray's single glance of stony-faced disapproval had done
to her. Laura was sure she would have stood up to the
Murrays in defence of others. She would have been ready
to champion anyone else's right to an independent moral
code, yet she had so easily been made to feel a sluttish
outcast. I suppose really, deep down, I must agree with
them, she thought.

She decided to be frank with him. ' I want to ask you
something. Have you a wife? '

' No.'

' Then you must have some sort of regular friend. Someone you're going to marry, you've never spoken about.'

' She is not important to me.'

At that moment they were passing under a lamp. It
showed her his face, weakened by its expression of guilt.
He was no longer handsome.

' A woman spat in my face the other day,' she said.

He produced a routine blasphemy; a filthy, meaningless
expression she had heard a hundred times before, but which
now displayed the exact composition of its ugliness.

' You should have warned me,' she said.

' I say she has no importance for me.'

When a man mouthed this kind of betrayal he was always
at his most unattractive, she thought. He would go on if she
let him. The darkness covered the fleeting meanness in his
face again.

' I've been too humiliated,' she said. ' It's impossible for
me to see you again. You understand that? '

He took a breath. The weakness had left him. ' It must be as you wish.'

To love a woman from the outside world was to play the most dangerous of the games of chance—a game only to be recommended to a good loser. And he had been trained to be a good loser by his fisherman's cultivated habit of stoicism. The fishermen were fatalists to the core; imbibers with their mothers' milk of the opium of resignation. The danger was that, broken in as they were to the changes of fortune, they were prone to a too easy shrugging off of defeat. All that was good was rare and impermanent: the instant of the festival rockets' reflections scorching out to them across the water; the swordfish cornered once in a lifetime in shallow water; the marriage night terminated for ever with the dawn. The fiesta was linked with the black tail of mourners winding up to the cemetery; the sea's womb emptied itself and remained empty for a year; love expired unnoticed. But total despair was held at bay by a wary appraisal of joy.

She held out her hand to him, and he took it.

' Till some other time, then,' he said, refusing by this formula to accept the finality of her decision.

They walked down silently together until their ways parted at the end of the Street of the Viceroy where she left him. Toniet turned back towards the fishing village. He was less than half deceiving himself by a device to lighten the heaviness of his spirit. Of course it's her mood, and that's natural enough. It's all Luisa's doing. The sly whore! And she said nothing about it. Imagine that! He would have to speak to Gabriel about it, and really insist that he took her in hand.

As for Laura—he consoled himself—with foreigners one never knew. A bird had only to unfold its wings to fly away. But just as easily it returned.

CHAPTER 3

THERE were no signs of discord on the surface of life in Vedra. Outwardly all was tranquillity. Seen from the air from a plane flying at high altitude between Las Palmas and Tangiers, the island looked like a scorched leaf floating on the sea, which was a luminous green at the leaf's crinkled edge but instantly darkening to the cobalt of deep, clear, wind-ruffled water. The veins of the leaf, which had escaped scorching, were valleys, planted as thickly as jungles with bananas. Eighteen villages sparkled in folds and creases of black earth. A lustreless hexagonal shape, devoid of villages or of any evidence of cultivation, was Tur's abandoned estate known as the salt-marsh, or Salina, of Sagral.

The tranquillity of the Vedran scene stood up fairly well to a close quarters' inspection. Foreign visitors who had discovered the island and went there for the winter season found themselves charmed into a happy torpor. The people they came into contact with smiled, bowed and made themselves useful, without obtruding their presence in any way. Calm, dignified, gracious, were the adjectives they called to mind. The climate was all one could ask for; nearly always sunny, rarely intolerably hot. Architecturally the town was a pure joy, and in spite of frequent fires, many of the ancient wooden houses dating back to the seventeenth century were still standing. The cathedral, the prison, the Palace of the Inquisition, were all of them magnificent buildings. Every street had its herbalist, its apothecary, its ancient wine-shop. Visitors snapped fishermen who squatted all day mending their nets along the sea front, the frequent processions of penitents chanting ' *Dios te salve Maria* ', the shy peasant girls, the gory poetry of sharks being dismembered on the quayside, the old wooden schooners on the harbour with their angel figureheads, and the cyclopean battlements that purposelessly encircled the town, never having kept out an invader. The conflicts were there, but they were kept out of sight. No one's peace of mind was disturbed by any signs of discord. The terrific problems of water shortage, land scarcity, pressure of population on the island's resources, and governmental inadequacy, got no publicity. Nor did the immediate and terrible crisis threatening the existence of the fishermen, whose poverty to the outsider was so picturesque.

With the exception of Tur himself who stood apart, of thirty-two smaller landlords, of a miscellany of a few hundred shopkeepers, mechanics, blacksmiths, soldiers, doctors, merchants, foreign residents, policemen of four sorts including the secret kind, and of the civil servants who attended to the island's book-work in their inefficient way—the population was four-fifths peasant and one-fifth fisherman. Tur saw himself as the father of the peasants, and—with outrageous self-deception—as a father who inspired love rather than fear. But the peasant element of the population was slowly bettering its lot, and escaping his parental solicitude. A small minority had managed by hook or by crook to buy a little land and set themselves up as petty farmers. Others found that their secondary skills, developed in entirely self-supporting communities, had a high market-value in the town. And when the worst came to the worst they had always been able to take refuge in emigration to Cuba.

The situation of the fisher-folk was far more unsatisfactory. They were seen as a race apart, temperamental, uncontroll-able, and unpeasant-like in every way; squanderers of money when they had it, too inclined to adventure for their own good. The Church disapproved of them as irreligious, and the authorities found them all too dangerously accessible to the new ideas that floated to them from over the sea. From the mere fact that no one had ever devised a means of buying and selling the sea, the fishermen had always been able to cling to a little dangerous independence. But although they called no man master, as it turned out they were worse off than the peasants. The fishermen had never known what it was to have a landlord on their necks, but they were always engaged in a war of survival. They fished inefficiently. Their boats were too small and too old. They needed engines and nylon nets. The sea swarmed with fish that were beyond their reach because they were only equipped to fish in coastal waters. For weeks on end they were prevented by rough seas from doing even this. These inadequacies had all been observed, and they were now about to be involved in a tougher fight than ever before—a worse battle than they had ever fought with the Algerine pirates of old. This time their adversary was a fishing combine in Las Palmas, who proposed with the co-operation of the Port Commandant of Vedra—whose palm had been properly greased—to eliminate them for ever from the Vedran scene.

Like anyone else who could possibly find the time to spare, the Port Commandant had been there to see the ship arrive, but unlike the majority of the crowd, he had not gone off to a meal and a siesta at roughly two in the afternoon. He was a loose-uniformed, gold-braided, untidy mountain of a man, with the face of an enormous baby, an expression of brutal good-humour, and a collection of large warts on his cheeks which danced about or even moved in small circles as he grimaced, chewed at an olive, or yawned. He was waiting for the delivery of the price of his support for the Las Palmas company—a new Volkswagen car, at present in the hold of the *Almirante Cervera*.

Two-fifteen. The Port Commandant sat twisting his glass and stared down at the olive, a small, green, lively planet rolling and bobbing about in its bottom. The human noises around him were dying down. A bicycle passed with the tick, tick, tick of a loose spoke. A wooden ship eased its muscles, groaning faintly, against the rope fenders suspended from the quayside. Racing flies threw their quick monotonous lariats of sound over him. At any other time he would have drowsed off, but now he was nervously alert.

The Port Commandant had finally been able to rationalize his conduct in the matter of the fishermen, the Las Palmas company, and the new car, into a piece of constructive benevolence on his own part. *Sea fished-out within ten miles of the port. Otherwise out of reach. Hard life. At sixty a man's finished—strained heart—rheumatism. Never taste meat, half of them. Chicken soup made from the head and guts on Sunday—if they're lucky. Things getting worse every year. Why encourage them to go on fighting? Act of mercy to bring in the company's trawlers. Means that in the end they'll go to work for the company. When they get used to idea. Wages low but at least security. Car or no car, had to be done one day. Car there, so may as well take it. Certainly no inducement.*

And another thing. The fishermen had let the town down and had exposed him to the Bishop's grave censure, through the mouth-piece of Don Firmín, in the matter of their failure

on the previous year to support the annual marine procession
of the Virgin, and the subsequent ceremony of the blessing
of the fishing fleet. Not only had they failed by dereliction,
but by actual sabotage. Surely some sort of punishment was
called for for this disgrace?

The service the Port Commandant had rendered to the
company had been an easy matter enough once he had made
up his mind that he was justified in taking the company's
side. The Vedran fishermen possessed long-established
fishing rights which the Las Palmas company wanted
abrogated, so that they could move into Vedran waters
with their up-to-date trawlers. They were particularly
interested in the melva-fishing season, which started early
in September. This was at its best in the whole of that part
of the Atlantic off the Vedran headlands, and hitherto it
had been reserved for the local fishermen as the mainstay
of their economic life. Every year an official lottery was held
to determine which boats should have the exclusive rights
to fish certain favourite spots. The Port Commandant, on
the lookout for broken regulations that would enable him
to take action against the Vedran fishermen, discovered that
the law compelled the fishermen to display their nets, if
called upon to do so, at the time of the lottery. He discovered,
moreover, a regulation that had always been overlooked—
as so many always were—that the nets had to be of a
certain minimum size, with a mesh of a determined gauge.
In the previous year, then—after the débâcle of the maritime
procession—nothing had been easier than to demand the
production of the nets, to measure, and to disqualify them
all for one reason or other. The company's trawlers had
gone into action a month later, fishing efficiently where the
Vedrans had always fished inefficiently before, but they
had withdrawn in the face of violence. But this year the
Port Commandant knew that they would be back in force,
and this year, backed by the authorities, they would be

ready for anything, and the Port Commandant was quite
sure they would come to stay.

By two-thirty what was left of the crowd was thinning
quickly, melting away into side streets; but the Port
Commandant still had nearly an hour to wait. He was
hungry. He ordered a ham roll with an extra filling of
ham. When the waiter brought it, he opened the roll, put
in the extra slice of ham, neatly tucked in the small pieces of
protruding meat, and began to munch quickly, the moles
leaping about on his cheeks as he ate. Small white tusks
of bread crust appeared suddenly at each corner of his
mouth and were withdrawn. Within less than a minute the
roll had disappeared. He flicked several crumbs off the
lapels of his uniform, stabbed with his finger-tip at a particle
of meat that had dropped on the table top, and put it in his
mouth. After that he wiped his fingers secretly on the
outside of his trousers where they were normally covered by
his tunic, and settled himself to wait.

The Port Commandant still had a little less than one
hour's wait for the consummation of a plan, the details of
which had been worked out roughly a year before. He was
very anxious indeed for it not to become known that he was
the owner of a new Volkswagen. In the first place it would
be quite obvious to his superiors that he could not afford
such a car, especially when the Alcalde was carried to his
official functions in a 1930 Opel, and the Governor himself
rode in the oldest Hispano-Suiza in the Spanish possessions.
Secondly the Port Commandant foresaw the possibility of
grave trouble with the fishermen when the Las Palmas
fleet put into port again in two or three weeks' time. If
ever he ventured to appear in public with his new car, he
preferred this to be postponed until the dust had time had to
settle. Not that it greatly mattered to him if he finally
decided never to allow himself to be seen at the wheel of his
Volkswagen. A good half of the Port Commandant's

personality had never wanted to grow up. As a child he had always refused to give up the toys he had grown out of. The Volkswagen would simply be the latest and most wonderful of these, and the Port Commandant did not object to the prospect of being condemned to years of polishing it in secret.

The plan was simple enough when one knew as much as the Port Commandant was bound to of the working of the port. After he had come to his arrangement with the fishing combine, he had carried out observations for several months to decide when—if ever—the car could be unloaded from the *Alimirante Cervera* with positively no one, outside the members of the unloading team, to witness the operation. The Port Commandant discovered that the only time when the port could be said to be totally deserted was not—as he would have supposed—in the small hours of the morning, but at three-thirty on any afternoon in August, the year's only really hot month. August was out of season—the dead end of the year—and mornings of cool breezes which tempted people to tire themselves by taking more exercise than they normally did were followed by afternoons of a quite predictable stifling calm. These were the hours when the weight of limbs suddenly doubled, and the eyelids were dragged together as if by magnetic attraction. It was the time of day when food and drink seemed to have been doctored with barbiturates—when sleep after the soporific midday meal was a hundred times more ensnaring than at night. It was the hour when the sun seemed to swell up and vibrate in the sky, and a fleecy curtain of silence fell on the town. At three-thirty on this afternoon, when the Port Commandant expected that Vedra would look as though the whole of its population had been carried off by sea-raiders, the ship's derricks would reach into the hold, pluck out his Volkswagen and deposit it on the quayside, and the Port Commandant would leap into it and drive it away to the stables on the town's outskirts where it would be hidden for as long as necessary—if need be, for years.

Three-fifteen. The strategic moment was close. Not a single person remained in sight outside any of the cafés. Scavenger dogs loped unconcernedly through the tables, on the alert for scraps. Three sagging taxis waited hopelessly in the delicate shade of a tamarisk close by, but their drivers had gone. A Civil Guard who was there to keep his eye on the ship had fitted himself, with the Customs man, into another small island of shade, and the Customs man was pressing back his yawns with a white-gloved hand. The ship's derricks had stopped work, and the dock workers would be away until nearly five o'clock. From where the Port Commandant sat, slumped in his chair, which was raised on a low, boarded platform outside the town's principal café, the Solimar, he could look into the harbour. The water was like dimpled oil, with bleared lights creeping lazily about its surface. The light's brilliance hurt his eyes. At any other time he would have drowsed off.

At three-twenty the Civil Guard and the Customs officer went off together. The Port Commandant was left alone with a soft, raised eyebrow of cloud in the sky, a couple of comatose seagulls perched on the quay's edge, and the urban street-cleaner's mule wilting, eyes closed, in the shafts of its cart fifty yards away. He clapped softly, but no waiter appeared.

The Port Commandant got up, took a last-moment look up and down the road, glanced up at the row of shuttered first-floor windows above the cafés, and was just about to cross the road, making for the gang-plank, when he heard the distant, waspish sound of a two-stroke motor-cycle. In a moment it came into sight, and he recognised with dismay that its rider was Don Felix.

Don Felix was the last man in the world that the Port Commandant wanted to see at that moment. This dry, keen, ageless man, noted for his almost diabolical mobility, was generally supposed to be a member of the secret police. Nobody had ever been able to offer the smallest piece of concrete evidence in support of this supposition, it was just that Don Felix had a manner, an air, a special kind of quiet confidence, a sinister inner serenity, that seemed to set him apart. People quite naturally referred to him as Don, although he had none of the usual property qualifications entitling him to this mark of respect. Above all, Don Felix, hurtling through the town's streets on his Moto-Guzzi, seemed endowed with the devilish power of being in more than one place at the same time. He was unrelentingly sociable too, and if any small groups of intimates chanced to pull their chairs together outside a café and start a spontaneous argument about any subject under the sun, they could be sure that Don Felix would soon join them, easing the intrusion with his usual charm, his proverbs, and his ready flow of small talk suited to any occasion.

There was scant hope that Don Felix would not stop. Don Felix always stopped, and now in fact—when he was still two hundred yards away—the Port Commandant knew by the sudden wane in pitch of the motor-cycle's exhaust, that he had been marked down. He looked round for somewhere to hide, got up, and dashed into the café's lavatory. Bolting the door, he heard the Moto-Guzzi putter to a standstill. He waited, half expecting Don Felix to come into the café, intent on hunting him down. He tested the lavatory bolt. Silence. The Port Commandant looked at his watch. The passage of time seemed to have speeded up. He climbed on to the lavatory seat and peered into the shafting sunshine through a small, cobwebbed window. Don Felix sat there, at the kerbside, astride his machine, his face raised a little, alert, like some rodent

animal that has caught a faint sound betraying the presence
of its prey.

The lavatory seat wobbled dangerously as the Port
Commandant shifted his weight. He climbed down
uncertainly and sat on the seat. The minutes were flying
away now and the lavatory's sharp ammoniacal stench
had begun to affect his bronchial tubes, causing him to
wheeze with each intake of breath. Three-forty, three
forty-three . . . The foreman would be waiting with his
gang of stevedores in the hold. He would be late. Soon
they would give him up and go off back to their bunks. In
less than half an hour the siesta would release its hold on a
few of the town's most restless citizens, who would then move
in the direction of the cup of black coffee they were accustomed to drink in one of the sea-front cafés to freshen themselves for the second half of their day.

At a quarter to four, the Port Commandant heard the
snap of Don Felix kicking down at his starter. The engine
started up, a clank from the gear-box, a rasping crescendo
of the exhaust which quickly faded, revived and faded again,
and he was free. He bundled out of the lavatory, across the
street and up the gang-plank. The foreman was waiting for
him at the top and they went down into the hold together.

The car squatted there in the gloom, a small, spine-
curving antediluvian monster, plated with gleaming green
hide. For the Port Commandant the catalogue had not done
justice to the beautiful reality. The car had been pushed
forward on to a pair of nets—one under the front wheels,
and one under the rear. The nets were attached to ropes
which were in turn bolted to steel cross-pieces, and the
whole arrangement would be raised and lowered by the
winch's single steel cable, like a parcel in a string shopping
bag. The man who manipulated this primitive device sat
sweating at the controls of a donkey-engine in a small
glass-walled box, fifteen feet above the deck and thirty feet

above the Port Commandant's head, and the Port Commandant glanced up at him anxiously before he turned his attention to his Volkswagen.

He bustled quickly round it in the poor light, on the lookout for scratches or dents in the bodywork. Then he opened the door and lowered himself into the driver's seat, noticing with a small pang that someone in greasy overalls had already sat there and left a dark smear on the tartan seat-covers. Happily he took into his lungs a fusion of odours of fresh leather, new rubber, of amyl acetate, engine oil, and the clear grease used to protect chromium surfaces all blended into the spiciness of a brand-new machine. The Port Commandant had read all the literature issued to promote the sales of the car. " Bred from success in countless international events, air-cooled engine, starts promptly on frosty mornings, cannot freeze, cannot boil," he was murmuring to himself as he ran over the controls. From a repeated and meticulous study of the instruction book, which had been sent to him in advance, he was as familiar with the lay-out of the instruments as he was with his own typewriter. He pulled out the choke, switched on the ignition and turned the key. The engine came to life—deafeningly in the iron-enclosed spaces of the hold. The foreman standing by was shaking his head in admiration, but the Port Commandant was startled by the tremendous noise, which it seemed to him must surely rouse the sleepers in the town's nearest houses. He switched off.

The car could be off-loaded, the foreman told him, in less than five minutes.

' Wait till I give the signal,' the Port Commandant said. He hauled himself up the iron ladder to the deck, went to the ship's rail and looked over the side. He shuffled down the gang-plank, reached the quayside and stood there, inspecting in turn the four quarters of the horizon. Whiteness. Silence. Nothing moved. All the town's eyes were

closed. He listened to the faint wheezing of breath through
his bronchial tubes, brought on again by the effort of
climbing the ladder from the hold to the deck. A pair of
swifts dived down over his head in ecstatic, screaming chase
of each other—a startling sound against this background of
noiselessness. The Port Commandant raised his hand to the
foreman, the foreman nodded to the man on the donkey-
engine; the donkey-engine began to chug, the pulley wound
up the steel cable, and the Port Commandant's car came
into sight.

The winch hoisted the car clear of the hold. It held it
for a moment, while the car rotated a few degrees on the
cable; then the donkey-engine man pulled a lever, and the
winch swung the car out over the quayside. A pull on
another lever; the Volkswagen dropped a few feet, then
stopped. The foreman was shaking his head and writing
something on the sky with a gesticulating forefinger. The
car had continued its slow rotation until its tail now over-
hung the ship's rail by a few inches. Two stevedores had to
be fetched, running. They pushed the Volkswagen's tail
away, but the clearance was not enough to satisfy the foreman
and the winch had reached the limit of its side-swing. A
rope now had to be tied to the rear axle and the two men,
standing on the quayside, tugged on this while the car was
being lowered.

These manoeuvres devoured time. As soon as the
Volkswagen's four wheels were securely resting on the
quayside, the Port Commandant rushed to throw himself
into the driver's seat. But there was still an interminable
delay while a spanner was first remembered, then found,
then brought, to unbolt the ropes holding the nets from the
metal cross-pieces. Meanwhile the Port Commandant
fumed and fretted, switching the engine on and off, shouting
his exasperation out of the window, getting out of the car to
go through the gesture of prayer, getting in again. Finally—

just as the last bolt had been withdrawn—the Port Commandant saw the first signs that the town was coming to life again. The blindness of the sun-bleached façade of walls facing the sea was no longer complete—a single shutter had been opened. At exactly the same moment, a man appeared at the end of the sea front. He was carrying a stool and a fishing rod.

The Port Commandant, now freed at last, started the engine again, engaged bottom gear, drove clear of the nets, then swung the car round in a U-turn. He preferred not to be identified by the fisherman, whoever he might be. It was his intention to approach the hideout he had prepared through a succession of derelict lanes skirting the back of the town. He had just reached the end of the sea front, without incident, and was in the act of turning off, when he almost collided with Don Felix on his motor-cycle, who was coming in the opposite direction. The Port Commandant wrenched on the wheel of his car, avoided Don Felix, turned the corner, accelerated.

He drove up the lane through the cactus, the scuttling pigs and the white dust. Had Don Felix had time in the emergency of the moment to recognise him or not? Their eyes had not met. On the whole he was inclined to believe that he had had an incredibly lucky escape.

CHAPTER 4

VICENTE TORRES FERRER was seen
as the most unpromising man in the Ministry, and in due
course he had been rewarded with the most unpromising
job—the governorship of Vedra. Vedra was a dumping place
of the Government for men they wanted to forget about—
men like Ferrer. After centuries of oblivion and neglect, it
had only forced itself on the authorities' reluctant attention as
a result of reports that it had become a breeding ground of
political disaffection. The Government was particularly
sensitive to reports of this kind at a time when it was coming
more and more to be realised that the sceptre must one day
fall from His Excellency's grasp, and when everyone was
beginning to wonder what was going to happen then.

The new Governor's most pressing problem was to discover
how much truth there was in these rumours of plotting and
sabotage, and insurrections in course of preparation. It
was a huge, complex, shapeless task; an operation in which
hard facts were hidden under mountains of triviality, in
which the haystack of hearsay had to be sifted through, straw
by straw, to uncover the needle of truth. In this the Governor
was obstructed by an army of incompetent and lackadaisical
subordinates, and by his own mental sluggishness. The

Governor read, talked and thought slowly, his ideas trudging painfully after each other like prisoners shackled together in a chain gang. For all that, he was a hard worker. As soon as he arrived in Vedra he set to work, and after three days and most of three nights at his desk, the pile of reports on the adverse political situation had been reduced to those relating to two episodes.

Episode number one concerned the open refusal of the fishermen—as it had been reported—to take part in a religious procession on the Feast of Epiphany. Tur himself had come to Ferrer's aid in this matter, supplying a cynical account of what had really taken place. Traditionally, Tur explained, the fishermen's annual holiday with its sea procession of decorated boats had always been celebrated in June on the feast of their patron, Saint Peter, and then they had been ordered to change this to the date in January, which was at the height of the winter season, so that the fiesta could be added to the list of tourist attractions. The Governor had press-clippings and a series of photographs of the procession as it got under way after leaving the church, and wound down through the streets crowded with sightseers towards the port. There was the town band, undoubtedly playing its standard bullfight tune, the priests in their canonicals under the Church banners, the penitents carrying the Virgin's image on its platform, the shopkeepers' wives in what Tur had mentioned were fake local costumes, the soldiers of the garrison swinging their arms over their chests as if brushing their way through thick cobwebs, the tourists squatting, cameras held to their eyes. And then the crushing anti-climax had happened, when the procession had arrived at the port only to find that the boats that should have been there awaiting it had not appeared. The story was that someone had cut the anchor-rope of the leading boat when it had been anchored outside the port, that it had drifted out of sight before its absence had been noticed, and that the other boats had gone in search of it. The image had been carried back to the church, deprived for the first time of its sea excursion, and the secret police had begun their investigations.

So much for the incident of the procession, reported in due course as the work of international agents, but which the Governor was inclined to see as little more than an effective revenge planned by the fishermen on Don Firmín, the Bishop's secretary, for his insistence that the law should be implemented which forbade fishing on the Sabbath Day.

Episode number two had proved more disturbing. In the previous year a trawling fleet from Las Palmas had appeared, and had begun to fish in Vedran waters. Certain fishing rights—which were not really rights at all, because they were without legal foundation—had gone by the board, and following this some trawlers had been sabotaged while lying in Vedra harbour. Once again the Governor couldn't draw any political inferences from the incident. Slogans were supposed to have been chalked on the hulls of the boats, and political leaflets distributed—although so far no one had been able to produce an example of the leaflets. The question was, had the fishermen formed any illegal organisation or not? If two or three fishermen had had too much to drink and then decided to go out and smash up the boats, the thing could be forgotten. If on the other hand there had been any discussion, any element of planning and premeditation in which ' five or more ' persons had been involved, then it was quite a different matter. In this case it became an act of rebellion.

The situation had been obscured by the quality of the information received from the island. Like all other government employees on Vedra, the secret police were the poorest of their kind, and well-known for what they were, the Governor discovered, by the local population, who were careful to keep them at arm's length. The information

supplied by these low-grade spies seemed to Ferrer to be
largely guesswork, and it was with the idea of improving the
quality of his intelligence reports that he summoned Don
Arturo O'Neill of the Civil Guard to his office.

The Governor faced Don Arturo across the top of a massive
table supported by brass gryphons. Sixty-nine of his
predecessors, represented either by portrait busts or huge
murky oil paintings, looked down on the scene with super-
cilious eyes. These were the faces of men not merely with
right on their side, but who *were* the right. The Governor
tried to convince himself that he was one of them now, tried
to absorb some of their power with which to counteract Don
Arturo's perfectly fitting uniform, his row of decorations,
the dignified repose of his face, which was as expressionless
as a carnival mask, beautifully made out of papier-mâché,
the cool appraisal of Don Arturo's glassy blue eyes. The
Governor's fingers closed for assurance in his pocket over a
confidential assessment of Don Arturo's character, supplied
by Don Felix, regretting that—as in this case—his information should so often be gossipy and anecdotal rather than
detailed. ' Vain and lazy ', the report summed Don Arturo
up. ' A heretic. Self-styled Commander of the spurious
Order of the Red Eagle of St. Cyril of Jerusalem. Runs after
girls. " An aged ram has been known to trip over its own
genitals." '
   ' Six trawler engines effectively smashed up by hammers,'
the Governor said. ' " Long live Russia " chalked over
the hulls. How would you interpret that kind of action? '
   Don Arturo extended the tapered fingers of his right hand
like a fan, and inspected the finger-nails.
   ' They don't know where Russia is. It's one of the
advantages of our system of education. We go as far as the
mother country and its ex-colonies—and then only with

selected pupils. For all they know Russia's an island, like
Cuba.'

'What steps have been taken to apprehend the culprits?'

'The normal investigations have been carried out,'
Don Arturo said, alerted now, and as nervous of the Governor
as the Governor was of him. The Ministry had done its best
to spread what it believed to be quite a false report of the
Governor's zeal and efficiency. Don Arturo had accepted
this on its face value. He was inclined to assess him as a
shrewd fellow who concealed his intentions under a clownish
exterior. The Governor for his part was quite taken in by
Don Arturo's cultivated and totally spurious phlegm of
manner. Even the reputation for laziness and vanity might
be a cover up for a cold, unsuspected inflexibility of purpose.

'And what were the results of the investigation?'

'At the moment, negative. We're still following certain
leads.'

'I've been running through some of the past year's work,'
Ferrer said. It caused him the greatest embarrassment to
take a policeman to task like this, particularly a policeman
of Don Arturo's magnificence. 'So far I've gone over the
papers in connection with more than a hundred cases. The
majority seemed to me to deal with cigarette smuggling, the
black market in paraffin, breaking the regulations relating
to the observance of the Sabbath Day, appearing in public
indecently dressed, improperly disposing of rubbish, and
shooting partridges out of season.'

Don Arturo waited blandly. A small extraneous grain
of concern had invaded his mind. While abstractedly
polishing his finger-nails on his thigh he had suddenly been
aware again of what seemed a slight numbness of sensation.

'There's a tremendous amount of paper work involved.
One gets the impression of men hard at work.'

Don Arturo nodded his agreement.

'And yet during the same period there was a record

number of deaths by violence of one sort or another, all apparently dismissed as misadventure. Eleven people disappeared without trace. Simply vanished.'

'Almost certainly illegal emigration,' Don Arturo said. 'A man gets fed up with his wife and family and he just packs up and goes off to Algeria, or somewhere like that. It's becoming a plague.'

The Governor rustled a paper. 'There's a case I have details of here of a farmer falling down his own well. A heavy stone managed to dislodge itself from somewhere above and falls on his head. His brains gushed out of his ears. Finding: accidental death.'

'They're careless,' Don Arturo said. 'And fatalistic. The old oriental attitude towards death probably comes into it.'

'I find here twenty-six typewritten sheets of evidence devoted to the case of a man charged with illegally hunting rabbits with a ferret,' the Governor said.

Don Arturo nodded. 'On the one hand the fatalism of the orient, and on the other a strangely western sense of fair play. I know. It permeates even the police force.'

'To get back to the question of the boats,' Ferrer said. 'I'd like to have your personal opinion as to what was behind the sabotage.'

'Hunger—or the prospect of it,' Don Arturo said, slyly reaching down to rub at another area of his leg.

'The trawling fleet's due back in a few weeks. That means more trouble.'

'It might. It well might.'

'And in the meanwhile this canning factory's gone up. I hear there's a great deal of resentment felt about it. Faced, as we are, with the possibility of new outbreaks of violence, what are we proposing to do about it?'

'Redouble our vigilence,' Don Arturo replied mechanically.

A shirker, Ferrer summed him up. From what he could see, justice had practically ceased to exist in Vedra. This man, and the feudal landlords with Tur at their head, and Don Firmín who controlled the old Bishop and preached that poverty was inevitable and might even be desirable—these were the really effective forces, the unintentional shock troops in any fight for Communism that might be secretly in course of preparation. These were the forces that would send the pendulum swinging violently from one extreme to the other if something was not done quickly to check their power. Whether or not organised opponents of the régime actually existed among the island's malcontents, the Governor knew that the real fight so far as he was concerned would be against these three extremists and their followers. He knew too that it was a fight for which, with his slow brain and lack of training, he was poorly equipped. The Governor was only too well aware that he was considered third-rate, and that he had only been given his appointment as a result of his father's string-pulling. As a beneficiary of the corruption he was coming to loathe, his only justification and excuse would be, somehow or other, to carry the job through.

' I feel I shouldn't conceal the fact from you,' the Governor said. ' We're both likely to find ourselves out of a job if there are any repetitions of the incidents of last year. How much time have we to play with before the autumn fishing season starts? '

' Three or four weeks. Perhaps more. Perhaps a little less. It all depends on the fish.'

' We must find the trouble-makers before then. We mustn't leave a stone unturned.'

' Of course not,' Don Arturo said.

' The ringleaders.'

' The ringleaders. Of course—that's understood.'

' And how do you intend to go to work? ' the Governor
asked.

' Well, in the first place we shall pursue our present line
of enquiry with redoubled vigour.'

The Governor saw that he was not to be spared proposing
a solution of the problem by the method he had first learned
of only a few days previously in an agonizing last-minute
rush of self-preparation for his new post. In between the
bouts of sea-sickness, confined to his stifling cabin in the
Alimrante Cervera the Governor had read several times
through a short technical work entitled, *A New Manual
of Police Procedure and Investigational Techniques*. He had
been astonished and appalled by this book, written in
a spare, classical style, and with certain archaisms, which
added almost scriptural overtones. The cruel cynicism and
the hideous deceits had seemed all the more shocking for
being wrapped up in this pseudo-liturgical prose.

' There are times,' the Governor said, ' when we're
confronted with a situation which resists all direct attacks.
When that happens we're compelled, in the nature of things,
to look round and see whether indirect means don't offer
a better chance of success.'

Don Arturo waited, his expression falsely complacent.
He was chilled by something about the Governor that was not
quite human. He was an Iberian, a fanatic, an inquisitor.
Don Arturo claimed, on the basis of his Irish great-
grandfather, a nordic temperament for himself. He was
slightly abashed, too, by the grandioseness and the appurten-
ances of the room, which were intended to instil a reverence
for the Governor's authority.

The Governor would have liked to be able to quote the
exact passages of the book in which reptilean guile was
dressed up with such dignity, under the section-heading,
' Recruitment of Informants '. He fumbled for words.

' I'm not quite certain how best to put this.' Shame lay in
wait for him, and was not to be avoided.

He took the plunge. ' It seems to be accepted—I mean
by people who've devoted thought to this kind of thing—
that circumstances do exist when the law can collaborate
with propriety with—shall we say, delinquent elements? In
the long-term interests of justice and order it goes without
saying.'

The Governor paused, waiting in the hope that Don
Arturo might relieve him of the burden of developing this
line of thought; this proposition of the means and the end
that gave suck to all evil statecraft.

Don Arturo remained implacably uncomprehending.
What astonished the Governor was that while he himself at
this moment should feel terribly abased, invaded by shame,
should feel himself physically cringe, should feel slyness
enter his face, his palms become sticky, and his breathing
noisier and slightly faster—should in fact recognise himself
attacked by the symptoms of a sort of disease—Don Arturo
after a lifetime of exposure to contagions of this kind could
appear so strangely detached and serene.

The Governor wanted to emphasize the ultimate purity
of his intentions. ' Necessity makes strange bedfellows,'
he said. He threw Don Arturo an anxious look, which
seemed to be ignored.

' I've read somewhere that the principle's commonly
employed in dealing with the smuggling fraternity on the
Pyrenean frontier—and of course, in the case of illegal
political organisations.'

' The principle? ' Don Arturo continued to be blandly
obtuse.

' It amounts to a man who's been in trouble being anxious
to be on the right side of the law. That's to be understood.
And this in turn means that in certain cases pressure can be
brought to bear. With advantage.'

This was the way the manual said that things were arranged—but surely not in a setting such as this? Surely not under the patrician eyes—and the expressions—all too narrowly removed from scorn—of the sixty-nine governors who had preceded him? All round the frieze were inscribed in Roman lettering the words God, Duty, Fatherland. . . . God, Duty, Fatherland. . . . He half expected Don Arturo to leap from his chair with a cry of horror.

But Don Arturo was relieved. The Governor's suggestion had broken the tension between them. He was human after all. The magnificence that had dominated him had leaked away. The brass-faced gryphon supporting the Governor's huge table top was no longer fierce, but foolish.

' You mean someone anxious to please,' Don Arturo said. ' That's what we call them. There shouldn't be much difficulty in arranging that.'

CHAPTER 5

Tur was badgering the Governor again about the labour crisis on his estates. The Governor did his best to listen, to understand, to hold on to his flagging interest. The tides of sleep were threatening him, smashing dully somewhere against a breakwater at the back of his consciousness. For a week he had averaged five hours' sleep a night, and had put in sixteen hours at his office desk a day. Fatigue had now accumulated in his system, dragged at his feet, doubled the weight of his head and his limbs. Thoughts were beginning to escape him; to transform themselves into quick, shallow, pointless dreams—sometimes even when he heard his own voice go drawling to a stop in the middle of a conference.

'They seem to be infatuated with the mere idea of living in a town,' Tur said. 'Even in slum conditions. Some unscrupulous individual comes along and offers them double the agricultural rates to go and work as carpenters or masons. The motive's always selfish and irresponsible, because naturally these jobs don't last. It's sheer exploitation.'

Somehow the Governor's will—itself drugged—forced his mind back to attention. Tur had cornered him in the land-owners' club called The Cultural Peak where the

Governor sprawled half-paralysed, eyelids flickering, in a
wicker armchair in an ambience of worn linoleum, spittoons
and hat stands. Something seemed wrong with what he had
caught of Tur's last remark. He had a quick, anomalous
vision of a peasant armed with set-square and chisel. Had
he been dreaming again? Tur read his thoughts and
explained how the apparent anomaly came about.

' They build their own houses in this part of the world.
Everything from digging out the foundations to putting
on the roof tiles. A woman won't marry a man until he's
built her a house to live in. I'm speaking of the peasantry
now—not the townspeople. And in their way, believe me,
they're the salt of the earth.'

Exploitation. The Governor gave his drowsy consideration
to the word. Does he really believe it? Can hypocrisy
become such a permanent habit of mind that in the end a
man's quite ready to believe black's white? Tur's trouble
was that at last his peasants had been touched by the
twentieth century. They were slipping through his fingers
and going off to work for high wages in the town. Once
again Tur was trying to put pressure on the Governor to
resuscitate some obsolete, but still enforceable regulation
which restricted wages. Don Flavio Tur. The Governor
had allowed himself to be reluctantly amused for once by
the irrelevancies of Don Felix's evaluation. ' Graduate of
Cambridge. Counsellor for three years at the London
Embassy. Tries to behave like an Englishman. English
manservant, well known as pansy. Pays his sharecroppers
ten per cent less than anybody else, but they cheat the rest
out of him. Atheist and freemason, although favourable to
the régime. His father married a prostitute, supposedly as
the result of a wager. He himself once celebrated for his
harem of servant girls, but nowadays losing his grip. " Everyone cuts firewood from a fallen tree." '

' In a matter of weeks a man finds his savings are gone.

And then where is he to turn?' Tur waved his arms in an indignant but un-English fashion. 'Where *is* he to turn? Please answer me that.'

The Governor's senses swam away from him and came back. For a startled moment he had imagined himself in the process of an audience with His Excellency, strangely dressed in a dark suit of foreign cut, his face, as the Governor remembered it, at once imperious and melancholic. The national face perhaps? The features of inherited pride, plus long years of heavy meals taken late at night immediately before going to bed.

'Reform.' Tur said. 'Urgent reform is what's needed.'

Once again the word with which they all bombarded him, each man meaning by it something quite different from the next, yet all seeing it as some sort of necessary action in defence of their own interests. Don Firmín too, now in control of the Bishop's senile will, was determined on reforms. Don Firmín's projected reforms turned their back on child mortality, illiteracy and wooden ploughs, and proved to be a matter of closing cinemas and straightening out the morals of the foreign visitors. The priest had actually handed the Governor a list of residence permits he wanted revoked. This the Governor had intentionally mislaid.

Tur was talking again, his words floating shapelessly on the surface of the Governor's mind. The Governor raised his hand to the back of his neck and dug with the long nail of his little finger into a muscle. The pain cleared his brain.

'A wonderful relationship is being broken up,' Tur was saying. 'We've always lived for our people . . . Seen them as one big family . . . A matter of mutual respect for obligations . . . One big family—all pulling together. All that's necessary is to apply the law before it's too late.' He flashed on the Governor the smile of a card-sharper inviting a country visitor to find the lady.

'Wouldn't it be feasible to put up wages?' the Governor asked. 'In fact to raise the standard of living?'

Tur's smile shattered itself. He would have expected this kind of suggestion from a half-educated schoolmaster. In the mouth of a high functionary, supposed to have some comprehension of economic realities, he found it depressing, and perhaps symptomatic. Another of the anchors of his world had dragged a little. He was afraid now that the Governor was, after all, just what he looked. A foolish fellow.

'We sell all our bananas to the English,' Tur said, in the coaxing, exaggerated simplicity of manner of a man speaking to a young child. 'They buy them for one reason only—because they're cheap. If we paid more wages prices would go up. That means the English would go elsewhere for their fruit. In addition to that we'd have inflation. And — as everything would cost more — our wage-earners would be no better off. It's a matter of simple economics.'

Standard of living. Tur considered the phrase. How strange it was that his ancestor Don Nemesio had been able to see through this vulgar fallacy a hundred and fifty years ago—had rejected it, exposed it for the impostor it was. This was the new label for the prize, the bubble that the lugubrious French had seized, while the vanquished had been left happily to take no heed of the morrow. Hadn't Don Nemesio emphasised in a hundred letters that prosperity is indigestible to the human soul? Tur only knew his astute forbear through his letters, and from his portrait by some low-grade church painter, who had shown him as a kind of Saint James of Compostela, grabbing a crucifix, his face sicklied by an imbecile piety. He had been a pig-dealer, a cheat, and a traitor, and he had been a century and a half dead, yet how infallibly he had understood the nature of the trap materialism had set for humanity. If only he could have

been here now at Tur's side to explain to this fool the fate
of those the gods cursed with riches.

The conversation was broken off by the appearance of
Don Arturo. Tur changed the subject, preferring Don Arturo
not to know that he was attempting to by-pass him by
making direct representations to the Governor over a matter
which really came under Don Arturo's jurisdiction. The
Governor took this opportunity to make his escape, and Tur,
to avoid having to listen to a long account of Don Arturo's
recent illness, went to sit by himself on the balcony. When,
as on this occasion, he was depressed, he preferred his own
company. That morning he had received another anonymous letter, accusing his daughter of misconduct with an
Englishman, and had absorbed some of the poison of the
first paragraph before he had realised what he was reading,
and destroyed the letter.

Here on the balcony his privacy was protected by the
rusty fronds of the club's potted palms. The club was
bisected by a stained-glass partition decorated with a
design of Scotch thistles. Beyond the partition sat the club's
ordinary members; gross, sedentary men who possessed a
qualification of nine hundred acres of land—consisting in
most cases of bramble-filled craters, cinder-fields spewed out
of volcanoes extinct for a thousand years, stinking salt-
marshes, and pigmy deserts—real saharas in miniature, even
furnished with their population of stringy camels. Tur's
section of this somnolent valhalla was reserved for the real
holders of power, notably Tur himself, Don Firmín, Don
Arturo, the absent Garrison Commander, the Judge, who
was also on leave, and the Governor. The holders of power,
unlike the minor landowners, were lean to a man, as it
was unnecessary in their case to proclaim their power by
sheer physical bulk. All the members of this governing
clique with the exception of the Governor and the Bishop's
secretary had been to school in England, and a tradition

had grown up that on the rare occasions that they found something to say to each other when on the club's balcony, English should be spoken.

Once again, it was the day of the ship; a day of excitement, restless longings and idle dreams. The balcony of The Cultural Peak overlooked the sea-front, now crowded with people—largely peasants—who were streaming purposely in all directions like excited ants whose nest had been destroyed. Tur had been strong enough to impede the building of roads and bridges, he had kept out the motor-cars, he had bought up or crushed by devious means the small, weak, industrial concerns that had tried to get a foot-hold in Vedra; but the shipping company had been too much for his strength. Tur's influence in Madrid had even been powerful enough to prevent the harbour's dredging being undertaken by the government, but he had not been able to block the action of a private company, the identity of whose backers was concealed behind nominee shareholders.

The ship whose advent they had prepared was a micro-cosm of the outside world, overspilling with the contagion of unrest. It lit fires and put out fires of its own making. It carried a new invasion of the germ of syphilis and new medicine for its treatment; it smuggled in dangerous thoughts and brought modern inquisitors on the search for political heresies; it provided new incitements to the flux of life in the form of stimulating fashions, books and films, and a variety of ingenious methods previously unknown on Vedra for cutting off the flow thus stimulated. In the first year alone came the complete equipment for two cinemas, a fleet of taxis, the petrol to run them, and the pipes, seats and pans for several hundred of the almost indecently commodious lavatories that fashionable city-dwellers on the mainland now installed in their houses. The ship disturbed the thoughts of the people of Vedra who travelled in it by the vision of Babylons by the shores of alien seas. In the ship came speculators who bought up whole streets of Vedra town for ' development ' in the interests of a future Tur could not bear to contemplate. It had carried the machinery for the canning factory—now almost ready to go into action—which would shortly disinherit the island's fishing population for the benefit of a few rich men in Las Palmas. Most recently of all, the ship had carried to Vedra the representatives of the Anglo-Spanish company with forty-nine per cent British shareholding, but all-British management. These men had offered Tur a fantastic price for land that was of nothing but sentimental value to him, and had smilingly refused to take no for an answer. The ship had arrived like a sudden and dreadful change of climate that freezes or drowns in slime the mastodons of another age. Yet never a week passed without Tur being there with the others to see it steam into port.

Tur turned his attention to the street beneath him. He was obliged to admit to himself that there were few things in life he enjoyed more than to sit where he was on this day of every week, a spectator of this turbulent, excited crowd. The peasants were there by their hundreds; half of them *his* peasants from *his* villages—truants from *his* land. On almost its first visit the *Almirante Cervera* had arrived with a hold full of bicycles, and since that time Tur had never had proper control over his labour again. The merchant who had imported the bicycles had sent his agents into every village to demonstrate the possibilities of this new mobilisation, and he had sold the whole shipment in a few days. The peasants had bought the bicycles, and they had pedalled away through the jagged lava fields, up the sides of mountains, and down the ravines; they had carried their bicycles across rivers and swamps, and then ridden on;

and at the end of a hitherto impossible journey, now demolished by the bicycle in a matter of five or six hours, they had at last seen the town, and the sight had disintegrated their lives. The first view of the town to peasants fresh from a village of five houses and a church was like raw alcohol absorbed through the eyes. It knocked them silly. And in Tur's opinion it very often turned them into scoundrels and animals—a fate from which he saw it as his life's mission to protect them.

The ship's siren shrieked, and the crowd in the street below bubbled up at the sound. Tur had noticed that the waterfront seemed to have a curiously exaggerating effect on the people to be seen there, apart from the peasants. The rich were more arrogant and the poor more abject. Women came here to flaunt an intense femininity, parading as thick-lipped as negresses, bodies uncorseted, breasts and buttocks aquiver, while their husbands, coarsely masculine, scratched and fumbled at their crotches as they walked along. Children seemed noisier and more wastefully energetic than ever, here on the sea-front. The old, on the other hand, were sadder, more dried-up and corpse-like in this setting. Beggars and cripples, who were rarely seen elsewhere in Vedra, congregated in numbers in this street to display their deformities. The inoffensive-looking Urban Guards managed to put on a hint of menace in this setting; priests here were more introspective and cadaverous, tarts more impudent, the prim-stepping virgins more aloof, and the young bloods who followed them lewder in their suggestions. Or so it seemed to Tur.

Tur hissed for the waiter.

'Show me the menu.'

He took the card from the man's hand and grunted. Lamb-chops, pork-chops, bifstek—why the devil can't they spell it properly? *Assiette anglaise* . . . 'Has anything been done about livening up the quality of the *assiette anglaise*? I see the price has gone up.'

'The chef's included a new speciality, sir. Straight off the ship. Canned luncheon meat with spices.'

'Canned,' Tur said. He threw a malevolent side-glance in the direction of the new factory.

'What else?'

'Stuffed olives, of course.'

'Tinned ones, no doubt?'

'Yes, sir.'

'Amazing,' Tur said. 'And as ever, sardines. In fact it's all out of tins.'

'It's what the members ask for, sir,' the waiter said.

'Well, I don't,' Tur said. 'I don't ask to be poisoned. Do you know what tinned foods do to a man in the long run?'

'No, sir.'

'They reduce his vital forces. They conduct an insidious attack on at least half-a-dozen of the glands. All the ones that matter most. You can take the menu away, I shan't bother to eat today.'

He dismissed the waiter just as an aged steward clawed his way through the emaciated palms, croaking softly, 'Don Flavio! Don Flavio!'

Tur signalled him to come forward and took a letter from the tray. He tore open the envelope and skipped through the contents '—in consequence of which I am duly authorised by our board', he read, 'to increase our offer to—' then came the figure that only a month before would have seemed so astonishing. This was the second letter the company had sent him in one week. For each caballería of thirty-three acres they wanted to give him more now than his father could have raised on the whole of their estates—more than his great-grandfather would have had to pay for the whole island. A manoeuvre to acquire this part of his land by compulsory purchase—on the grounds that it was not being put to use—had failed, in consequence of which a new humility had entered the tone of this one-way correspondence.

He tore the letter up and let the pieces drop to the floor, and the steward scrambled after them like a dog snuffling up crumbs. Tur allowed himself a little grudging amazement at the wonders of modern science. These people actually proposed to turn that vast and useless part of his patrimony known as the Salina of Sagral into an enormous vegetable garden. Nothing grew in this area but a tough and practically indestructible thorny scrub, which sheltered mosquitoes by the million. Tur's grandfather had had the idea of introducing fox-hunting to the island and he had brought over a number of foxes from England and let them loose in the Salina. But they had quickly removed themselves from the flat, bare terrain where they could have been hunted, and were now firmly established in inaccessible ravines, from which they issued forth at night to prey on the surrounding countryside. Nothing could live in the Salina, not even foxes, and nothing could be done with it—or, at least, could have been done with it until now. But Tur loved his wilderness, and its arid black earth under its icing of salt, and he could think of no inducement that could persuade him to part with it.

This, after all, was the real difference under the skin of pretence between the aristocrat and the peasant. A peasant's life was shaped exactly by his possession of land—of which he never had quite enough—and on the basis of these iron-walled limits he calculated his existence—always furnished so sparsely with pleasure and indulgence. The land-owning aristocrat, freed from obsessions with land, could afford to love it. Tur could squander his acres as another man threw away money at the card-table. To hold on to the Salina in the face of this incredible offer was a piece of

magnificent folly that at once defined both Tur's character
and his standing as Vedra's leading citizen.

But the satisfaction Tur felt when he occasionally
contrasted his lot with that of the average peasant was apt
to be marred by a single unpleasant reflection. There was
one aspect in which the division between overlord and
underling was an imperfect one. Peasants had a limited
sense of family. They had no ancestors, and lived com-
placently with the certainty that they themselves would
quickly be forgotten by their descendants. This view of
human society as a kind of recurrent crop that came up,
withered, and vanished without trace, offended Tur. He was
an agnostic whose only hope of a secretly hankered-after
immortality lay in the continuance of his line. And this,
at the moment, seemed unlikely. Tur had six known
ancestors, the details of whose lives he had studied with
loving absorption, but only one child born in wedlock—a
daughter, who herself was childless. He was convinced he
had procreated other children although he had known none
of them. He had shared his paramours with husbands, or—
so he had assumed—with other lovers, and he had taken no
interest in their progeny. So the sons that might have been
his had become the sons of others. There was one exception,
he had come to believe, to this melancholy rule of
squandered paternity, and it was this, and the beguiling
illusion he had created around it, that induced Tur to
spend more and more of his time on the verandah of The
Cultural Peak waiting for a glimpse in passing of the young
man he was now quite sure was his son.

Tur sat there more and more eager and more perturbed
as the clock's hand sagged slowly towards the hour when the
streets would empty for the siesta. The Governor and Don
Firmín had long since gone away. Across the verandah

Don Arturo had captured the nondescript temporary-Major Perez, acting garrison commander, and was going through a familiar dramatisation of his recent illness, which ended with a quick, lop-sided canter through the palms to demonstrate the miracle of his complete recovery. ' Divided right down the centre,' Tur heard him say. ' A line drawn by a ruler, you might have said. Clean through the bridge of the nose, the Adam's apple, the breastbone, the navel—even the sexual member. You can't imagine a neater dissection.'

A vigorous hubbub of young male voices from below distracted him from Don Arturo's performance. A group of fishermen went past. They were fresh from the sea, carrying between them in their shallow baskets what seemed to Tur a meagre catch. Tur got up and went to the verandah's edge, his eyes hungrily following the young man he believed to be his son, until the party was out of sight. The most unlikely evidences of paternity had become for him the most convincing. That walk, that swagger, he thought. The way he holds his head up. Charges ahead and lets the others get out of his way. Obviously he can't help it. In the blood. Tur contrasted Toniet's bold carriage with what he saw as the depressed and shambling gait of the other young fishermen. They were inheritors of nothing but the bitter monotony of the war against the sea. *His* son was by nature a free man, who could even wear the accident of his bondage lightly.

Toniet was the son of Tur's servant of old, Brigida, who had been widowed in tragic circumstances just at the time when Tur had succeeded in possessing her, and, as he now believed, begetting Toniet. He had taken her as a matter of course within a few days of her coming to work in his house, just as he had taken a succession of presentable servant girls. It had been at a time when his wife was still alive. The only thing that Tur was quite certain about was that he had had intercourse with Brigida on many occasions; but of

these furtive conjunctions of the body he could remember
nothing: neither time nor place, tears nor joy. He could not
separate the memory of Brigida's caresses or of her flesh
from all the other memories. What remained was a vague
composite image of sensuality refined by time of its heat and
lust. When Brigida had found herself pregnant she had gone
away. They were the harsh days of the Civil War when Tur
had been astonished to find himself hated by his dependants.
She had lived on somewhere out of sight, and Tur had had
few further thoughts about her. Now she was dead. It was
too late to go to her and force her to admit the truth of what
he knew was certain.

Seized by an impulse, Tur rushed out of the club, found a
horse-cab, and had himself driven home. There was nobody
about the place. The housekeeper and the girl who did the
washing would by this time be locked in their rooms,
wrapped up in their afternoon cocoons of sleep. Tur went
banging and kicking at doors and ringing his handbell until
his manservant Smith appeared. Smith had been Tur's
servant since Tur's student days at Cambridge had ended in
1921, and outside a brief holiday visit paid to his birthplace
before the Second World War he had not left Vedra for
over thirty years. Both men, and for roughly the same
reasons, regarded each other with a kind of affectionate
contempt.
  ' Clear a space on the table,' Tur said. ' I want to show
you something. Get your spectacles first. You know you're
as blind as a bat.'
  Tur went to a shelf in the dark cluttered kitchen in which
he and Smith spent most of their time, lifted a clock and
found a photograph. He put it down on the table, pulled
another photograph out of his pocket and laid it at the side
of the first. The photograph Tur kept under the clock was

one of himself at the age of twenty-one extracted many years before from a group which had appeared in one of the University magazines. The second photograph was a portrait of Toniet which Tur had seen displayed in the local photographer's shop.

'Well,' Tur said, 'what do you think?'

Smith, who would have tapped his head meaningly for the benefit of anybody else who had happened to be in the room, said, 'I don't think anything.'

'What I mean is, do you see any resemblance between these two photographs?'

Smith picked one up and then the other. He held them so that the light fell on their surface. The one of Tur was extremely faded and blurred. It showed the wraith of an introspective, sickly-faced youth, with a slightly rodent expression. The face was pock-marked all over with the enormously enlarged screen of the newsprint. The other photograph was sharp in detail, and starkly black and white. In it Toniet wore a stiff collar and tie supplied by the photographer, his thick black hair had been slicked down and parted in the middle, and he had been encouraged to put on a silly bridegroom's grin.

'Am I supposed to see any?' Smith said.

'I didn't ask you that. Do you, or don't you?'

'No,' Smith said.

'But you do. Of course you do. Why don't you use your imagination?'

'I'm using my eyes. My imagination doesn't come into it. I've seen this young fellow somewhere. I recognise him. The other's you, isn't it? Where's the resemblance supposed to come in?'

Tur snatched the photograph away.

'You're a fool, Smith. That's the trouble with you. That young man's my son. The other picture was taken of me when I was his age.'

Smith, offended, shrugged his shoulders. ' Your son,' he said. ' What are you talking about now? '

' You won't be aware of this, but I had a short-lived affair with his mother in the days when she worked in this house.'

' Aware of it,' Smith made a sour face. ' I was aware of a lot of things you got up to. Nobody could help being aware. You made it only too plain. Not that anybody thought any the more of you for it.' He would have liked to add, ' And not that you were the only one in the picture, most of the time.'

' Who *was* his mother? ' Smith felt that the question was expected of him.

' Brigida. Poor Brigida.' Tur pronounced the name in a voice of the deepest melancholy.

' Which one was that? ' Smith asked.

' You must remember her. In thirty-six. She was a woman of great natural distinction. Quite unrepresentative of her class. The face of a madonna.'

' The fisherman's wife you mean, don't you? ' Smith said. ' Hardly a madonna, I'd have said. Surely madonnas are fair? ' Pictures of all the Tur ships of the past century were assembled in the dark harbour of the kitchen's walls. They were shown, fifty or more of them, in all their diversity of antique rigs, under full sail on seas of agitated green milk. Smith found his eye drawn to a particular ship.

' Wasn't there some mystery about the husband's death? '

The remark was malicious. An ugly rumour had circulated in the island at the time, which Tur hoped had at last been forgotten. The feline element in Smith's character was only too ready to bare its claws when Tur paraded his self-delusions—as he so often did—about his progeny.

Tur preferred to ignore this question. He got up to put the photograph back under the clock.

Smith was determined not to let him escape. ' Of course, I remember now. He was one of those who went off in the boat.'

' I believe he did,' Tur said. He put his ear to the clock which had been stopped for some days, picked it up, rocked it and put it down again.

Believe he did! You know as well as I do he did, Smith thought. I wonder if the old villain really did stage-manage the whole thing after all. Nowadays he was all hypocrisy and benevolence, full of the virtue and repentance of failing glands—in some ways he reminded Smith of the régime itself. But twenty years ago he was capable of anything. They're savages at bottom, Smith thought, even the best of them.

' I can see him as if it were yesterday,' Smith said. ' Rather a fine young fellow I thought. An improvement, I should have said, on the wife.' Smith believed that southern women in general were less to be relied upon, less worthy of his esteem than the men. The two-thirds of his life spent in Vedra had left him little of his English background intact, except the national prejudices. To these he had eagerly added what local fallacious beliefs he had been able to pick up. Savages at the bottom, they were. Cruel people—the women as well as the men. The Tur of old would have been quite capable of killing a man to get his wife. Yet surely even Tur in the days when he openly boasted of always taking what he wanted would have thought twice at the idea of doing away with a whole boat-load of fugitives?

Tur was still busy with the clock. ' Only a month since it was overhauled,' he said. ' It doesn't say much for modern standards of craftsmanship.'

' I wonder if we shall ever know,' Smith said.

' Ever know what? '

' What happened.'

' What are you talking about? ' Tur asked, irritation

pitching his voice a couple of tones higher. ' What happened to what? '

' To the famous boat-load.'

Tur mastered a sudden flash of the old spirit showing itself in an impulse to throw the clock at his servant's head.

' We do know,' he said quietly. He felt his anger remodelling his mouth and jaw. ' We were told officially what happened. They ran into a storm, that's all. Have you any special reason to doubt the truth of the official statement? '

' No,' Smith said.

' Well, please be quiet then.'

' I will be,' Smith said, as angry now as was Tur. ' I will be.'

' As things turned out, it would have made no difference one way or the other,' Tur said. ' We knew by what happened elsewhere they'd have been done for if they'd have stayed here. Far better the way it was. At least they had a chance.'

It suits you to say that now, Smith thought. Lost in a storm indeed! Smith happened to remember the weather as being exceptionally fine and calm at the time. Remarkable it was that within a few hours of His Excellency's insurrection getting under way in Tenerife someone should have quietly passed the word to all the known Republicans in Vedra that their night of the long knives was at hand, and that they should have been permitted to decamp in Tur's least seaworthy barquentine, mysteriously made ready for a sea voyage. As brilliantly conceived and economical a piece of mass elimination as Smith had ever heard of—if in fact the thing had been planned. Vedra's right-wing extremists had kept out of sight, had been relieved of the slightest possibility of danger to themselves, letting their enemies escape without molestation. Watched by a wondering but undemonstrative crowd on that bright July morning

in 1936, Tur's boat the *Elvira* had carried the fugitives
chugging out of the harbour into the sinister peace, the
silence and the oblivion of the sea; and nothing more was
known of them. But Tur's reputation had never quite
recovered from the slanders of those who saw themselves
as bereaved by treachery.

Savages at the bottom, Smith was thinking. All of them.
An English education and the passionless years in the North
had done nothing to change the old animal. The women
too, in their way, were no different. Half of them were
what did they call it? He couldn't remember the word.
Couldn't be left alone with a man—any man—for a few
minutes without something happening. Tur's mother had
been one of them—a famous example—and in Smith's
opinion his daughter Basilisa if given the slightest rope would
be exactly the same. Hadn't they had to marry her off to a
husband they'd never have looked at in the ordinary way
because she wasn't a virgin? Nobody else would have her.
Nobody would touch her. Smith had heard she'd allowed
herself to be seduced in a lavatory. Disgusting. Nothing but
an animal. Yet Tur couldn't see it. He wouldn't see it.
Any other girl in this country would have been thrown out of
the house as a whore, but she was Tur's daughter so somehow
she managed to be still virtuous. So far as Tur was
concerned, at any rate. And now the ridiculous obsession
with that other harlot Brigida's boy. Smith felt a new
pang of jealousy, which he quickly disguised as natural
indignation at the thought of his employer making himself the
laughing-stock of the island over someone else's son. His
fury suddenly boiled up. ' Excuse me,' he said, ' but if you're
so certain this young fellow belongs to you, what's the next
step? You'll be thinking of calling in the lawyers, won't
you? '

' Yes,' Tur said. ' I suppose that's the logical action.'

' What's Basilisa going to say about it? '

'I haven't given thought to the matter.'

'Shall I tell you?'

'I don't think I'm particularly anxious to hear your opinion.'

'She's not going to like it,' Smith said. 'And that's putting it mildly. If you ask me she's going to be very angry indeed. I'd say you're in for a rough time.'

Tur sighed.

'It's a pity her husband isn't capable of giving her a child.'

'Please mind your own business,' Tur said. He picked up the clock and rushed out of the room.

CHAPTER 6

It was a foregone conclusion that Tur's daughter Basilisa would fall in love with the first young Englishman she came in close contact with. She had been to boarding-school in England, still corresponded with one or two of her old school friends, read nothing but English magazines, chose her intimates among the wives of the English colony. England was her spiritual home. After her return to Vedra her life had been crushed into a mould of excruciating boredom. Nothing but the sterile episode of her marriage had happened to her for ten years until she went to Beckett's studio for the first sitting for her portrait.

Basilisa's tragedy was that she should have been the child of Tur's middle age. By the time her mother died, leaving Tur with the full responsibility of her upbringing, the liberalising influences of Tur's youthful surroundings had already died out. With the years he had ossified into a traditionalist. He still liked to wear English clothes and speak English whenever he could, but within, nothing remained of the man who had been so receptive of foreign ideas, who had been so eager to adapt himself to the alien society in which he had spent his most impressionable years.

Basilisa was away at school between the ages of eleven and sixteen. Tur had originally intended that she should go to the Sorbonne, or to one of the Swiss finishing schools, but long before the time came for this he had changed his mind. Instead, he put her in the care of one of his sisters, who lived in a farmhouse on a mountainside in the island's interior. It was so isolated and the roads so bad that the aunt could only find the energy to make the journey to Vedra Town once or twice a year.

The reason for this brusque change of policy was that Tur had relapsed completely into the spiritual attitudes of a typical islander, including his reactionary view of the position of women in society. At the age of fifty-five Tur was quite ready to fall in with the view that thought it on the whole best to keep womenfolk under lock and key, and—failing that—subjected to the strictest security measures.

This frame of mind was fed by memories of an unhappy family experience. Tur's father had married a woman popularly credited with a special island affliction—politely known as ' the weakness '. Such women were the descendants—so people believed—of mixed marriages between Vedran peasants who had gone to Cuba to work in the sugar-cane fields and the mulatto women of that country. The wives brought home by emigrants who returned to Vedra sometimes looked white enough, but the children of the union were apt to show their Negroid blood in skin, lips and hair, and the girls—it was alleged— were often visited with a demoniacal sexuality. To avoid the dangers involved in marrying them, a category of experts came into being, who would examine prospective wives for a fee, and either go away shaking their heads, or issue a clean bill of health. The upper class was supposed to be contemptuous of this kind of nonsense, but they went in for it in secret. Tur's father had actually married a woman with ' the weakness ' partly out of bravado, but also attracted by their reputation for incomparable prowess in bed. The marriage had turned out a catastrophe.

Basilisa spent two drab years on the farm. Her aunt was a puritanical virago, who had clearly inherited none of the dreaded predispositions of Tur's mother (' the weakness ' was supposed to be transmitted, a kind of sexual hæmophilia, affecting females only, from mother to daughter). Neither did it seem likely by the docility of her behaviour that Basilisa had done so. With his father's awful fate in mind, Tur had picked out for himself a little blue-stocking of a librarian from Madrid, a northerner, whose efforts— complicated by miscarriages—to produce a single child, had exhausted her and eventually caused her death. Basilisa was a quiet girl who took after her mother—so Tur thought. While Tur was looking round for a suitable husband for her—a problem complicated on Vedra by the paucity of its ruling class—Basilisa worked. The farmhouse was like a small, squat fortress. Its walls were eight feet thick, and the windowless rooms enclosed either night or a candle-lit twilight full of stark shadows and the sober smell of earth and clean linen. The aunt, like Tur himself, believed in the ennobling effect of a peasant existence, and she saw to it that her family lived, and worked, and ate like peasants. Basilisa spent several thousand hours embroidering bed-covers and napkins. She was only allowed out of the house on Sundays to climb five miles over the mountain to go to Mass. One day an urgent message reached Tur, telling him to come and take his daughter away.

' But how on earth can it have happened? ' Tur asked when he arrived. ' Is it the custom here to allow a girl to go running about the place at night? '

' She has to answer the call of nature, doesn't she? ' the aunt said. ' This isn't one of your grand town houses.'

'And you're quite sure of it?' Tur said. 'I'm not interested in suppositions. You're absolutely convinced that it's come to the worst?'

'I saw the man run out of the latrine. Is that enough for you, or do you want to call the doctor?'

'No,' Tur said. 'Never mind about the doctor. The poor girl will be upset enough as it is without that. There's no doubt about it, some wretched scoundrel has taken advantage of her innocence.'

The mechanism of self-delusion was already working smoothly. He roared with indignation when his sister suggested that Basilisa might have given some encouragement to a lover.

Tur took his daughter home and treated her with greater affection than she had ever known before. A week later he appeared with a quiet, sharp-faced young man, who was about ten years older than Basilisa. He wore a stiff suit, specially made for him by the tailor in twenty-four hours, and he carried a soft hat lent him by Tur, and a pair of gloves. The young man smelt of violet-scented hair oil, and Basilisa noticed that in walking he took quick short steps like a man carrying a heavy weight on his back.

'This is your husband to be,' Tur said.

Basilisa, who had surmised the worst, clenched her teeth to prevent herself from crying. 'I don't want to get married,' she said.

'I'm afraid there's no option, my dear.'

'He's a peasant, isn't he?' Basilisa said through her teeth. She had seen all she wanted to of the young man, and avoided looking at him again.

'Of peasant stock if you will,' Tur said. 'An exceedingly respectable family. In the near future, he'll be a landowner. Quite one of the most talented young men I've ever met. He's also in love with you.'

In this interview lasting ten minutes, the bridegroom-to-be said nothing.

Within the month they were married. Tur gave Valentin, his son-in-law, a handsome present in hard cash, which Valentin put into a highly confidential scheme that had just been proposed to him, of which Tur was told nothing. For her dowry Basilisa got a considerable tract of land belonging to Tur's estate at Sagral—the famous Salina. Tur saw this as a cunning move on his part. The land comprised in the dowry was practically worthless. He proposed to settle valuable agricultural land on Basilisa under a deed of trust in such a way that she would always be independent of Valentin, but he was surprised and a little disappointed that Valentin should allow himself to be fobbed off in the matter of the dowry with a lot of what was undeniably tenth rate. Tur's high opinion of his son-in-law's intelligence suffered a temporary slump. Tur successfully proposed Valentin for membership of The Cultural Peak, although with what Tur considered becoming modesty, Valentin never put in an appearance at the club. There were a number of small points that were easily settled. Like most peasants, Valentin had an unfortunate family name: Escoba—meaning 'yard-broom', but he was quite in agreement with his father-in-law's stipulation that the children of the marriage should bear the name of Tur. The old man had forced himself to be philosophical about the disparity in social status of the young couple. A surgical measure had been called for and Tur had taken it.

There had been one further stipulation; providing for an arrangement which proved most obnoxious to Basilisa. While still quite convinced of Basilisa's basic chastity, Tur wished to protect her from any possibility of further victim-isation by unscrupulous males. He made Valentin, a

relatively broadminded man, agree that an impoverished
relation of Tur's, a cousin twice removed, should enter the
new household and act as a lady's companion to Basilisa.
This was an example of the way Tur's mind worked now
that he had become a total reactionary. ' Ladies' companions ', as they were now called, were nothing more than
the formidable dueñas of the last century under a new
name—domestic gaolers who inevitably bred bitter rebellion
in the luckless women to whom they were attached.

Augusta had been with Basilisa for ten years now; a
grey, voiceless wraith that never imposed itself, had no
opinions, put up only the most feeble of defences when
attacked—*but was always there*. Basilisa frequently had
daydreams involving murder by subtle poisons. And then,
one day, she made the great discovery in which she saw her
eventual salvation. Augusta had become a secret drunkard.
From that moment on, her course was set.

On the morning of Basilisa's assignation with Beckett she
called to Augusta. ' Get ready. We're going out.'

No reply. Basilisa went into the room where Augusta
sat with inflamed eyes and running nose, working on her
picture. Basilisa looked over her shoulder and shuddered.
For two years Augusta had given all her spare time to a
needlework picture, ' Christ Risen from the Dead ', and
within the limits of her medium she had achieved a horrific
realism. The picture was in its last stages and Augusta's
Christ leaped from the tomb with macabre vitality. This
face of a revenant was still divided by death from humanity,
putrescence glowed in all the cells of his body, yet the
staring eyes were re-awakened to the memory of agony.
The broken, murdered body exhibited its gore-blackened
wounds to the beholder. Of all the samples supplied by the
nuns, the original of this, inspired by Murillo, had appealed
to Augusta. From the creation she gave to it came all her
joy in life. ' This is my lover,' she would whisper with her

cracked lips. Sometimes the emotion she felt translated itself into a pain in the womb, like a sharp peristaltic twinge that preceded the release of wind.

'We're going out,' Basilisa said. 'Please get ready. I don't want to be kept waiting.'

'I thought we were staying at home today. You know there's never anything worth having in the market on a Monday.'

'Who said anything about the market?'

'What else is there to go out for in this heat? Do you want the sun to ruin your complexion?'

'My complexion is my own affair. I've decided to go and have another sitting for my portrait.'

'But you were going on Wednesday.'

'Well, I've changed my mind. That's all there is to it, so please put that thing away and get ready.'

Muttering, Augusta pushed her needlework aside. Then suddenly her nostrils caught the familiar, stale, sweaty, rancid odour. She's on heat, she thought, of course that's the answer. And now she's off to the painter. She can't wait. Augusta was panic-stricken. She foresaw the ruin of all her plans. She's off her head. She's mad with it. How am I going to get a message to the master? Her mouth filled with water as the horror of the situation came over her. Never, never again when this is over she promised herself. When this was over she would leave Valentin's service and go and work for the nuns.

Augusta's hate for Basilisa was on a higher and sublimer plane than the animosity that Basilisa felt for her. Basilisa's fury was regularly relieved in small oppressions and acts of spitefulness. Augusta's hatred, constantly generated and never given satisfaction, overflowed in all directions, a dark vitriolic flood that spared only Valentin out of gratitude for the animosity Augusta sensed that he, too, felt for his wife. When 'the weakness' took possession of Basilisa it

made Augusta ill to be with her. Her throat became
inflamed, she ran a temperature and found it difficult to keep
her food down.

This was a country in which only a beautiful woman
could hope to marry, and Augusta had not even been
considered worth watching. In her late thirties Augusta's
body and soul had begun to fade and diminish. Her breasts
vanished, the nipples finally existing as no more than
roughnesses in the small folds of skin over her protruding
ribs; her womb shrivelled away till it was a dried ball of
sinew hardly bigger than a walnut; she became the victim
of a complex of distressing allergies; her voice turned thin
and sharp, her features—vague and poorly defined, like an
old fading photograph—took on a catlike expression. She
had been thrust away out of sight, among the old, patient,
faceless crones whose lives had withered after the brief
flowering of their childhood and who now awaited death
in the shadows of their fathers' houses. From this dusty
attic of souls she had been rescued by Tur. By the terms of
her service, Augusta never left Basilisa's side outside the
house. Her detestation of her mistress had been born of
Basilisa's flaunting of the things she had never possessed, and
those she had lost: the breasts, the buttocks, the hair, the
teeth, the thighs, the tight, creamed skin, the musky,
sickening aroma of an ovulating female in the full tide of
her womanhood. Augusta's horror of the sexual instinct had
developed through the years of her servitude until she was
overcome by faintness at the sight of dogs copulating in the
street. Her bitter mania even drove her to creep out secretly
in the early mornings and smash down the mud beginnings
of the nests the martins always attempted to fix under the
eaves of the house.

'What's the matter?' Basilisa said. 'You're not sick
again, are you? Why are you always sick when I want to go
out?'

' It's not my fault if the food doesn't agree with me. I think I'll run down to the pharmacy and get something for it. I shan't be more than ten minutes.'

' I haven't time to wait,' Basilisa said. ' Take a drink of water. The trouble is the way you bolt your food.'

' It's passed,' Augusta said. ' I'm better now.'

' If you want to pick up something from the pharmacy,' Basilisa said, ' we can stop on our way. In the meanwhile go down to the wine cellar and see if there's anything we need to order. Here's the key. I'm going to get dressed.'

The key of the wine cellar was a component of Basilisa's broad strategy. Augusta, she knew, would take it and open the wine cellar and pick up the nearest litre bottle of wine and drink a half of it in a couple of gulps. By never allowing Augusta more than a thimbleful of wine with her meals, Basilisa believed she could count on the accumulation of Augusta's thirst being ready to serve her purpose.

Augusta took the key. As soon as Basilisa left the room, she rushed to scribble down the note to be left with the pharmacist, who was another of Valentin's men. Then Augusta went down to the cellar, unlocked the door, and groped her way into the small, dark chamber full of wine fumes. She opened a bottle, put it to her lips, took a mouthful, and held the wine in her mouth, rinsing it round her teeth, making sure the odour would remain on her breath. After that she poured most of what remained of the wine down the sink. She felt dizzy and had to clutch at the edge of a shelf to save herself from collapsing. It mustn't fail, she kept saying to herself. Please God don't let it go wrong. Please dear Christ don't let anything happen to stop the master being there in time. Our Lord, please. Please, dear Jesus.

Meanwhile Basilisa had gone to the bathroom, where she undressed. She stood in the bath and sponged her body down, shivering as the cold water trickled down her belly and thighs. She looked at herself in the mirror. When this mood took her, she was able to see her body with a kind of ecstatic detachment, almost as the body of a stranger, a lover. These ardours directed inwards upon herself had sometimes reached an intensity keener than she had ever experienced in her brief, furious contacts with the fieldworker in the outhouse on her aunt's farm. Basilisa found that her breathing had gone rapid and shallow. She touched herself and felt a shuddering thrill of pleasure radiated to every nerve-end of her body. She got out of the bath quickly, guiltily dried herself and began to dress.

She opened the door of the bathroom. 'Augusta! Augusta!' she shouted down the stairs. 'Where are you? Why do you keep me waiting? What ever is the woman doing now?' she added in an angry undertone.

A few minutes later Basilisa was dressed. Augusta was waiting for her at the foot of the staircase. Basilisa could smell the wine. Good, she thought, she's been at the bottle. No doubt about that. She'll only have to sit down and she'll go right off to sleep.

There was something strange in Augusta's expression that Basilisa had never noticed there before. Those staring eyes in the wasted, bloodless, waxen face. There was something about them that reminded Basilisa of the eyes of the risen corpse in Augusta's picture.

While the taxi carrying Basilisa and Augusta groaned up the hill towards Beckett's house, Beckett stood at the street door with the girl he had picked up in the Mirasol on the previous evening. The girl was holding his hand, and this in itself embarrassed Beckett. He had felt himself threatened by a certain possessiveness that had entered her manner since they had got out of bed, and Beckett, who couldn't think of anything to say, would have liked her to go.

She let go his hand, and began to fiddle with the Mexican straw hat that was beginning to lose its shape.

'Well,' she said, 'once again, thanks for everything.'

'Not at all,' Beckett said. 'Thank *you*.' He was suffering from his usual morning-after-the-night-before revelation, which forced him to notice the disproportion in the lower part of the girl's face; the heaviness of the jaw. Never in his life had he made love to a girl without something of this kind happening to him.

'And you're taking the ship tomorrow,' Beckett said.

'I suppose so. I've got an option on a cabin until nine o'clock.'

'You were lucky to get one. At this time of the year. Everyone's travelling. People like to get away in August.'

Leaning against the wall, she shifted her weight from one foot to the other and pushed her fingers through the crack in the hat-brim.

'I'd better make up my mind quickly, hadn't I?'

'Your mother will be glad to see you,' he said.

'She thinks I'm still in Gibraltar—imagine that.'

'And there's nothing else that you want?'

'No,' she said. 'And thanks again for the money.' Beckett had contributed ten pounds towards the fare. He wondered who the other subscribers had been.

'Do you want me to come back this evening?' she asked.

'I'd love you to, but I'm going to be tied up until awfully late.'

'I see,' she said, her voice gone flat. 'Well, in that case I won't.'

Beckett preferred to withdraw ambiguously rather than brutally from the situation. 'I tell you what. I'll be in the Mirasol at about nine.'

'Yes, all right,' she said. 'We'll leave it at that.'

She gave him a rather sad, sour little smile and went off. When she got to the corner, she turned and waved, and

Beckett waved back. He was just going in when the taxi came into sight. Beckett was afraid that Basilisa might be in the taxi because it was the one she always hired, a veteran Panhard, with a speaking tube and a brass dragon in flight on the radiator cap. He waited, uneasy. He was not in the best mood to carry his adventure with Basilisa another stage forward towards its logical conclusion. Why on earth should she have come on the wrong day? He wondered whether he could put her off without offending her.

The taxi stopped, and as he had feared, it was Basilisa with the inseparable Augusta. Basilisa seemed agitated. She was pulling at Augusta's arm. Augusta lay back in what appeared to be a faint.

'She's been sick in the taxi,' Basilisa said. 'Please help me to get her upstairs. The pharmacist gave her something for her stomach, but it's only made her sick.

'And she's as drunk as a pig,' she said fiercely in Beckett's ear. She squeezed his arm, and he was amazed at the strength in her fingers.

CHAPTER 7

BECKETT went through the ritual of putting on his white smock. Surreptitiously he lit an incense cone and put it under the belly of the brass Buddha. He took a brush out of the rack, tested it with a finger-tip; shook his head, frowning, and exchanged it for another. His secondary personality had entered into action. Now he was the bohemian, the temperamental painter of fashion his clients expected him to be. It was a role that Beckett was secretly ashamed of, but he was compelled to cater to an addiction for make-believe. All his sitters were idle upper-class women, unsettled by their lives in the no-man's-land between two traditions. The latest craze was to have one's portrait painted by Beckett—a foreigner, who lived in a romantically dissolute fashion, and looked the part. Beckett, after a brief research into local myths, had cluttered the cool spaces of his studio with stage properties and surrealistic bric-á-brac; with African masks, mobiles in wire, idols, leopard skins and oriental stools. Large canvases, awaiting completion leaned against the wall: faces tranquillised in the sweet coma of Beckett's art. It was good business, but alien to his nature with its affection for tidiness and the exactitudes. With the memory of hard times Beckett swallowed his scruples. He had been as much a failure as a painter as at everything else until one day the previous governor, a friend of his father, had commissioned him—more as a charitable gesture to an old friend than anything else—to paint his wife. Beckett, as a kind of despairing joke, had painted her as a girl in her twenties, wearing a Chinese mandarin's coat, and had instantly become famous.

Basilisa had been seated on a gimcrack throne of gilded wood and plaster to face the easel. She was feeling the heat. She had happily agreed to be painted in an eighteenth-century Venetian brocade gown, and this—magnificent as it was in its faded way—was inappropriate to a stifling August day in Vedra. Augusta had been guided to a divan on the other side of the vast room, and had been left, half-recumbent, her back propped up with cushions, and her head had fallen sideways like that of a newly cut-down suicide. She was breathing heavily—a dog-like snuffling that Beckett hoped might mean she was asleep. But Augusta, although exhausted by her sickness and excitement, was not asleep. To be sure, Beckett signalled to Basilisa, nodding in Augusta's direction, a finger placed over his lips, then went to the kitchen and poured out a glass of water. He came back, went over to Augusta, listened for a moment, then nudged her gently and put the glass in her hand. Augusta held the glass, staring into the water with a clairvoyant's absent stare. She sipped a mouthful and gave the glass back. The tip of her tongue darted out suddenly like a small, grey lizard, flickered over her lips and withdrew. Then the eyelids, pale, withered leaves of skin, fluttered together. Beckett tiptoed away back to Basilisa.

He picked up his brush, tilted her head slightly and examined her face from the new angle. She was magnificent, with a kind of almost barbarous beauty Beckett only remembered seeing before in the two years he had served in the Colonial Service in West Africa, before the colony he had been posted to had been given its independence. The

cruel joke was that all he so much admired about Basilisa
he would be called upon to suppress in the interests of a
spurious nordic refinement which was the ideal of every
Vedran woman. This was not even the usual matter
of ignoring lines and wrinkles, enlarging and brightening
eyes, cleaning up the curve of a chin, straightening a nose,
seeing black hair as brown hair. Here all the exuberant
vitality of Africa stamped in a face had to be obliterated;
nothing of it must be allowed to show. He had to turn a
woman who for him was a Negress into one who was
impeccably white, and the result had to be recognisable.
For his own pleasure, Beckett would draw Basilisa as he
really saw her—a sketch which Basilisa would never be
allowed to see. It was such surreptitious sketches as this
made of his sitters—in which all the true facts censored in the
main portrait were re-inserted—that had become Beckett's
atonement for what he saw as his artistic parasitism. Ironically, it was his clients' hunger for the unreal that had cured
Beckett of false pretences as an artist, turned him into a
realist, and in the end, into a good painter.

'Darling,' Basilisa whispered. He smiled, and stroked
her cheek with his finger-tips. He wondered whether he was
falling in love with her. How remarkable, he thought,
that by her sheer presence she should be able to neutralise
the essentially ridiculous imposture of gown and throne.
For some reason he thought of Laura. Laura's beauty would
have ceased to exist in this room, dominated by the beauty of
Basilisa—the embers of a fire quenched by the sun. Basilisa
took his hand and drew it gently down to her neck. Beckett
saw that her expression had changed. Her breathing was
faster. He found himself faced with a slightly alarming
conclusion. This was the reason why she had come to him.
She was ready for him to take her. Without further preliminaries. With Augusta there—certainly still in earshot,
wherever they went.

Everything about the circumstances abashed him—went against the grain. It was hardly past nine o'clock and the air was full of crisp morning sounds; bells clanking tonelessly in half a dozen belfries, street-cries, hoofbeats, alerted dogs, the clattering passage of a cart, the busy ecstasy of pigeons everywhere in space beyond the half-open window shutters against which hot yellow sun was pounding. All the world had done with the night and its passions. Love had already emptied him. He was sluggish and devitalised, the victim of conscience and satiety. And Augusta was there, not thirty feet away, asleep, he hoped, but how deeply he could not tell. Beckett wanted to put off this moment, to be allowed to prepare in his own way for the soft crepuscular grappling he had always imagined as awaiting him at the end of his pursuit. Basilisa let go his hand and he picked up his brush and added a few strokes to the canvas.

Basilisa looked up at him in perplexity, the shadow of disappointment falling near. He had made none of the overtures she had awaited with such tingling anticipation, and a dreadful doubt about the strength of her attraction for him had been born. Augusta had fallen into a drunken sleep, and the moment had come when she expected Beckett to make some further move towards the end implied in the small initiatory liberties he had allowed himself a few days before. Having fallen in love with Beckett, Basilisa saw no reason for delaying the consummation of that love. She was quite ready to be Beckett's slave. Apart from the furious juvenile maulings and couplings in the outhouse ten years earlier, Basilisa had never known love. Valentin from the day of their marriage had always been a husband, never a lover. Valentin was the archetype of a husband, slyly moderate in all things, with a refined, monastic absorption in his own affairs. Beckett had promised to be the embodiment of the lover; flamboyant, generous, and obsessed with her. Each man occupied his own niche in the opposite categories of humanity; the one in the dry mediocrity of the familiar, the other among the dangerous excitements of the unknown.

She held out a hand. Beckett put down his brush again. She pulled him closer.

'It's stiflingly hot,' she said.

Watching him, she took away the hand that had been holding the gown together at her neck, and it fell open. Beckett saw her breasts fully displayed. He had never seen breasts like them before. They were firm, smooth, long and slightly pendulous. The nipples were invisible, and in their place were dark, rounded swellings. Basilisa's breasts were the living version of those of the ebony statuette from Dahomey that squatted gloatingly on a low table nearby. So under her clothing she really *was* an African native. The spectacle was completely devoid of excitement. It was too strange. All Beckett felt was intense curiosity. Basilisa waited for him to touch or caress her, and her bewilderment deepened. Then Beckett got up, found a sheet of paper and pencil, and began his sketch.

Beckett drew for fifteen minutes, and at the end of that time he knew that this was one of the best portrait sketches he had ever done. For once in his life he had been totally successful in capturing a reality that waited, unrecognised, behind the blind windows of flesh and bone. The slight aesthetic shock, with the tiny injection of revulsion, that the sight of Basilisa's breasts had given him, seemed to have finally liberated his inspiration from the crippling habit of banality forced upon him by his means of livelihood. Beckett had drawn Basilisa quite frankly as an African, playing down what was European in her features, dwelling with enthusiasm on what he saw as her Negroid characteristics: the flare of the nostrils, achieved in a series of most delicately interlocking curves; the subtle retroversion of the top lip with the petal-like veining of the membrane beneath; the eyes, elongated, pointing like narrow spears at the temples, and clouded with the burdens of subconscious sorrows; the long gourd-shaped breasts.

She had remained seated and still, perfectly unself-conscious when she saw him put down the pencil; she was anxious to be shown the result. Beckett was embarrassed. His drawing would seem to her nothing more than an insulting caricature. He picked up the sheet of paper, held it at arm's length, shook his head at it with pretended exasperation.

' I'm sorry,' he said. ' I made a mess of it.'

She got up from her throne, insisting, and tried to take it from his hand, and he backed away from her, the drawing held behind him. When she followed him he quickly slipped the paper into a pile of sketches. Basilisa started to search the pile and he put his arm round her and dragged her away. In this instant of unsought and unpremeditated contact, the sensation of the nakedness of her twisting, struggling body heightened by its thin sheath of silk, Beckett was caught in an upsurge of sensuality. Awakened at last he tried recklessly to steer her in the direction of the curtained alcove where the disordered bed of the night before awaited. But she resisted, shaking her head and tapping her watch. He saw that hardly five minutes were left of the hour she always stayed. Beckett pleaded in whispers, searching her body with his hands for a way of breaking down her resolve, but she was firm.

Just then a groan from Augusta, as deep-throated and powerful as the sound of a man in pain, drove them apart. Augusta had rolled over to face them, and her eyes fell open, unfocused. She was genuinely ill now; prostrated by nervous tension and her disgust. Her throat had become so tight that she could hardly breathe, and her forearms and shins tingled painfully as though she were being given powerful electric shocks. Her mouth seemed to be choked with rotting fur. She levered herself to her feet, and creakingly straightened her back. Hand held over her mouth, she began to stagger towards the window. Beckett moved forward to help her, but she waved him away.

Augusta reached the window, and passed through it out on to the balcony. Her sickness had built up into a swinging tide, but she was determined not to vomit. Her heart was beating like a hammer at her ribs and sometimes between the hammer blows came a flutter that brought faintness with it. Beneath her, she had a myopic vision of the town as a white bosom decked with necklaces of streets. Black points like specks of soot danced over the whiteness of the houses. Each black point was fastened to her eyes, rocking like lead weights as she tried to focus her vision on the street below. At a corner fifty yards away she thought she could make out the figure she had hoped to see seated at a table outside a small general store.

Augusta held up her hand, waved and made a negative sign with her forefinger. Immediately a man got up and began to walk away. Augusta went to the balustrade and leaned against it, breathing in and out as deeply as she could, purifying her lungs. Then she went back into the room.

Basilisa and Beckett were finishing their leavetaking.

'Next time?' Beckett whispered. He knew that one didn't leave questions unspoken with Basilisa.

She nodded, smiling.

CHAPTER 8

Don Arturo waylaid Tur on his way home from the club, and climbed into the cab with him.

'Do you mind giving me a lift as far as my office? My car's given up the ghost.'

'Delighted,' Tur said. 'I imagine it's not often you have to fall back on the horse.'

'To tell you the truth, I'm addicted to all leisurely forms of transportation. But in these hectic times——' Don Arturo reached for his handkerchief. The ancient victoria, known affectionately to the townspeople as The Galleon, carried with it a peppery cloud of molecules released by the decaying leather that made him want to sneeze.

He blew his nose, and put the handkerchief away. How ever am I going to break it to him? he wondered again.

The old horse had blown itself up in the long hours of immobility, and now the day's first exercise was having its usual effect. Don Arturo was distracted from his purpose by an enormously prolonged and creaking deflation, which inconveniently began as soon as they reached the Mirasol. He waited for the interruption to subside.

'What on earth are they doing to that building?' Tur

asked, as soon as silence came again, and before Don
Arturo had time to speak.

' They're restoring it.'

' Restoring it to what? '

' To its original fifteenth-century condition.'

' Its fifteenth-century condition? What do they mean by
that? It didn't exist in the fifteenth century. There isn't
a house in the town that goes back to the fifteenth century,
so how do they know what a fifteenth-century house even
looked like? '

' I can only pass on what I've been told myself,' Don
Arturo said.

' And in any case, what are they going to do with it when
they've finished putting all those carved beams together? '

' It's going to be one of our principal attractions. The
Palace of Columbus.'

Tur blew out a small explosion of disgust.

' It's part of the Syndicate of Initiative's programme to
focus interest on the town's historical aspects—in the
interests of tourism, of course.'

' This town hasn't a history,' Tur said. ' Unless you call
being burned down by the Algerines a few times, having
a history. They wanted me to allow *my* house to be called the
Palace of Columbus, but I turned it down. Where, in the
first place, did they get the idea that Columbus even visited
the island? '

' From Don Fidel's history, I expect.' Don Fidel had
been Don Firmín's predecessor—a priest continually in
trouble with the Bishop for his neglect of routine duties in
the Cathedral in favour of his historical studies. These
provided the material for a number of works, all of them
inspired by an unscrupulous romanticism.

' High time we stopped going in for this kind of fraud.
In attempting to delude others, we end up by deluding
ourselves, and that's a sad business.'

'I'm entirely in agreement with you,' Don Arturo said.

'One's either a realist or one's not. As it happens, I am. It's something I can't help. I don't delude myself.'

'I think it's a very admirable state of affairs,' Don Arturo answered mechanically. He was still racking his brains as to how best to approach the painful subject that had necessitated the encounter.

'This business of tourists,' Don Arturo said, 'seems to be provoking a conflict of opinions. On the one hand you have the Governor and the Syndicate of Initiative, who seem to be prepared to go to absurd lengths to attract them. On the other hand you have the Bishop and his supporters, who would send them all packing if they had their way.' He had a brainwave. 'And apropos of that, I was wondering if you could perhaps help with a problem that's turned up?'

'I very much doubt it,' Tur said. 'We usually find ourselves on different sides of the fence when it comes to these problems of yours.'

'In the strictest confidence,' Don Arturo said, 'Don Firmín's just handed me a list of foreigners he wants action taken against. Two in particular. The first needn't concern us, because it's a most charming young lady who—alas—has already left us of her own volition. The second happens to be a tenant of yours.'

'Well?'

'Again in strict confidence, I've already had a word about this with the Governor, and he's opposed to extreme measures. That's to say he agrees with me that you don't attract people to the island with deportation orders.'

'And what does he suggest?'

'He seems to be of the opinion that it would be far more sensible simply to make things difficult for the man. He might then decide to go of his own accord.'

'And where do I come in?'

'As his landlord, you could revoke his tenancy agreement. It's almost impossible to get accommodation these days.'

' On what grounds? '

' That's entirely left to you. He's a nuisance to his neighbours, for example. We've had more than one complaint of his habit of playing his gramophone at all hours of the night.'

' I won't do it,' Tur said. ' The trouble with his Lordship and Don Firmín is that they want to turn this island into a rest home for incurables. So far as I'm concerned the man can do what he likes, so long as he pays his rent and doesn't smash up my furniture. Personally, I don't want tourists—they put up the cost of living; but let's be fair. What's his name? '

' Beckett,' Don Arturo said. ' He's regarded as a scandalous person.'

' If you listen to Don Firmín, everybody's a scandalous person. I am. You certainly are. What do you mean by scandalous? Let's get down to facts—what's the man done? Is there anything definite against him? Or is this the usual priests' twitter? '

' People are constantly seen leaving his house in a state of inebriation.'

' That's because they're English. We're just as bad, but we take care to keep out of sight.'

A bend in the road brought the canning factory into sight. Tur saw it and looked away quickly; his indignation boiled up.

' I'm simply not prepared to do anything. It's all too trivial when there are so many other things on this island that want looking into. In any case our English colony's unique. The people on Herrera may have the biggest volcanic crater in the world, but we've got our English. They're a feature of the place. As a matter of fact I'd go out of my way to make extra concessions to an English tenant, if it happened to be necessary.'

Don Arturo sighed, taking in as he did so much of The Galleon's atmosphere that he followed the sigh with two violent sneezes.

' The house in question was raided yesterday,' he said.

' A house belonging to *me* raided—what on earth for? '

' We received a report of a minor girl, alleged to have been taken there for immoral purposes. It turned out to be a false alarm.'

' Of course it did.'

' The girl proved to have been legitimately employed as a laundress.'

' What did you expect? '

' More than half the raids the police make turn out to be a waste of time,' Don Arturo said. ' The people responsible for these denunciations are only too often silly or vicious. In this case it seems to have been pure jealousy on the part of a discharged domestic. The point is that in the course of the routine search of the premises, certain things happened quite by chance to come to light which—well— we feel you should know.'

' Well, tell me then, man. Tell me.'

Tur waited while Don Arturo juggled with alternative approaches to the crux of the matter. After all, what could be the most unpleasant thing to have happened in his house —since at least it hadn't been burned down? Why, undoubtedly that Beckett—wild in the way, Tur had to admit to himself, that most foreigners were—had run amok and smashed up the furniture. In a matter of a couple of seconds while Don Arturo went through a convulsive nervous manoeuvre with his hands, shuffling the fingers as he stared down at them, then spreading them out as if to invite Tur to draw a card from a pack, Tur ran through a mental inventory of the few objects of value in the house.

The Olot bed and linen chests, painted with rosy-limbed, rustic-faced angels, winging out of heaven like a flight of pigeons; the carved romanesque saints salvaged from the ruin of a Pyrenean chapel. Tur pictured ribald, possibly obscene additions to the baroque absurdities of his decorated furniture, and the saints perhaps hacked in pieces to stoke the cooking fire. The cab jerked to a standstill. ' Ah, here we are at the station,' Don Arturo said. ' I wonder if I could trouble you to come in for a moment. There's something I should like you to see.'

Tur raised his hands, palms outwards, in a gesture of mystified submission, and followed Don Arturo into his office. ' I must say I find all this most extraordinary,' he said. ' I really don't know why you can't come to the point.'

While Don Arturo was fiddling with a bunch of keys, then unlocking a cupboard, Tur wandered round the room studying the portraits of wanted criminals, admiring the obvious qualities of resource, tenacity and originality that most of the faces seemed to him to display.

' I wanted to show you this,' Don Arturo said. He had unrolled a drawing, and now spread it out on his table top for Tur's inspection.

Tur stared down at the drawing in silence.

Am I doing the right thing after all? Don Arturo was wondering as he awaited the explosion. Some men could never allow themselves to pardon the bringer of bad news. Might he eventually soften to gratitude under the stiff incrustation of pride. Who could say? Who could say? This was all that could be expected to come out of an excess of foolish zeal. Don Arturo had instantly rewarded his corporal—and at the same time sealed his mouth—by banishing him to the island's most godforsaken village, where his energies would be properly absorbed in continuous investigations of bestiality and black magic.

' Well,' Tur said, ' and what is this supposed to be? '

'It was found by my corporal when he carried out a routine search of the house.'

Tur picked up the drawing, held it close, then at arm's length. He twisted it round, held it upside down, and laughed. 'Modern art,' he said. 'And all very well in its own way, I've no doubt at all. I suppose I've only myself to blame if I say it doesn't appeal to me. Is this young lady supposed to be anyone we know?'

Don Arturo was flabbergasted. Was he play-acting? Or couldn't he really see—bad as the picture was—who it was meant to represent? He braced himself.

'It's supposed to have some sort of resemblance to your daughter.'

Tur turned on him with amazed eyes. 'And do you think that it has?'

Don Arturo coughed into his hand, and turned coward. 'Well, hardly.'

'Why waste my time, then? Why show it to me?'

The sudden brusqueness of his tone rallied Don Arturo to a show of self-defence.

'Your daughter has been visiting this man to have her portrait painted. That we've definitely established. The corporal reported that there was a recognisable picture in a half-finished condition of her on the premises, as well as this indecent affair. The point is that the lady—whoever she is—certainly seems to be wearing your daughter's necklace. At least I'm personally under the impression that it closely resembles the one Señora Escoba was wearing at a cocktail party I attended the other day.'

'Don't be an idiot,' Tur said. 'In any case, all modern jewellery's the same.' He unrolled the drawing mechanically and glanced at it again. The necklace, he thought. The necklace. I've certainly seen one like that somewhere. Old-fashioned in fact. And rather pretty. You don't see necklaces like that every day of the week. It's the best part about the thing. He studied the face. The necklace. The face. I've seen the necklace before. I could swear I've held it in my hands. But how can that be? Can it be—? Can it be— But this is a Negress. He shut the appalling thought —this debauched parody of probability—out of his mind. A moment later he had recovered.

Firm-mouthed, Tur handed the drawing back to Don Arturo.

'Truly, my dear friend, I'm surprised at you. And may I suggest you find some discreet way of returning this to its owner.'

CHAPTER 9

Next day Tur, who had been nagged all night by returning doubts, paid a visit to his daughter. He sat sipping lemon tea, uncomfortably gripped by the haunches in a deep chair, designed for another climate, that took too much effort to get out of. He watched Basilisa bustle about the room. She was nervous, highly-strung, continuously manufacturing excuses to be on the move. Tur was consoled by this wholly nordic aptitude for unrest, and at the same time the sight added a little to the sensation of fatigue always induced by these surroundings. This house was the showcase of restless lives. So much in this seemed to gesticulate at him, to demand attention. Sitting there, Tur had an illusion of the distant growl of traffic, of the presence of crowds rooting endlessly, like truffle-hunting pigs, after motives for action. Tur had only to visit Basilisa to realise that age had readmitted him to the cloister of the traditional Vedran existence. Ah, for a house like his own, graciously and majestically void, aflow with rivers of dim light, a carapace for a tiring human body and soul.

Basilisa had jumped to her feet once again to bring him an English magazine from the rack. The ship had brought a fresh bundle for her the day before. The magazine

contained a photograph of a girl she had been at school with,
who, still seemingly in her late teens, bony-faced and boyish,
appeared at the back of a well-dressed group of people round
a buffet. They were all smiling widely at the photographer,
and several of them were making a gay pretence of raising
food-laden forks to their mouths. With a second or two of
nostalgic rejuvenation Tur realised that the rich scent of the
paper had remained preserved in his memory for at least
forty years. Dutifully he read the genial, low-brow commen-
tary. Basilisa kept up with all these distant triumphs of
her friends.

' Does the name of Beckett mean anything to you, dear? '
Tur asked.

' Very much,' she said. ' You mean the painter, don't
you? He's the man who's painting my portrait.'

Tur tripped over his thoughts. Minutes seemed to pass.
' I don't seem to remember your telling me about it.'

' Didn't I? '

He watched her expression. She seemed quite unconcerned. ' A surprise for your husband, I suppose? ' Tur
said.

' No,' she said. ' It was his own idea. Everyone has to be
painted by Beckett these days. It's all since the article
about him appeared in *Blanco y Negro*. I expect you saw it.
All the girls at the club are having their pictures done now,
before the prices go up.'

Tur rushed to seize the small hope of escape from his
prison of suspicions and doubt. Couldn't the drawing
possibly be of someone else after all? There were half a
dozen dark, extremely exotic-looking girls whose husbands
took them to the English Club.

' What were you going to say about Beckett? ' Basilisa
asked.

' It appears he lives in one of my houses,' Tur said. ' He's
managed to make himself unpopular with the neighbours

in some way. I'm having pressure put on me to cancel his tenancy agreement.'

' How disgusting some people can be. What are you going to do about it? '

' Nothing,' Tur said.

' I'm glad,' she said. ' It's only jealousy.'

' Jealousy? ' he said quickly. ' Why jealousy? '

' Oh, I don't know. People are like that. They go behind other people's backs.'

' Yes,' Tur said, ' I'm afraid it's one of our less pleasant characteristics here. You don't know anything to his detriment, I suppose? '

' No,' she said. ' I don't know anything about him. He's a painter, that's all. He's quite nice.'

' Is he a good painter? ' Tur said. ' I mean a really good painter? '

' They all say so,' Basilisa said. ' I think he's good too. You'll be able to judge for yourself when you see the result.'

' He's a lucky man. I can think of worse ways to spend a life than painting pretty girls.'

' He makes you look very romantic,' Basilisa said. ' That's probably half the attraction. I'm a Venetian princess, against a background of the Grand Canal. And gondolas.'

' That's a charming idea,' Tur said. ' I'm sure you'd have made a most attractive Venetian princess, my dear.' A white skin, he thought. Olive at most, if she exposes herself too long in the sun. More typical of a classic Italian style of beauty than Spanish, he would have said. Beckett was obviously no fool. Italy was the land of romance for Tur. As a background to his relief there was a feeling of shame that he should have allowed his faith in his daughter to be so easily shaken. Can I be a naturally suspicious man? he wondered. He made a pact with himself that he would never again harbour even the hint of such a cruel, libellous doubt about his daughter.

' I'm being painted in a wonderful old gown,' she said.
' A real Venetian one. I'm wearing all my jewellery. All
my rings and bracelets. I know it sounds vulgar, but actually
it isn't, because it's all in period.'

' Of course,' Tur said. ' They went in for a great deal of
display in those days. Especially the Italians. They weren't
afraid of magnificence.'

' Remember the necklace you gave me for my eighteenth
birthday? I'm wearing that too.'

' The necklace? ' Tur said.

' You brought it back from Lisbon. The pearl one.
Don't you remember. That very delicate necklace. It's
always been my favourite.'

Tur, half-dazed, feeling a sensation of concussion as if
from a blow, had not heard the last sentence.

' The pearl necklace. You must remember it. All the
pearls were in little separate pendants.'

' I recall buying you a necklace,' Tur said, ' but no more
than that. It's a long time ago now. I'd like to refresh my
memory, if you can put your hand on it easily——'

' I can't show it to you now,' Basilisa said, ' because it's
at the jeweller's. A pearl fell out of its setting. I was terribly
lucky to find it. I'm going to have all the settings
tightened up.'

' Yes,' he said. ' That's a wise precaution.' But she's
always taken after her mother, he was thinking. After her
mother, not after me. Certainly not after her grandmother.
Absolutely not. There's not the slightest possible similarity
anywhere. ' Tell me,' he asked, ' is Augusta here? '

' She's about the house somewhere. Probably working
in her room.'

' How do you and she get along these days? '

Basilisa made a face. ' You know my views on the subject
of Augusta. Why—do you want to see her? '

' No,' he said. ' I don't want to see her . . . When did you say Valentin would be back? '

' Tomorrow. He's staying at the *fonda* on the estate.' How strangely he's behaving suddenly, she thought.

' Tomorrow afternoon? Tomorrow night? '

' I'm sure I don't know. I never expect him to give me an account of himself. If he's not home tomorrow it will be the next day. Is there anything wrong, then? '

Tur put down the cup and saucer and levered himself to his feet.

' No, dear, there's nothing wrong. I want to see him about some business, that's all. But it's nothing of importance. It can perfectly well wait.'

Tur's visit to the jeweller's was made under the excuse of asking for the bill for the repair of his daughter's necklace to be sent to him. He had the opportunity of confirming his fears. He then set out immediately for his estate in Sagral. This was Tur's normal reaction at a time of crisis: to go off without warning, to cut himself off from his daily affairs and bury himself in the depths of the countryside where he could be alone with the situation whatever it was, and either learn how to live with it, or work out a plan for mastering it, as the case might be.

A taxi took him the first three miles, which was as far as the road went. Here he too became the victim of the dead hand of his own family in the matter of island communications. From this point one either walked, rode a bicycle as the peasants now did, or hired the services of hammock-men in the medieval style which had fallen into disuse in the other islands for hundreds of years. The trouble was that even the hammock-men had felt the lure of town life and were now scarce, so that the villages of the interior were more isolated now than ever. On this occasion all the hammock-men were away, having by coincidence been engaged earlier that day by three other travellers to the Sagral area. Tur waited in the farmhouse at the end of the road through the heat of the afternoon, and at five o'clock, as the hammock-men had not returned, he set out to walk the four miles to Sagral.

The heat was still intense and the path rock-strewn, steep and shadeless, but Tur, obsessed by considerations of destiny and survival, hardly noticed these things. His feeling was that his future had been amputated—or rather something infinitely more than his future—the future of his family. Until this moment he had held on tenaciously to a last shred of hope that Basilisa might some day have a child, but now he gave in, obliged to admit to himself that there could be nothing but hatred between her and her husband by the time she had done what she had done. So there remained one alternative, now both urgent and unavoidable, if his line was to be saved. He must recognise Toniet as his son.

This business of the survival of the family, Tur thought, was an instinct. It was the substitute for self-perpetuation in a man like himself, who had remained instinctively unresponsive to religious doctrine, and who rejected the idea of the survival after death of the human personality as both crude and incredible. This flimsy, incoherent ancestor-worship of the Turs seemed immensely more real and solid to him than the feebly-coloured, unimaginative fictions of Purgatory and Paradise. He must act, act now, to fight off the silence and oblivion that threatened him. Otherwise his family would vanish. Within twenty years all the streets and squares called Tur would be renamed after the politicians of the day. Within another twenty years, if not before, his beautiful old wooden ships would long have been dismembered in the breaker's yard. By the end of the century the Tur Hospital and School would be pulled down and replaced by the impersonal buildings of the future. In the end his name would survive only in the hasty, perfunctory professional mumblings of the tired nuns of the Convent of the Assumption—the annual mass paid for by a foundation established by one of his ancestors. And the Turs would have returned to the dark textureless humus of humanity from which they emerged.

Tur was decided on his course now. He would claim Toniet as his son without further delay, and he would settle on him his estate in the Salina—the Salina, because although it might be virtually unproductive of revenues, it was also devoid of problems. There were no ancient, inherited, and never-settled legal disputes, no squabbling share-croppers, no trouble over water—there being no water—no boundaries, no rights within rights, no taxes to be paid. The lord of the Salina pocketed the few pesetas the peasants paid to graze their animals there in spring, and turned his back on the place for the rest of the year. A settlement of land was a necessary accompaniment to an act of recognition. Tur would see about a provision of remunerative land— land that would keep a man and his family in comfortable style—at some later stage, when the lawyers had had time to unpick some of the legal tangles.

He reached Sagral, tired out, his clothes and skin clogged with dust, shortly before sunset. Sagral was a matter of white-washed walls bespattered with the yellow stains of sunflowers, an inn, a church, silence and heat. Tur kicked away the last of the baleful dogs that had trailed him through the village and limped into the inn. The innkeeper, a double of the amiable soak on the extreme left of the quartet in Velazquez's painting, 'The Drunkards', came rushing out of the black bowels of the inn to kiss his hand, and then fell on his knees to take off Tur's boots. Nothing had changed

at the inn of Sagral for three or four hundred years. The
occasional guest was still called ' Your Grace ' and enveloped
in a great unproductive flurry of medieval servility. The
innkeeper scuttled ahead of Tur, leading the way to his room,
shouting ' Water for Don Flavio! A towel for Don
Flavio! . . Muck on God, where's the maid? ' Presently the
maid, dirty-faced and giggling, brought him half a pint of
amber-coloured liquid in a jar, a ragged-edged cloth, and a
slab of green pumice soap. Later when Tur groped his way
into a nearby thistle patch to relieve himself, he noticed that
the inn radiated a perfume of unwashed bodies. He was
already feeling rested and refreshed, and was able to make
allowances for this. Water was as precious as wine in Sagral
at this time of year.

By the time Tur sat down to supper he had fully recovered,
and was ready to tackle whatever the Middle Ages had to
offer. The meal was a huge anonymous bone, swimming in
greasy liquid, to which some stringy meat adhered. Probably
camel, Tur thought. He knew that in Sagral no peasant
could afford to let a worn-out camel die a natural death.
Tur champed away philosophically, resolutely entering
into the spirit of the thing; pretending that he enjoyed the
new, cloudy wine tasting of the goatskin in which it had
been kept; carelessly flicking cockroaches off the table.

Peasants were playing cards or ludo in an adjoining room.
The people of Sagral and of all the other villages in this
part of the island were passionate gamblers, and Tur had
been informed that they sometimes staked their houses and
even their wives on the turn of a card. He knew by
experience that they staged tremendous scenes in the inn
every night, accusing each other, with terrible oaths and
menaces, of cheating. Soon Tur heard them beating on the
table top with their fists and howling blasphemies at each
other. It was nothing, he knew. Nothing more than a
nightly letting off of steam, the natural reaction to lives of

excessive predictability, when—outside the hazards of
sickness—people knew exactly what was going to happen to
them day by day and week by week, and so on, without
variation, year in and out, until the end of their days. Sagral
was a place where people still rushed out of doors, clutching
at each other, to see a plane fly over, and Tur remembered
that when about fifteen years previously a villager had come
back one day from Vedra with a battery-operated wireless
set and had switched it on for the first time, he had later
been stoned for having dealings with the Devil.

And yet people lived here, as Tur believed that Providence
had intended they should live. They built their houses
with their own hands, clothed, fed, and more or less governed
and policed themselves, without outside assistance. Hard
work kept them pure in heart. The people of Sagral asked
help from no one, drank their own piss for the jaundice,
cured their children's coughs with soup made from rats,
married late to keep the size of their families down—and
in this way kept real hunger at bay. Tur admired their
wonderful natural cunning, their malicious humour masked
by a fake simplicity. He was always coming across sly old
fellows who pretended to believe that the nation's watchword coined by His Excellency, was not ' United, Great,
Free', but ' A Great Hare', which, admitting the fact that
libre became distorted to *liebre* by the local accent, was an
excusable error in a half-wit. ' We're all great hares these
days,' they would say, grinning and winking. The hare
was thought of as the most stupid of animals. There was
no doubt about it, Tur thought, these people were as much
a product of their surroundings as the laurel forests that
once covered the island had been.

He sat for an hour after his supper drinking enough of the
goaty wine to ensure that sleep would come easily, then he
went to bed. The bugs that had been waiting to feed on his
blood came trooping out of the cracks in the wall-plaster,

but Tur, who kept his own private supply of insect powder at the inn, was ready for them. He killed a dozen moths as big as bats that were flapping about the room. Then he got into bed and blew out the lamp.

Beneath him, through the floor, he heard the peasants crashing about, kicking the furniture over and screaming at each other.

How they enjoy themselves, he thought with envy.

CHAPTER 10

I N the morning a deputation of villagers wanted to see Tur. This was a normal feature of his visits to Sagral. The peasants manufactured quarrels as another device to relieve the tedium of their lives. Most of the peasantry belonging to the seven small villages in the neighbourhood were tied economically to Tur's interests in one way or another, and they lost no opportunity of calling Tur in to arbitrate in these inter-village squabbles that took the place of theatre, cinema, club and popular press.

Tur surveyed the assemblage genially, fascinated as ever by their wild, eager, tribal faces, enlivened by malice and cunning. Each man reeked of the sweat or of the dung of the animals he lived among; of pigs, goats, camels, hens, more frequently of the guinea-pigs the peasants bred in cages in their living-rooms for conversion into stews on high feast-days. It amused Tur to play mental tricks with people's appearances. In his imagination, he padded their hard bodies with fat, hung jowls from lean jaws, filled in the hollows under cheekbones with pouchy cheeks coloured with a purpled suffusion suggestive of blood pressure, and finally clapped round paunches over each iron-muscled stomach.

Instantly he had turned them into members of His Excellency's cabinet. He was delighted.

The complaint was that the peasants of the nearby village of Hondos had killed all the hunting dogs of Sagral by the cheap, effective, and prevalent method of leaving out for them sea-sponges that had first been dried and then fried in olive oil. The Vedrans had a superstitious aversion to killing dogs by outright violence; in this case the dog's stomach burst some hours after its meal, as a result of the sponge's swelling up as it filled with the digestive juices. There were, as usual, two sides to the story. Tur soon found out the people of Hondos had taken action in revenge for a trick played on them by those of Sagral. They had been taking a body to the cemetery for burial, and instead of going by road, had cut across land cultivated by their neighbours, thus creating in perpetuity a sacred right of way.

Tur thoroughly enjoyed occupying himself—or pretending to occupy himself—with these trivialities. But his good humour was destroyed by one single disturbing fact that came out of this meeting. An independent peasant, one of the rare small freeholders in the Sagral district, had acquired a tractor, and immediately—as Tur would have foreseen—the balance of nature had been upset. He was flabbergasted. A disquieting rumour had already reached him of a shipment of agricultural machinery observed to have been dumped on the quayside from the holds of the *Almirante Cervera*, but Tur had not believed it possible that any of this could have been within reach of a peasant's pocket. The villagers explained what had happened. The man had been given three years' credit by a company called La Palomita, whose agents had been going round the villages. Most of the men who made up this deputation were share-croppers of Tur's, and now, shiftily, ready to cringe, yet with a suggestion of a new, impudent confidence in their manner Tur had never noticed before, they wanted to know if he were prepared to do something to help them get tractors too.

He dismissed them wrathfully, afterwards regretting his abruptness. There was no one to open their eyes, to show them the world as it was, to make them see how much better off they were as they were. They were eager to become the victims of usurers, of the financial bloodsuckers who were a feature of modern times. For once in his life Tur remembered with affection an aspect of the Inquisition's work. The Inquisition would have known how to deal with people who lent out money on usury and deluded peasants into spending three years in paying for a tractor—which in any case, would be quite wasted on a field the size of a pocket handkerchief.

This business about the tractor put Tur in mind once again of the present wave of what he called ' desertions ', and now he was at Sagral he decided to take the opportunity to see whether there was anything that he, personally, could do to halt the process.

The villages of the interior of Vedra had always been famous—even on the mainland—for their clairvoyants, who combined their practice of the occult with a valuable specialisation in a whole range of psychosomatic illnesses; in particular conditions of the skin, headaches, melancholia, and the locally endemic nymphomania. They had survived five hundred years of energetic opposition on the part of the Church, but in recent years had come to suffer severely from the competition of a hereditary caste of water bailiffs. The primary function of these men was to apportion communal water supplies, but they had successively set themselves up as adjudicators in inheritance disputes, and from that become money-lenders, and even dabblers in the black arts on their own account. Tur had always been impressed by the old clairvoyant of Sagral, notwithstanding her occasional failures, and, a little shamefacedly, he sometimes consulted

her on his family problems. If he had any soul at all, Tur
knew that this woman looked into it. He had often used his
influence, throwing in his weight on the side of Don Arturo's
natural apathy to any form of action, to protect her from the
attacks of Don Firmín. In return, the clairvoyant had shown
her gratitude by working on the superstitions of the peasants'
wives to keep their husbands' noses to the grindstone. But
now, after a reign of twenty years, in which she had defied
the local priest, the Bishop, and latterly even the energetic
Don Firmín, this woman's prestige had been shattered
overnight by a singular circumstance. She had sold at its
face value of twelve pesetas and fifty centimos the tenth part
of a lottery ticket which had won a million-peseta prize.
Disillusioned by this evidence of the collapse of her
premonitory powers, her supporters had deserted her. Tur
lost a powerful supporter, and the process initiated by the
ship and the original cargo of bicycles began to speed up.
In the ordinary course of things the natural ally to whom
Tur would now have turned should have been the priest,
Don Claudio, but as it happened this extraordinary man
could be expected to do nothing to advance his cause. Don
Claudio was virtually a dwarf, and when he had first been
sent by the Bishop to Sagral, the villagers, regarding themselves as slighted, had refused to accept him. They sent a
petition to the Bishop, but asked to be allowed to withdraw
this as soon as they found that Don Claudio lived openly with
a mistress. Peasants who had previously never allowed their
wives to go to confession for fear of exposing them to the
inflamed sexuality of a celibate priest, relented with Don
Claudio. Don Claudio also announced as soon as he arrived
that he proposed to earn his keep like any other man and,
taking off his cassock, he worked in the fields with the
peasants when labour was short. His sermons were poor,
bluff and short. These, and other actions and attitudes
had earned him the reputation, not only in Sagral but in

half a dozen neighbouring villages, for something like
sanctity. Tur toyed for a moment with the idea of going and
looking Don Claudio out. He knew that he could expect to
find him not in church but in a field somewhere, helping to
drill a well, or keeping an eye on someone's pigs, and that
Don Claudio would wipe his hands on his thighs with the
intention of shaking hands with him, and then change his
mind. It was a piece of intolerably bad luck that the one
priest on the island, perhaps in the whole country, who would
never in any circumstances side with a landlord, should
control the spiritual welfare of so many of *his* peasants. Tur
decided to keep out of Don Claudio's way.

Instead he went to see the water bailiff, and found—
as he assumed would be the case—that this man had quickly
stepped into the shoes of the deposed clairvoyant. He
turned out to be a surly fellow who didn't even trouble to
remove his hat to receive his visitor. Tur recognised him
immediately as an opportunist and a mountebank, who had
seized his chance to take over a ready-made business for
which he lacked any possible qualification. Where his
predecessor had been subtle, and in some ways disturbingly
convincing—even to Tur—in the manipulation of the stage
properties of her trade, the new incumbent was merely crude.
He had nailed a chart up on the wall of the kind one saw
outside the booths of fortune-tellers at village fairs. This
showed a plan of a huge, bald, human head, drawn in
profile in violet ink, the whole area of the cranium being
ruled out in sharp divisions in which mental and emotional
attributes, such as intelligence and malice, had been stacked
in containers like the hams and cheeses in a grocer's store-
room. But there was a more sinister addition to the room's
decoration in the form of a presentation calendar issued by
—for Tur—that now baleful enterprise, La Palomita, which
depicted a dove carrying in its bill an olive branch, to which
several one-thousand-peseta notes had been pinned. Along-

side the calendar was a framed certificate announcing that the man had been appointed agent of the company. Tur realised that he could abandon hope of any co-operation in this direction.

The purpose of Tur's visit—in so far as there had been a purpose—having failed, he borrowed a mule from the innkeeper, proposing to make the best of what was left of the morning by riding to his estate, the Salina.

Within a few minutes of leaving the village, the cultivated fields began to get smaller and stonier, and bamboos, half-throttled by the blue and purple trumpets of morning glory, began to oust the maize and the beans from the landscape. He soon reached the point where the peasants had given up the struggle against the black sands of the Salina. Thereafter it was all wilderness. In winter the Salina was turned for a few weeks into stinking, saline morass, in which the Turs for generations had been willing to feed the mosquitoes with their blood in the hope of shooting a few brace of duck. In summer, it was the Sahara in miniature, complete with wind-blown dunes of blackish sand, and gristly, desperate vegetation of spine-armed bushes. Coming in sight of it, Tur found it hard, once again, to understand what could have induced Valentin to agree to a share in this desert providing the bulk of Basilisa's dowry.

In the remote past the Salina might have had some value, as it had been wooded and fertile. Tur had read an account of the area by one of the island's conquerors—an account now preserved in the town's archives. This man, a Breton soldier of fortune, had in fact described that part of the island now called the Salina as being covered by the densest forest he had ever seen. His mention of the fact arose out of a catalogue of the difficulties he and his companions had encountered in their work of exterminating the aboriginal inhabitants. Unable to ride their horses into the trees in pursuit of the fleeing Guanches, the conquerors had burned the forest down, to produce the Salina in its present form. In other parts of Tur's estates which he had thought fit to leave uncultivated, the peasants had come closing in, moving the boundary stones a few feet a year in the way they did— 'digesting' the land was their expression for the process. But there was no water—everybody knew there was no water—so they kept away. They had never troubled him, not even in the last days of the Republic, when so many landowners' lives had been made unbearable by the encroachments and occupations of the peasants. But Tur knew that had the Republic been allowed to survive, there would have been trouble sooner or later. It would only have been a matter of time.

Tur urged his mule up a track leading to the summit of a small hill, from which he expected to be able to see any signs of human activity for a radius of several miles. He was entranced by the inhumanity of the scene, and proud and happy that this should have been part of his patrimony. Fresh from the sterile order of the town, Tur could not remember ever having been so impressed before by this majestic desolation. Whirlwinds, like skulking ghosts wrapped in cere-cloths of black dust, wandered hither and thither across the landscape, materialising, moving away, vanishing again. An outrageous sun had scourged the earth, reduced leaf and branch to ashes, and even the fertile, leafy soil he knew must once have been there, to crackling, briny grit. Even the sky had a bruised and scrofulous look, yet this scene composed of iron, coal and emeralds and jagged stone, quivered like flesh with the fierce vibrating life poured into it by the sun. Five miles away at the edge of the

black land, the sea was like a bar of molten metal. Two or
three camels were coming up from the shore, looking
like pale insects on a dark, rumpled, mangy hide. Tur knew
that they would be laden with seaweed—the only fertiliser
ever used on Vedran land. To be the master of these empty
acres gave Tur a momentary surge almost of ecstasy. It
was like possessing an unscaleable peak, remote and undefil-
able. There's nothing like this anywhere in the world, he
thought. And it's ours.

It was for such possessions, Tur thought, that wars were
fought—their own war included. It had not been fought
in support of His Excellency's watchword for the nation,
because the country had been as free and as united at that
time as it had ever been—freedom and unity didn't come
into it. As for the greatness—well, that had long since
departed for ever, as anybody but a complete fool would
admit. The war had been fought, in Tur's opinion, in
defence of several hundred Salinas, for the glory of
indomitable acres that stood out against the processes that
turned a country into a mixture of slag-heaps and cabbage
patches. The men on Tur's side, in Tur's view, had shed
their blood not for ideologies—whether of Dr. Goebbels and
Rosenberg, or of Karl Marx—but for a past they loved, for
a country freed from the shadow of agrarian reform laws,
for a Spain where the rivers were still full of fish, where there
were bears in the mountains, and the eagle and the fox had
the right to exist.

Suddenly he felt faint. The heat, he thought. He had
hardly noticed it, yet here in the shadeless fury of the sun,
it must have been almost beyond endurance. There wasn't
a tree, not even a bush that could offer a square foot of shade
for miles, and the wind coming in puffs from the direction
of the African shore was like the heat released from the open
door of a furnace. Tur took a mouthful of foul-tasting water
from his bottle, turned his mule's head, and began the ride

back to the inn. By the time he arrived it was nearly midday, and the first thing he saw was his son-in-law, Valentin, at a table which had been brought out and stood in the shade of a huge old vine. Two strangers were with him, and as Tur rode up, the three men rose politely from their seats.

The innkeeper came out and took away Tur's mule and he sat down. He was not in the slightest surprised to see his son-in-law. Tur had developed premonitions where Valentin was concerned. The two men were introduced: Piercey, Griffin—Englishmen. One of them was large and nimble, sandy-moustached, skipping like a boxer as he went for a chair, one of those men, Tur judged, who had mastered the art of concealing purpose with affability. The other wore a beard like a coconut on a strange jaw that flapped open and then shut abruptly whenever he spoke. Tur immediately assumed that these interlopers were travelling representatives of the nefarious La Palomita—doubtlessly engaged in laying some dark scheme with Valentin.

The feeling Valentin gave Tur—whenever he saw him—and which at this moment he felt with exceptional acuteness—reminded him of the sensation he experienced at the sight of a beautiful snake. Tur admired snakes but had always been prevented from developing a wholehearted affection for them by one troubling thought—poisonous or not? Was Valentin an enemy? Tur's intuition told him that he was. Valentin sat there, sipping his raspberry-flavoured mineral water, not thinking, Tur believed, in the way other men did, but deep in cogitation beneath a shallow pretence of attention; dressed and manicured like a Greek shipping millionaire; dark-spectacled eyes readily alerted; almost certainly in alliance with La Palomita.

' You're the agricultural machinery people, aren't you? ' Tur asked Piercey.

' Well, not quite,' Piercey said. ' They're chums of ours, of course. Another division of the organisation. All part

of the same parent company—Morgan's. I expect you've
heard of us. Rio Santo. We're in the estate business.' He
bubbled a routine laugh under the sandy moustache.

Rio Santo. Now Tur remembered. It was the company
who wanted to buy his land and—of course—they had
written once again, asking him to see two of their representatives arriving by the ship that had docked on the previous
day.

'We got in yesterday from Las Palmas,' Griffin said.
'Just having a look-see. Señor Escoba's been kind enough
to take us under his wing.'

Tur knew what it was Griffin reminded him of—a
ventriloquist's dummy. He had a dummy's goggling eyes
and high-pitched voice, as well as the strange, snapping,
lower jaw.

'Most fortunately for us,' Piercey added, with another
laugh.

Valentin, the man all the foreigners went to first, Tur
thought. Known as ' the lucky one ' back in his own village
in the old peasant days. Lucky in the first place because in
the lottery conducted for the division of the family property
at his father's death, he had drawn the only field with a
well, and then, finding the strength to turn his back on his
brothers' and sisters' entreaties for water, had soon been able
to take over their land too, for a few pesetas. And what
of it? All Valentin had done so far as Tur was concerned was
to demonstrate that he had purified himself from sentimental
servilities implanted in childhood. Tur could appreciate
these ferocious transactions straight out of the Old Testament
for what they were worth—the trickeries which it only
needed success and the passage of a little time to hallow.
Great names were founded in great treacheries. Hadn't
the man commonly known as the country's second citizen,
the patron and protector of the arts, the sciences and the
Church, the financier of His Excellency's Movement, started

life as a tobacco smuggler? Hadn't Don Nemesio, his ancestor, the second citizen of his own day, made his money feeding his country's enemies? It was not this aspect of Valentin's character that puzzled him.

'A wonderful, wonderful place,' Piercey said. 'I was saying to your son-in-law, I can see it becoming another Capri. It's got everything that Capri's got, and a great deal that it hasn't.'

'Except that it's too far from the centre of things,' Tur said. 'If you're referring to this island and its attractions.'

Valentin spoke in English. 'But then in ten years' time, distances will mean very little.' He had a soft voice, but people listened to him. Nobody ever interrupted Valentin. Recently he had developed a mannerism much disliked by Tur of putting his point of view, then looking from face to face of those present, as if to exact a tribute of assent from each member of his audience in turn.

'After all, we're annihilating space,' Valentin said gently. Tourism, he was thinking. The greatest industry of the future. His thoughts automatically switched to German, for Valentin was an excellent linguist, and English was the language of business, but German of tourism. *Romantische Zigeunerfeste mit Gitarenmusik, Stierkämpfe, Ferienhäuschen mit herrlichem Aussicht zu vermieten.*

'Absolutely right. The world's shrinking every day,' Griffin quacked. Tur saw that he had transferred himself for the moment to a new ventriloquist.

'In a few years' time no place on earth will be more than two or three hours from one of the great centres of population,' Valentin said. And, for the adventurous spirit of course: *Tropfsteinhohlenerforschung, Unterwasser Fischerei, Wasserski, Tintenfischfang bei Nacht im Lampenlicht.*

'No trouble at all in putting this place on the map,' Griffin said. 'Given the right publicity.'

Tur, still a little dizzy, had lost touch with the argument.

He shifted his chair farther into the shade of the vine, and drank a little water mixed with red wine.

'But at present it's remote,' Tur said, 'and we may as well face it—undeniably primitive.' He invited them with a gesture of deprecation, hoping there was no trace of a smile on his face, to examine their surroundings. Sagral, elbowed into its cramped corner of the landscape by the vast emptiness of the Salina, was busy in its usual rustic fashion with its affairs. A peasant woman sat at the door of her hut, carefully, almost lovingly disjointing the wings of live chickens, for easier transport to the market. Monkey-faced children were playing in the street nearby with a croaking, terrified bird they had captured and tied by the leg. Half a field away, an old farmer dragged a train of luminous dust after a plough from Ur of the Chaldees. Through the sharp scent of the geraniums in their pots all round the inn, Tur caught an occasional sour, earthy whiff, recognisable to him as the odour of human excrement, sun-rotted almost to humus.

'Primitive,' Piercey said, 'but that's just the point. That's what people are looking for these days. That's what they're prepared to pay for. Everything's absolutely perfect here. Just as it is. Don't let anybody touch it, though. Above all, don't let anybody touch it.'

Griffin let out a sudden squawk. 'A camel.'

A camel, mountainously piled with its load of seaweed, had just come into sight from between the houses. It plodded towards them and passed, grunting with ill-humour, and with a clicking of arthritic joints. It was a scrofulous beast, and the skin, rucked loosely under its patchy, moulting hair, and its bulging, bloodshot eyes, gave Tur an impression of evil senility. Tur was more interested in the peasant with the camel than the animal itself. He had a sun-blackened face and a mad expression, and his lips were drawn back from his mouth exposing his teeth permanently, reminding

Tur of the most valuable example in his collection of Guanche mummies. Seaweed collectors were the lowest of the island castes, the knowledge of whose existence injected a flavour of privilege into the otherwise total humility of the peasants.

The Englishmen watched the passing by of these two untouchables with the excitement of children at the zoo.

' Camels in Europe,' Piercey said. ' I suppose this does count as Europe? Just imagine that. Camels—and being carried about in a hammock. All you need here is an airfield, and the tourists will start pouring in by the thousand. Wouldn't you say so, Griffin? '

' I would,' Griffin said. ' I would indeed.'

Tur, troubled by waves of dizziness and even more by the onset of a vague nausea, could still appreciate the irony of the situation. Now a pass had been reached when the obstacles he had so carefully set up against the world's intrusion on his peace had been transformed into attractions. The reaction had set in. People had had enough of being coddled in the upholstered guts of their motor-cars, and they were actually on the look-out for holes and corners like this, where they could surrender themselves to the night of the Middle Ages. Suddenly he lost patience. What did they want with him? What was Valentin up to with these fellows? They hadn't come to sell tractors. The estate office, Piercey had said. That meant land, didn't it? They were nosing round after land. But whose land?

Piercey appeared to read his mind.

' I'm under the impression some correspondence has passed between you and the company, sir.'

' What company? ' Tur said peevishly. ' I don't understand all this business about divisions and sub-divisions. What is your company? What does it do? '

' It's really quite simple,' Piercey said, ' although it all sounds dashed confusing. We're Rio Santo. We were

originally spawned off by Morgan's—that's the parent
company of the group—to take care of the property side.
In other words, to acquire suitable agricultural properties.
The basic idea, of course, is to secure outlets for Morgan's
fertilisers—but I needn't enter into that.'

'And what's your company's real interest in acquiring
my land? As an outlet for fertilisers?'

'The parent company's possibly—in a somewhat indirect
way. Our own is more complex. As you know, we're
connected with La Palomita—through a recent takeover.'

'What's the relationship in this case?'

'The relationship? Ah well, now, that's a little difficult.
Theoretically they'd be considered a subsidiary of ours, but
owing to the reconstituted financial structure of the
company, there's been rather a shift in the centre of gravity
and inevitably a reslant in policy.' Piercey produced the
gestures of a man running his hand over a fine piece of
sculpture. 'Consequent upon this—at least for the moment
—we're in the position of being harnessed to La Palomita's
chariot. In other words, a case of the tail wagging the dog.
Of course it isn't half so complicated as it sounds.'

'I haven't replied to any of your company's letters,' Tur
said.

'Of course not,' Piercey said equably.

'In the first place because I rarely reply to letters.'

'Not at all a bad idea. I'd have done the same thing in
your case.'

'—Secondly because their proposition isn't of the slightest
interest.'

Piercey shook his head. 'I wonder if that's quite what
you mean?'

'I assure you it is,' Tur said.

'The way I see it is, it's not a bad thing to keep them
waiting. In fact, it's an excellent thing. It helps to wean
them from the highly erroneous point of view that they can

always expect to have things their own way. Don't you think so, Griffin?'

'I do,' Griffin said. 'They get above themselves. Up in the bloody stratosphere half the time.'

'Personally,' Piercey said, 'I feel the greatest respect and admiration for someone who stands up to them. It's better for us all. May I make a suggestion?'

'Please do, if you wish,' Tur said. He had a strange sensation of being detached from the conversation, while being able to register in a mechanical fashion what was being said—which, in any case, was not of the slightest importance.

'My suggestion,' Piercey said, 'is simply this—that when you're ready—assuming you do have second thoughts —you get in touch with me personally. It's the personal touch that counts. Quite frankly, between you and me and the gate-post, half the trouble with organisations of the type that provide Griffin and me with our daily bread is this lack of contact between individuals. One tends to feel oneself too much at the mercy of the machine.'

Tur, breathing deeply, as if to draw some of the vine arbour's shade into his dry lungs, found that the trend of the argument had slipped away from him again. What were they talking about now? Why did they go on like that?

The innkeeper's gargoyle face appeared, fixed on to the black opening of the inn's doorway. Ice, Tur thought. Ice for my forehead; and then remembered they were in Sagral. Ice was a precious rarity in Vedra itself. He called the innkeeper over, and told him to bring a cloth soaked in vinegar.

He found himself staring at Valentin. Their eyes met— Valentin's mild and unchallenging. Valentin's lips were moving slightly as if in silent prayer, or perhaps in some mathematical calculation: two blocks of flats—three rooms —usual offices—mains water supply (intermittent in summer), equals one soap factory plus three sailing barges. From this subtract the island's total independent tomato crop purchased speculatively in advance, and what do you have? And what do you do with it when you have it? . . . Shall I tackle him about the picture now? Tur wondered. And if so, how best to approach the question noncommittally, so as not to incite or increase his suspicions. " But do you find that modern art awakens any real response in you? For myself, I must confess it's not always easy to understand the artist's intentions." *The artist's intentions.*

Tur's imagination had successively placed Don Firmín's head and then the Bishop's head on Valentin's shoulders. Valentin was essentially sacerdotal. Of the two heads, the Bishop's—had it been possible to rejuvenate it by thirty years and to restore the vagrant reason to the eyes—would have suited him better. Valentin's voice at all times resembled that of the Bishop, recalling in particular the vague, abstract charity of the Bishop's pronouncement of the benediction.

'. . . by no means,' he heard Valentin say. ' At least, for my part, I can't see any objection. There's nothing to be gained or lost. I expect Don Flavio feels very much as I do about it.'

' About what? ' Tur asked.

' Mr. Piercey has just made a suggestion that one or two test borings for water might be carried out here and there. Even though we're not ready to talk business, there can't really be any objection.'

' There is an objection,' Tur said. ' And a very strong one.' The innkeeper appeared with a vinegar-soaked cloth, and Tur took it from him, and clapped it on his forehead.

' I've already made it perfectly plain to these gentlemen that they're wasting their time,' Valentin said. ' Still, if they like to throw their money away——'

' It's not only a waste of time, it's an act of aggression.'

Valentin's motives were suddenly clear to Tur in every detail. He felt slightly drunk, and, whatever it was, this semi-intoxication seemed to have promoted an interlude of exceptional mental clarity. Valentin—he could see it now—was plotting to get his hands on Basilisa's dowry, and to sell it. This purpose could be achieved if there were to be a legal separation through Basilisa's adultery, since by Vedran custom all marriage contracts contained a clause allowing husbands to retain the property their wives brought into the marriage in the case of a separation on such grounds. Valentin, he saw, had coolly staged the setting for this act of domestic banditry. Hadn't Basilisa said the picture was his idea?

Tur pulled himself up straight in his chair, took the cloth from his forehead, squeezed it out over the ground, then put it on the table. He must take action. Immediate action. If it wasn't already too late.

And what was to be done? Why, logically, the first thing to do was to clear Beckett off the scene. To arrange for Toniet's legal adoption, and then organise Beckett's expulsion from the island. The latter operation meant the enlistment of Don Arturo's aid, and probably meant winning over the Governor too. He would call on the Governor next day, tell him that he had changed his mind about cancelling Beckett's tenancy agreement, and be ready with evidence—which surely Don Arturo could be persuaded to manufacture—of Beckett's unsuitability to continue to be a resident. Tur would even humble himself to call in Don Firmín, if Don Firmín's avowed hostility to his tenant could be harnessed to his cause.

He got up, but unable to feel the earth under the soles of his feet, sat down again.

' I wish to discuss this act of aggression,' Tur said. He fumbled mentally for a forceful way of bringing home to his audience the truth of his allegation.

' It's in the mentality,' he explained. ' Or rather—in
our mentality, perhaps I should say. The habits of mind of
centuries. And now, therefore, too late to change. What
really matters to the people who walk to the cemetery after
a man's coffin is what he did with his land.' Tur looked
round at his listeners. Piercey, with his policeman's sympathy, always on the victim's side; Griffin, naturally
acquiescent—even when it happened to be Tur who was
speaking; Valentin, tactically unresistant as a Japanese
wrestler preparing a new hold.

' I'll give you an extreme example of the attitude,' Tur
said. ' Without mentioning names, a farmer I know found
himself in low water with his wife dying of tuberculosis.
He couldn't afford to give her the attention she needed. A
neighbour—one of our foreign residents, who should have
known better—wanted to discuss the possibility of buying a
field from him. As a measure of charity, you understand.
The farmer threatened to set his dog on him. That, as I say,
is an extreme case.'

He thought again in the unresponsive silence. ' Now
take this village, for example. I have it on good authority
that only one boy in fifty ever manages to teach himself to
write. He's a prodigy, understand me. But what's the first
thing he does as soon as he can form the letters? He carves
his name on every tree trunk within a mile of the village.'

For Tur a most cogent argument in support of his view-
point had been linked with this illustration of prideful
conduct, but he had lost sight of it in a maze of irrelevant
reflections. And at that moment he was taken with a terrible
faintness—the sensation that his life was leaking away,
draining out of every bodily cell, every vein, every nerve-end,
to form a receding tide of vitality, that left him numb,
voiceless, almost blind—only still certain of being alive
because he was afraid.

The wave came swinging back, with a delusion of icy

air. Valentin, Piercey and Griffin were there again, in sharp focus, although distorted and over life-size, with the slightly bloated heads of carnival figures. Trivial objects obsessed him: a dog scratching itself continually with the action known locally as ' playing the guitar '; blue, glossy flies dancing on the table top.

Heat-stroke, he thought. 'I'm a fool not to remember I've got no hair left these days.'

He tried to speak, and to stop his teeth from chopping up the words. He wagged a finger at Valentin, and made a tremendous effort to say what he had to say. ' Now you see the fact is I have a daughter . . . a beautiful daughter——'

Piercey jumped up and caught him by the shoulder as he was falling.

CHAPTER 11

WHEN *el vomito*—the vomiting sickness—struck Tur down, it had already attacked, or was on the point of attacking, a fair proportion of the upper-class population of Vedra, as well as many foreigners. The name was a misnomer because people did not necessarily vomit, but they usually complained of an undulant fever, severe headache, stomach cramps, and diarrhoea. Local medical men explained that *el vomito* was simply a convenient title for every summer stomach disorder, and any undiagnosed fever. The lay population stuck to the opinion that it was a genuine speciality of the island, to be expected every August. It was clearly carried by water-borne microbes, because the vomiting sickness always made itself felt at the time when the wells began to run dry and people were obliged to use the stagnant water which had been drained off from the rooftops in the winter and stored in underground tanks. Very few people died of *el vomito*, but it had become so much an island legend—even a frame of mind—that many people got into their pyjamas at the beginning of August, switched to a diet of lemon-juice and dry biscuits, laid in a supply of the latest antibiotics, and kept out of sight until the month was over. The sickness also provided a good excuse for certain married men to banish their wives and families to large antiseptic hotel suites in Gran Canaria, while they themselves went off with pretty secretaries to discreetly located love-nests in the small islands: Palma, Gomera or Lanzarote. As Tur had enjoyed saying to Don Firmín, ' Morality is entirely a matter of what's seen. There's nothing immoral about a successful deception. If no one knows, believe me, God doesn't care too much.'

Tur, stricken as never before, spent a week in bed at the inn of Sagral. In his case the sickness had been aggravated by severe heat-stroke, and a weakening heart. Piercey and Griffin got back safely with Valentin to Vedra. Warned of the outbreak and the precautions necessary to avoid it, the two Englishmen were careful to substitute Vichy water for ordinary water, but were lost when they yielded to the temptation to cool their beer with ice—made, as was often the case, from an infected water supply.

El vomito appeared to favour the working population at the expense of those more comfortably situated. The fact was that the poor were obliged to be active, whatever the weather, and lived on a low diet that kept their livers in good order. Drinking, moreover, as they did, more or less infected water all the year round, they had built up a fair degree of immunisation to the microbes of the storage tanks. There were no cases of the sickness in the port, where the fishermen, caught in the doldrums of the year, awaiting the replenishment of the sea with fish, spent their time in the bars drinking cheap, raw alcohol that disinfected their stomachs.

Of the island notabilities, the vomiting sickness spared the Alcalde, Valentin, and Don Firmín—the men whose way of living most resembled that of the working class. Don Arturo was ill for two days, but made his indisposition an excuse to stay in bed a further week, reading books on occult matters. The Governor was sick too, but remained at his

post, working at a snail's pace, but still working. The
flow of anonymous denunciations had tailed off because
people were too busy worrying over the state of their health
to indulge in intrigue. Don Felix, overcome while riding his
Moto Guzzi, had fallen off and had been taken home in
an ambulance, his output of garrulous secrets tem-
porarily cut off; but following the Governor's suggestion
to Don Arturo, the regular police had succeeded in recruit-
ing a far more valuable informant from among the ranks
of the fishermen themselves. Reports received through
the man confirmed the Governor's fears that the fishermen were organising their resistance to the trawling fleet
from Las Palmas, which was expected to arrive at any
moment.

Beckett was ill. Having taken every conceivable precaution to avoid the experience of the previous year, he
had failed to prevent his cleaning women from using
infected water to wash up after meals. He had been struck
down on the very day arranged for Basilisa's last sitting.
She had come, Augusta with her, drunker, apparently, even
than before, hammered on his door while Beckett had been
sitting on the lavatory, and gone away. Basilisa herself had
had the vomiting sickness for seven years in succession. Each
year its grip on her was lessening, and this time she took only
a day to shake off the attack.

On the next day she was up as usual, with nothing more
than a not unpleasant floating sensation to remind her of the
flaring temperature of the day before. She was having tea
with Valentin, when Valentin, who normally showed little
interest in her affairs, suddenly asked about her picture.

' How is it coming along? Wasn't it to have been ready
by now? '

Basilisa started out of a daydream in which Beckett
had been playing a quite impossible role. Could Valentin

really be a thought-reader after all? Anything was possible with a man like that.

'It's in the last stages. You can never say for certain how long a thing like that is going to take.'

'And are you pleased with it? That's the main thing.'

'Yes,' she said. 'I think so. I think it's quite like me.' What was it about the atmosphere that had suddenly changed? Was there any detectable difference in his voice? —his look? Separated as they had always been by the tremendous gulf of their irreconcilable personalities, they were still joined by some subtle, finely-tuned cord of communication. Basilisa received a warning signal.

'You didn't go for your usual sitting last week, did you?'

'I couldn't. He was ill.'

'Yes, of course. I remember your telling me.'

Did I? she wondered. Basilisa couldn't remember, but if Valentin said she had, then she had. Valentin's mind contained a filing system in which the smallest trivialities were carefully recorded. He was never wrong.

'The usual trouble, I imagine?' He was balancing his spoon on the edge of his teacup, tilting it with his fingertip so that it dipped to touch the surface of the tea.

'The usual trouble,' she said.

'Foreigners seem more susceptible than we are. Have you had any news how his condition is progressing?'

'No,' she said. 'No, I haven't.'

'I've taken rather a liking to Beckett,' Valentin said. 'From the little I've seen of him.'

'He's quite pleasant. In a reserved sort of way.'

'Reserved?'

'Yes,' she said. 'I suppose you'd say he was a typical Englishman.

Valentin gave his teaspoon a final tip. It filled and sank. He took the spoon out and put it in the saucer. Now he

would drink his tea. Basilisa knew every one of his
mannerisms. Their tea-time discussion for the day was over,
and there had been nothing behind it. Nothing but her
imagination. Except on the days when she decided to
camouflage her boredom as sickness, they always had tea
together, and Valentin talked to her politely about a single
topic for not more than ten minutes. The day before
yesterday he had devoted a dozen sentences to the new
indoor, air-conditioned tennis-court he had planned. The
day before that, she couldn't remember what they had talked
about. Today it was Beckett. Now he would drink his tea,
wipe his fingers very carefully on his napkin, get up, go over
and smell one of the blossoms on the tuberose, and then he
would leave again for the office. Mercifully, she saw very
little of him. Valentin left for his office every morning before
Basilisa got up. On three evenings out of four he dined out
with business friends. They occupied different bedrooms.
They were virtually strangers . . . and yet united by this
delicate, almost telepathic mechanism she didn't understand.

Valentin got up, made for the pot plant, then turned
round.

' When's your next sitting? '

A little electric shock jolted her nerves. ' My next sitting?
Friday, I suppose. It's usually Fridays. That's providing
he's on his feet again.'

Basilisa had to do something with her hands. She
reached for her third bun. She raised it to her mouth,
watching him nervously over its frosted amber surface. She
assured herself that there was no significance in his questions.
A perfunctory attempt at politeness; a way of destroying
silence; no more. He was a man absorbed in private visions
from which she was excluded. She watched him pick up his
empty cup, stare absently into its bottom, put it down again.

Five-fifteen. He never stayed later than this. Now he would go.

Valentin, feeling his wife's eyes upon him, searched idly for an oracle among the tea-leaves. A small movement of her head released him. She had returned to the bun, and he was in time to see her teeth close in its side.

Valentin was easily able to interweave two streams of thought at the same time. At the moment he was thinking constructively about the Salina and about Beckett: the Salina, that rich wasteland—its exuberant vitality only awaiting release by the water coursing—he was quite certain—only a few feet below its surface; and Beckett, the instrument by which this wealth was to be unleashed. A vagrant consideration of Basilisa's present activity broke in. Excessive feeding. Inevitably mental processes slowed down. Blood drawn away from brain-cells to the stomach. Valentin's thought skipped away to flick through a quick mental catalogue of his wife's defects. He was as free as a practising Buddhist from acute likes or dislikes. She over-ate and was therefore inefficient, in the way that an engine with slack pistons was inefficient. One didn't feel any emotional aversion to an engine that used too much oil. One replaced it if practicable or necessary. Valentin did not wish at this stage to replace his wife. She had always been unattractive to him. He found that he couldn't think of her without picturing fat-larded intestines. But at this moment she was a necessary cog in an efficiently conducted life.

' I hear your father's still very much under the weather,' Valentin said.

' He has only himself to blame. He eats so little, and besides that he takes too much exercise. And of course he insists on going out in the sun. At this time of the year, of all times.'

Valentin crossed the room and stroked the polished,

empty wall surface over the mock fireplace. 'We'll hang the
picture here,' he said amiably. He didn't particularly want
to lose her. To have a wife attractive to others was an aspect
of efficiency, just as it was efficient to keep the bowels
regular, to eat light, well-balanced meals, to sleep soundly
for a minimum of six hours, to worship God in public.
Valentin wished to avoid a dislocation in the balance of his
existence, if at all possible.

'I had a stroke of luck yesterday.'

'That was nice for you.' Valentin's luck was a voracious animal that habitually fed upon the misfortunes of
others. Occasionally, in three or four brief sentences over
their tea and buns, he told her of passionless coups, of men
bought and sold, of competitors outmanoeuvred, absorbed,
or destroyed.

'Rio Santo made an offer for our part of the Salina.
About a hundred times the market value, I should say.
They must have money to burn. One supposes they know
what they're doing, but personally I don't see how they're
going to get their investment back.'

'I don't quite see where the luck comes in,' she said,
'when you had to turn the offer down.'

'I didn't turn it down.'

'But what's the point?' Basilisa said. 'You know you're
not in a position to accept it. Aren't you rather wasting the
people's time?'

'No,' he said. 'I don't think so. I try never to waste
people's time.'

'But surely you know Father's attitude? And also you
must know that he'll never change his mind.'

'Perhaps I haven't made myself clear. I'm talking about
our land, not his.'

'You're talking about my dowry.'

'Yes,' he said. 'Your dowry.'

'I'm sorry. I thought I'd already made it clear I won't

go against my father in a thing like that. I can't and I won't.'

Valentin had gone round the room in a semi-circle that took him close to the tuberose in its pot. He stopped to sniff at it, and was facing her again.

' Where is Augusta? ' Valentin said.

' In her room, I suppose, messing about with her dreadful picture.'

' Fortunately her hearing's not acute. I believe she's capable of eavesdropping.'

' After all, it's her profession.'

' What a pity. What a pity,' Valentin said. Shaking his head, he went to the door of Augusta's room, opened it, looked through, and closed the door gently again. He came back.

' I would really have preferred not to be obliged to remind you of certain circumstances.' He hesitated.

' Go on,' she said, pressing her lips together.

' Some ten years ago when I first met your father he was a very worried man. He was in a hurry to find you a husband.'

' And he made the famous bargain with you.'

' I repeat—I'm sorry to have to bring the matter up.'

' I couldn't have married anyone else. That's what you're saying.'

' I'm not saying that. Not at all. On the other hand that may well have been your father's opinion. I've found out since that certain overtures *were* made in other directions.'

' I don't believe it. My father would have told me.'

' It might have been better if these points had been cleared up before,' Valentin said. ' Overtures *were* made. To be exact, your father employed an intermediary to sound out several families.'

' Such as? '

' The Vidals, for one.'

' The Vidals? ' she said, bewildered. Who were the Vidals? She ran through a mental list of the names of the leading members of the English Club, the Yacht Club, The Cultural Peak. The Vidals?

' The big shopkeepers,' he said.

' And? '

' They asked to be excused. I still see no point in raking up all this old history.'

Basilisa tasted blood. She had been biting the inside of her lip. She touched her tongue, then inspected the small red smear on her fingertip. One eye had begun to twitch. She sat on her hands to stop them trembling.

' The circumstances being what they were, your father made it clear that he was prepared to arrange for an exceptionally generous marriage settlement. That, at least, was the intention expressed.' Valentin knew that he was handling the situation without finesse. He wasn't used to dealing with women. With a man it was different. Most of them were prepared to respect honest bluntness. ' Look here, the fact is I'm rather pressed for time. Let's cut out the preliminaries, lay our cards on the table, and get something settled here and now.' Women expected you to beat about the bush. He wondered if he should try bribing her first. A winter chalet in Las Palmas—a yacht.

' It's an opportunity that's chosen to present itself at this moment. I can double my investment in a few days, but I must have cash. At any other time I wouldn't have entertained Rio Santo's offer. As things are, I simply can't afford——'

Basilisa was thinking of the son of the Vidal family. Juan —it could only be Juan; a thick-fingered sluggish youth then, now prematurely middle-aged, who had earned for himself the contemptuous nickname ' Split-currant ', and had been designed in every detail of his being to be what he was—

a grocer. Not even the Vidals would have found room for her in their house that stank of stockfish.

Speaking again, she found that her throat had suddenly swollen up. ' I've been in prison for ten years,' she said.

' Through no wish of mine, I'm sure.'

' Continually spied upon by that witch of a woman. Sometimes I wish I'd have died.'

' Augusta was your father's idea.'

Basilisa wanted to smash something. She wanted to scream and kick over the furniture. She picked a vase up by the neck, and put it down again.

' I'd be as happy as you to see her go,' Valentin said. ' She was a part of the original pact. It was a very out-moded arrangement.' Valentin made a last effort to secure a bloodless victory. ' I suggest we go and see your father together. Lay our case before him. Talk things over as a united family. Try to get him to see we're living in the twentieth century, and that you're a responsible woman and not a silly girl who has to have someone to look after her. We'll tell him we want to send Augusta away. You can bring up the matter of the land at the same time. I'd prefer you to be the one to do that. It would come better from you. I'm sure you can make him see that in our day it is quite the normal thing for a husband to attend to his wife's business affairs.'

But Basilisa was beyond reason now. Hate possessed her entirely—a hate so intense and so composed that it presented itself almost as a kind of logic. Valentin had made the profound mistake of telling her of her rejection by the Vidals. After that any accommodation between them had become finally impossible.

' No,' she said. ' Not for anything. Not for anything in the world. Never. Never. Never!' The last word was a scream.

Valentin saw the case was hopeless. She and her father

were cast in the same mould. Survivors of the sociological remote past. Admirable, perhaps, in their way—but doomed by their inflexibility to self-destruction. A pity. A pity indeed. Valentin would have preferred to avoid the domestic explosion facing him now as the only alternative to the settlement he had tried to come to with Basilisa. Battles of this kind were enormously wasteful of the spiritual energy he needed for creative work.

There's nothing for it, simply nothing for it, Valentin said to himself on his way to his office. For once his notorious good luck had actually caught him off his guard. A year before he had used his influence with the then Governor to push through the permit for the building of the fish-canning factory, and had been slightly disappointed to receive as an acknowledgment of this service, twelve months' option on a large block of the company's shares at par. Since then the shares had remained inactive until the previous week. Then—with less than twenty days to go before his option expired—the news had been leaked to a few cronies of the board of directors that a contract would shortly be signed for the whole of the factory's estimated production at a price showing a profit of something like a thousand per cent.

Valentin wanted to take up his shares, and he wanted to buy more—all that he could get his hands on. But the price was rising every day, and all his funds were already tied up. He'd been taken by surprise. There was only one way of raising so much money in so short a time. He'd been left no alternative.

CHAPTER 12

Augusta's organs, her glands, her skin, were vulnerable to assaults from all directions. She was miserably incapacitated in various ways by a catalogue of causes. Her skin blistered, her eyes ran, and her throat swelled up on the smallest provocation. She was obliged to use a special pillow made of sponge rubber; the scent of flowers made her sneeze, contact with the foliage of almost any plant produced an itching rash; there were many foods that disagreed with her. Despite this, she was a glutton.

Basilisa had kept her short of food for two days in preparation for this meal, which was violently spiced, insidious and abundant. The first course consisted of black sausage, a rich and malodorous blending of various peppers with pig's blood, that was notorious for the strain it put on the most vigorous digestion. But the main attack on Augusta's stomach was to be launched with the second course—a stockfish stew seasoned with saffron. Basilisa knew that the smallest quantity of shellfish had a dramatic effect on Augusta's system, and had calculated that the stew's brilliant colour and anarchic flavour could be relied upon to conceal certain dangerous additions that would otherwise be rejected. As soon as the cook had finished her preparations and put the casserole on the fire, Basilisa sent her out of the kitchen on an

errand, and while she was away, got out a cupful of oysters
she had hidden in a cupboard, and emptied them into the
stew.

The meal started in silence with the usual salad. Valentin
would have been quite ready to show in any way he could
that the morning's conversation had been dismissed from his
mind, but he was preoccupied. Valentin paid Don Felix
a small retainer to pass on to him copies of the reports
Don Felix submitted to the Governor and to Don Arturo.
The report he had received that day—the first since Don
Felix had risen from his sick-bed—had dealt with the rapidly
increasing popular discontent with the presence of the
canning factory, now ready to go into operation as soon as
the trawlers could deliver the fish. Valentin regarded himself
as virtually a part-owner of this enterprise. Allowing for
any professional informer's vested interest in despondency,
he was afraid that this report contained its worrying residuum
of truth. Between several apathetic mouthfuls he resolved to
put pressure on the torpid Don Arturo to step up his security
precautions, and if necessary, to go over Don Arturo's head
to his superior in Las Palmas.

Now the maid arrived with the black sausages looking like
three engorged intestines lying in a pool of dark liquid.
Augusta, watching the dish, felt the saliva well up under
her tongue, and a sudden twitching animation spread from
her spine. Her stomach gave a soft, anticipatory gurgle.
Basilisa helped herself to the only small sausage on the dish,
leaving Augusta with the choice of two exceptionally large
ones. Augusta watched intently as the sausage was transferred safely to her plate. Swallowing her saliva, she picked
up her fork and pricked its skin. Instantly an infant's mouth
opened in its wall, bubbling and blowing steam. Valentin
was nibbling round the edge of a digestive biscuit. As an
ex-peasant, he detested these peasant messes, and would
only tolerate them on rare occasions, such as Augusta's

saint's day. Wrinkling his nose, he got up and moved the flowering plant on its table closer to him.

Delicately, almost with reverence, Augusta began her attack on the sausage. She curled back the skin with her knife. Gathering a little of the dark, steaming, mealy contents on her fork, she held it poised, as if waiting, her eyes raised towards Basilisa, for Basilisa's assent.

Basilisa nodded at her, smiling her encouragement. ' Freshly made yesterday. What's-his-name at the butcher's told me he went to the slaughterhouse personally for the blood.'

The first forkful went into Augusta's mouth. She felt a kind of spasm, a nervous, shuddering delight, dissociated from the mere satisfaction of hunger and gluttony. She began to chew quickly, like some small, furtive animal, with a smooth rotary movement of the jaw. A small gout of black liquid slopped on her chin. She plunged her fork into the body of the sausage again, releasing fresh pent-up vapours. Valentin looked up, found himself staring with an intense, flesh-crawling revulsion at the greasy adhesions at the base of Augusta's fork, ready to be plunged once more into the demolished sausage. He looked away.

The maid came in again, carrying the casserole with the stockfish stew, and Augusta found herself obliged to surrender her plate while engaged in the final satisfaction of scraping clean the hollowed-out sausage skin. She heard Basilisa say ' very little ', and glanced up to see her being served with half a ladleful of stew. A moment later the maid had reached Augusta's side. She ladled the stew into her plate, while Augusta's eyes swivelled sideways, oscillating slowly as they followed the ladle from bowl to plate and back. The maid stopped, but Basilisa nodded to her, and in slopped a final ladleful. Augusta's plate was now full to the brim with a sulphur-coloured liquid in which floated several greasy islands of boiled fish.

There had been a germ of hardly conscious doubt, a stubborn vestige of caution in Augusta's mind, heightened by the inexplicable generosity with which Basilisa had filled her wine glass. These hesitations were soon anaesthetised by the rich fragrance arising from her plate: the sourish, almost putrescent odour of the fish, an odour of which she was so fond, allied with and heightened by the slightly metallic fragrance of the saffron. Slyly, under her eyebrows, she watched Basilisa. Basilisa had raised her spoon to her lips, and appeared to be eating as she always did—her eyes a little uplifted. Listening, Augusta heard the faint suck of the intake of food. She curled her finger tightly round the handle of her spoon and plunged it into her stew.

Squinting slightly as she watched her spoon with its contents, she brought it to her mouth. Although accustomed to tasteless food, meal-times reanimated her, and in her desolate life only the act of eating now preserved the tiniest grain of the pleasure, the excitement, and the adventures of living she had once known as a young girl. Her lips closed firmly over the spoon, and she experienced a return, although now subdued, of the fleeting orgasmic delight induced by her first mouthful of the sausage. She withdrew the spoon, clean almost as when she had picked it up. Swallowing, she felt the scratching of small bones in the crevices of her throat. As usual, she thought, the cook had been careless with the spines in preparing the dish. She coughed to dislodge a bone, and took another spoonful.

Delicately balancing two trains of thought, Valentin found himself eating something he did not care for. He pushed his plate away and dabbed at his lips with his napkin. He remembered his pill, swallowed it, and washed it down with a mouthful of imported mineral water. Extraordinary that the Las Palmas company hadn't thought of building a canning factory in Vedra themselves, instead of being quite prepared to have their trawlers scuttle backwards and forwards from the fishing grounds to Las Palmas to unload their catches. They hadn't realised, either, that labour costs in Vedra were half those in Gran Canaria, until Valentin had pointed it out to them. Surprising.

Basilisa had been watching Augusta anxiously. Augusta had stopped eating. With her head cocked on one side, she appeared to be listening to sounds which Basilisa could not hear. Basilisa tried sympathetic magic. Every few seconds she scooped up a little stew, raised her spoon to her lips, then put it down again. Their eyes met. Basilisa was afraid that Augusta's appetite was flagging. She tried to smack her lips, compulsively, yet with decorum. In reality Augusta had only paused because she was on the point of sneezing. The slightly sickly odour of Valentin's tuberose in its pot was tickling her nostrils. She drew back her top lip and closed her eyes. She sneezed; her head jerked forward by a frantic convulsion, and a tiny fleck of stew that had been shot through the interstices of her fingers struck Basilisa in the neck.

Mastering her hatred and disgust, Basilisa nodded to the maid to bring the casserole again. ' Please eat all you can. It was made specially for you. It will be wasted otherwise.'

Valentin was pondering a series of related problems. A: Whether to put through a call to his broker in Madrid to instruct him to take a call option on any of the shares of Conservas Vedreras—the canning factory—he could get his hands on, at say a limit of 10 per cent over the nominal quoted price. B: Whether something could not be arranged to facilitate Basilisa's visit to Beckett's studio on the Friday? Valentin had informed himself that Beckett was now out of bed, and he had already gained the allegiance of the care-taker of the building, who as a matter of course held a duplicate of the various door-keys. If matters could not be brought to a head this week, in a way that would be productive of irrefutable evidence of Basilisa's lapse,

Valentin saw no alternative but to take the photographs
he had had made of the drawing of his wife, during the
few hours it had been left in his hands, to the Judge,
and to persuade him to try the case on this evidence
alone.

This introduced further problems. The Judge—like so
many Vedrans who could afford to do so—had taken his
annual holiday in the unhealthy month of August, and was
due back on the *Almirante Cervera*, arriving on Thursday,
the next day. He was a small, self-important, owlish old
intellectual; an ex-Republican who had been led astray
by too strong an affection for fat living on too lean a salary.
Valentin had bought this man—not in a single, brazen
transaction, but through a long, assiduous process of gifts
and favours, at the end of which Judge Peñaflor had found
himself trapped like a rabbit in a wire snare. The Judge was
therefore bound to be on Valentin's side. But in manipulating the give and take of the law in Valentin's favour
he could expect a head-on clash with Tur—something which
nobody had ever tried before and survived; and this also
meant, as Valentin foresaw it, the start of a civil war among
the island's ruling class. Tur would turn immediately
in this battle to the garrison commander, Colonel Rocamoro,
who also was expected to arrive back from his leave on
Thursday's boat. Peñaflor and Rocamoro, respectively the
heads of the civil and military courts, were traditional
enemies, and Rocamoro was a man of power and character.

Valentin could see the battle spreading. In any trial of
strength, man for man, the Colonel would wipe the floor with
the Judge, but the classic line-up would be completed, and
something like a shaky balance of power re-established, by
Don Firmín's entry into the fight on the Judge's side. Don
Firmín despised the Judge as a man, but in recent years a
silent, invisible, subterranean antagonism had come to
exist between the Army and the Church—each mistrustful

of the other's power—and this made the Colonel Don
Firmín's natural opponent.

Valentin had excluded Don Arturo as an effective
combatant in this conflict. Nominally, Don Arturo would be
on the Church's side too, but Valentin saw him as too
cautious a man to make an effective ally.

Valentin shied away from the violences and the disloc-
ations—the wasted expenditure of creative energy—implied
in this solution. It would have to be used only in the last
resort. The respectful repetition of his name recalled him to
the moment. The maid was at his elbow with the fruit
basket. He selected an orange. With knife and fork he
carved away delicately, producing a flower of ten identical
petals of peel, with the uncovered fruit at its centre. He
did this quite automatically almost blindly, having returned
to his plans and his visions.

Basilisa was watching Augusta with anxiety again. She
was slowing down and inclined to leave long ruminative
pauses between each mouthful. She showed no signs of
discomfort yet. Could it be that she hadn't eaten an oyster?
Unlikely, Basilisa thought. Augusta had eaten half the stew.
She picked up the carafe of wine, leaned across and filled
Augusta's glass. A nice mixture, she thought. Sour wine
and fish not quite as fresh as it ought to be.

Augusta looked up at her mistily. 'It's hot in here,' she
said.

Basilisa took courage. Surely the oysters were at work
now, churning their poisons in Augusta's stomach.

'Hot,' Basilisa said. 'I can't say I find it hot. Are
you quite sure you're feeling well?'

Augusta emptied her glass. She put it down and placed
the palm of her hand on her cheek.

'You seem flushed,' Basilisa said, once again falling back
on the power of suggestion.

Augusta picked up her spoon and put it down again. 'It's

just that I seem thirsty today. I'm thirstier today than usual.'
She looked in the direction of the carafe. Basilisa filled her
glass again. Augusta drank and her eyes watered.

'You don't feel well, do you?' Basilisa said. 'You're
as red as a peony.'

Augusta shook her head doubtfully. She put down her
glass, cupped her hand over her mouth and tried to belch.

'I hope your food isn't disagreeing with you,' Basilisa
said. In fact, studying Augusta, she was excitedly relieved to
see that her cheeks were swelling up as she watched. As
her cheeks puffed out, her eyes were disappearing. Her
forehead too had become spotted like a fungus. That was
what Basilisa's face reminded her of now—one of those
pink funguses, with white spots.

'I'm afraid you've a stomach attack coming on,' Basilisa
said. 'You should take something quickly. Go and lie
down.'

Augusta felt a bubbling tide surge into her throat. She
gripped the edge of the table.

'You're ill,' Basilisa said softly. 'I'm afraid you're ill.'

With horror now, and with a panic sense of being trapped,
Augusta saw Basilisa's white face, mistily, through a
firmament of bleeding stars. She saw the hatred there, and
suddenly connected it with the terrible fermenting tide in
her stomach, chest and throat. She pulled herself out of her
chair, struck out with her arms, fighting her way towards
the bathroom. Then as her legs folded at the knees and the
haunches, she went down; her head struck the floor, and
her body emptied, roaring through her mouth.

When she awoke it was morning. She was weak and light
in her body, and faintly alarmed by the sensation that she
was floating a little above the surface of the bed. She allowed
the morning noises to filter through her head unchallenged,

but alert for the slightest sound that might be of Basilisa.
Augusta heard Valentin leave for his office, with the
slamming of a car door and the rush of tyres. Five minutes
of the twittering of the birds, then came the rattle of the
handle of the telephone, and the dragging jingle of the bell.
She gathered herself, hissing and groaning under her breath,
like a broken wrestler, slid down from the bed to the floor,
and, half-entangled in the folds of her nightgown, began a
hands-and-knees shuffle towards the door. It was a struggle
to reach the handle, but in the end she turned it and pulled
the door open half an inch. She put her ear to the crack.
A faint jumble of words reached her, carried through by the
warm draught; a disjointed rambling stripped of meaning
in its passage through crevices, keyholes and partition walls.
She tried to poison me, I nearly died, Augusta said to herself.
She pushed open the door and listened with a passionate
concentration. Her hearing was the only sense that had not
yet showed signs of failing her, and Augusta's eavesdropping
was assisted by Vedra's dilapidated telephone system, with
its crossed lines, short circuits, and its permanent crackle of
static, that made someone two streets away sound as if he
were speaking under the worst possible conditions from South
America.

' To go to this address, and to wait an hour,' Basilisa said.
' To wait an hour, I said . . . An hour.'

She was ordering a taxi. That was all Augusta needed to
know. She dragged herself back to her room, and after
lying on the bed for a few minutes, she got her street clothes
ready. As soon as she heard Basilisa go out she began to
dress.

CHAPTER 13

BECKETT met Laura off the ship at nine that morning. He carried her luggage across to the Mirasol.

'Well, and how was life chez Susan?'

'Life chez Susan was fine. I always enjoy staying with her. I like Susan.'

'But you're back.'

'I never had any intention of staying for more than a fortnight.'

'Tenerife the same as ever?'

'The same as ever. I can't say it's a place I warm to.'

'You used to be full of it, all the same.'

'Did I? I suppose I must have changed. Nowadays I find it all rather grey.'

'I should have thought that would be the last thing anyone would accuse Tenerife of being.'

'It's grey by comparison. And really I mean the people and the atmosphere—not the place. Everyone goes about looking as if they had bank overdrafts and stomach ulcers.'

'This isn't grey too, by any chance?'

'No,' she said. 'Vedra isn't grey. And it's nice to be back.'

'You're looking absolutely wonderful,' Beckett said. 'I've come to the conclusion I've missed you badly.'

'It's nice to think somebody's missed me. Were you very ill?'

'Only a little worse than usual,' he said. 'You timed your departure rather well. The whole colony was laid low this time—Eastaugh, the Cartwrights, the Murrays—the lot. I only managed to crawl out of bed the day before yesterday.'

'You're thinner,' she said.

'Thanks to a diet of soup and lemon squash. I've lost nearly a stone.'

'I expect there's still time for me to get it,' she said. 'If there's any of it still going about I will. I always do.'

It was really wonderful, she thought, what a fortnight away from a place could do. Everything was fresh again, although nothing had changed. They sat at the same table littered with dirty cups, and were waiting for the same slovenly waiter to notice their presence. The same excited peasants had come to see the ship—she actually recognised their faces now. Ten minutes earlier the same band had shuffled up to the quayside in quick-step to welcome the arriving notables. All the regulars were in their usual places outside the Club Nautico next door—pieces in a chess game that never started. Tur's old schooners were berthed, as ever, opposite the Mirasol, the winged figureheads with the face of Tur's great-aunt staring benignly vacant at them from just across the road. Laura counted the number of ornamental gourds hanging from the vine outside the Club Nautico. There had been seven last time, and now there were eight; and in the blind white façade above, the two Pepsi-Cola signs continued to flower like scarlet camellias. Even the Governor's Hispano-Suiza had chosen to break down in almost exactly the same spot as when she last saw it, and now it stood, sagging slightly to one side, in the middle of the road, the sunshine exploding softly on the angles of its brass and nickel-plate.

Laura remembered that the car had carried the Governor to the quayside to meet the returning Garrison Commander.

' I met the Colonel on the boat,' she said. ' He's an old sweetie.'

' They had to fetch him back in a hurry,' Beckett said. ' Before his leave was up.'

' How was that? '

' The trouble over the fishing fleet from Las Palmas. They're expected any day now. The police are supposed to have got wind of some sort of plot.'

' Nice to have a char who gives you all the news,' Laura said.

' As it happens it wasn't my cleaning woman this time. Unfortunately I've been in a spot of bother over her since you've been away. You remember I told you I kept missing odds and ends. In the end it got more than a joke, so I had to invent some excuse to get rid of her. As it turns out, I don't know if it was a wise thing.'

' What else could you do? '

' The mistake I made was taking on a replacement without letting a decent interval elapse. The next thing that happened was the police raided the studio, which—considering my cleaning woman's husband was included in the raiding party—looks more than a coincidence.'

' How incredible. Did they give you any reason for raiding the place? '

' None at all. They just came in, turned everything upside down, asked the new girl a few questions, and cleared off. I can't see what it can have been other than spite. It does seem, though, as though I've made an enemy.'

' It does, doesn't it.'

He patted the back of her hand affectionately. ' Do you know something? I feel terribly happy to see you. More cheerful about things in general. Here comes the canary man. How about a destiny?'

'That's the last thing I want.'

'Don't say it like that. Aren't you happy to be back?'

'Yes. In a way.' She smiled weakly. A pair of guards went by, blue-jawed, dark-spectacled, canvas neck-protectors hanging from the backs of their hats, pistols in patent-leather holsters. Laura, who had sharp hearing, noted that they were talking about the price of eggs.

'Two new ones,' she said.

'Part of the precautions. They've brought in most of the police from the villages. Not that anything's going to happen, of course. Don Arturo wants people to think he's indispensable, that's all.'

'Do you know anyone who would take over my house?' Laura asked.

'Not off-hand,' Beckett said. 'It shouldn't be too hard to find someone. Why—you don't mean to say you've really decided to desert us, after all?'

'I think so,' she said.

'If you'd have said something in your letter, I might have been able to get someone lined up.'

'It doesn't matter. There's no hurry. Not for a few days.'

'I was beginning to think of you as a permanent fixture,' Beckett said.

'That's the way I was beginning to think about myself.'

'Why the sudden change of plans, then?'

'I don't know. Three years is a long time. I've been here three years now.'

'But on the whole, you've enjoyed it, haven't you? You've been able to work.'

'No,' she said. 'I haven't worked. It's all been a game of make-believe. I've pretended to work, and the time passed, but in the end nothing's been done. Sometimes I feel I don't exist at all. I don't feel real. Do you feel real?'

'I suppose so,' Beckett said. 'Off and on.'

'I think we should be real,' Laura said. 'It's not being real to pretend all the time. And yet how can we go on living if we can't pretend any more?'

'I don't know,' Beckett said. 'I've never given it a thought.'

'I'd like to work in a factory, or drive a tractor, or something like that,' Laura said. 'Anything to make me feel I really existed.'

'You exist,' Beckett said. 'There's no doubt about that, but I do suggest thinking it over before you do anything rash like getting rid of your house. Give it a few more weeks.'

'I don't think I could carry on for a few more weeks. I've stopped being able to fool myself about anything any more.'

'Surely that's a good thing?'

'No,' she said. 'No, it isn't. Not if you carry the process too far. I just feel empty and sick with myself all the time. Either I have to be real, or I have to believe in the pretence—and I've stopped being able to, that's all.'

'Your friends will be unhappy to see you go.'

'Have I any friends?'

'Have you any friends? What on earth's come over you? What a thing to say.'

'I'm tired,' she said. 'Don't take any notice of me. It's the journey. How are the Cartwrights?'

'They've been under the weather like the rest of us. Victor looked in only yesterday. He was asking when you were expected back.'

'They were rude to me last time I saw them.'

'My dear Laura, I simply refuse to believe it. I happen to know that they have the greatest possible affection for you. You're imagining things.'

'Perhaps I imagined it, then. Such a lot of things

happened just before I left that in the end I was ready to believe anything.'

'It's funny,' he said, 'that we should both have chosen the same moment to make our decisions. You're going and I'm staying. I've taken the great step at last, and applied for my naturalization papers.'

'That's rather drastic, isn't it?'

'I don't know. I came to the conclusion that as I look like spending the rest of my days here, it was the logical thing to do. Mind you, it was the business of the studio being raided that really clinched it so far as I was concerned. Residents don't have any rights. They could kick me out tomorrow, and it would mean having to make a start all over again somewhere else. A thing I don't believe I could bring myself to do.'

'You've done very well,' Laura said. 'You're the only one outside the business crowd who's done anything worth doing.'

'I've been lucky,' he said. 'I'd never have the same kind of luck twice in a lifetime.'

'Are you still painting Tur's daughter? She's beautiful, isn't she?'

'I am, and she is. I'm sorry you listen to scabrous rumours.'

'I'm sorry you do.'

'All right. Let's have our own non-aggression pact then, shall we?'

Laura suddenly pulled several snapshots out of her bag. 'This is Susan and Ralph, and their new house. Ralph had the beds made like ships' bunks. It's the latest craze in Tenerife. The dining-table folds back into the wall. It's a picture when not in use. That's highly fashionable, too.'

'Have you gone off your head?' Beckett said.

'Talk to me,' Laura said. 'There's somebody coming I don't want to see . . . This is Jane, their youngest. She's really a terribly sweet child, but her education's turning out a terrific problem, because they don't want to part with her, and the nuns at the local school pinch the children to make them behave. She says, slap a child if you must, but somehow she can't bear the idea of Jane being pinched. In cold blood, too.'

Beckett, dutifully bowing his head over the photographs, was also doing his best to see what little he could of the passers-by. From under his eyebrows he saw the skipping feet of a group of peasants newly released from the rough-going of their fields; the torn trouser-legs of a sauntering bootblack; the swirl of a priest's black skirts; a whore's buttocks jerking under her dress in exact time to the cracked convent bell; a big fish hauled by a muscled forearm, splashing water and scales on the pavement; the knife-edge crease of linen trousers, and under them clean canvas shoes dragged swaggeringly on the heel at each step. Beckett raised his eyes and saw the rest of Mila's back. The trouble was you had only to sit here for a couple of hours for the whole population of the town to pass.

Mila stopped suddenly, releasing himself from the current of movement. He turned his head and Beckett's eyes met his. Beckett, who knew him slightly, nodded, but Mila gave no signs of recognition, and Beckett checked his half-formed smile. Hope he doesn't get the idea I'm the boy friend, he thought. Nasty customer, but very interesting face. Most people's faces haphazard; accidental assembly of unbalanced, unsuited components. Mila's features all taken from same bold, emphatic stock. Would have made wonderful Othello. Beckett would have liked to paint him.

'The boy's in school in England,' Beckett heard Laura say, ' but they're not too happy about it. Susan said he was quite like a stranger when he came home after being away a year. She used to think he was too dependent on her. I suppose you can't have it both ways.'

The crowd had gathered Mila up again and carried him away. He heard Laura take a deep breath. 'What were we talking about?' she asked.

'About Susan's Jane being pinched by the nuns.'

'No, before that.'

'About your lunatic idea of going away, presumably as the result of a slight attack of persecution mania.'

She was brightly matter of fact. 'It's the climate I'm going to miss most. Just imagine Stockport in November.'

'To say nothing of December, January and February,' he said.

'Five months of winter.'

'Of course you won't stay. You've been away too long.'

'Perhaps I won't.' Laura put her hand on his and got up. 'I think I'd like to go home now, and get unpacked. I'm desperately tired.'

'Come swimming tomorrow,' Beckett said. 'No, let's make it Saturday. We'll make up a party with the Cartwrights and go to La Caleta.'

'With the Cartwrights?'

'They'll be terribly keen to see you again, I know.'

'All right,' she said. 'We *can* get a boat from here, can't we?'

'From here?' Beckett was surprised.

'What I mean is we don't have to go all the way down to the fishing port?'

Now he understood.

'No,' he said. 'There's never any difficulty on a Saturday. Always plenty of boats kicking about. No trouble about picking one up at the steps.'

'That's fine. All right then. Early, I suppose?'

'Say nine,' he said. 'Before it gets too sticky. I'll come round and pick you up.'

Laura was on her feet, bags in hand, already moving

away. 'Come round for a drink tonight if you can make it. I really must dash now.'

'Hold on a minute,' he said. 'What's the hurry? I'll carry those. Let me pay this and I'll come with you.'

He put a note under the saucer. 'What's all the rush?' he called after her.

Then he remembered. Mila would be on his way back now from his stroll to the end of the sea front.

CHAPTER 14

Beckett left Laura at the entrance to her dilapidated palace, among the servile hands and doffed hats of those who lived there rent-free, and went straight back to the Mirasol. Although the six unfinished portraits awaiting attention grimaced impatiently at the back of his mind, he could not bring himself to work that day. He was weak; drained of energy. The sickness had left its aftermath of depression, too.

Although Beckett had a weak stomach for strong liquor, this was the one time when he felt justified in ordering an alemana. Alemana was a local concoction of absinthe, so-called because it was supposed in Vedra to be a drink for which the Germans had formed a dangerous national addiction. The supreme virtue of an alemana was the speed with which it changed the face of the world. In a matter of minutes colours flowed into drab landscapes; mere noises rearranged themselves, with the slightest excuse, as music; the past ceased to admonish, and the future to threaten. But this was an euphoria, too, that could be carried to unmanageable lengths.

The alemana was served, with the usual half of a small, green lemon. Beckett squeezed the lemon into the clouded liquid, and watched with anticipatory satisfaction, as the droplets sank and spread their oily ectoplasms. Remembering that he had eaten nothing that morning, he ordered a packet of dry biscuits. He began to sip the alemana—the first he had had for months—and shuddered at its wry but sickly flavour of cough-syrup with an undertone of bitter herbs. The first glass seemed to produce no effect. How much of the famous kick was imaginary after all? he wondered. By the time, ten minutes later, Beckett had finished his second alemana, he still couldn't be certain he felt any better. Perhaps, if anything, a slight clarification of the processes of thought had taken place, but he was aware of no spectacular change in his outlook on life. He ordered his third. His main objection to alemana in the past had been that on more than one occasion it had made work seem unnecessary. As he had no intention of working that day anyway, what did it matter? The locals, on the whole, had a nervous aversion to alemana drinking. On the most extraordinary grounds, Beckett remembered. All the bald peasant women one saw about, for example, were supposed to be secret alemana fiends. What nonsense.

Beckett found himself absorbed in his plans for the future—in particular about the best way of dealing with the formalities of naturalisation. Naturally enough, he would require a sponsor and referees. But who? In the days of the last governor, the Governor himself would have been the obvious choice of sponsors, and Beckett supposed that it would have cost him a slap-up dinner. But the new man was rumoured to be unapproachable. It might, therefore, have to be Don Arturo, or the Judge; both accessible men, especially the latter who had never been shy in admitting to his delight in imported wines. Then if only Don Firmín would agree to sign the papers as referee, the outcome of his application could be taken as a foregone conclusion. In what way would it be correct to reward Don Firmín for such a favour? A pair of altar candlesticks? Beckett had no idea how one approached so delicate a matter with a priest. He would have to sound out the terrain.

For no particular reason, he laughed out loud. The sound took him by surprise. He looked round cautiously at his neighbours but no one was paying him any attention. Intoxicated? Beckett found it hard to believe it could be so. He tried to compare his present mood and sensations with those of a half hour before. The mental heaviness seemed to have lifted, that was all. Perhaps too he was abnormally conscious of what was going on round him. Possibly the special chemical—the ester or whatever it was—in the liquor possessed the power of neutralising the poisons of fatigue in the blood. Nimbly his brain had begun to pick up the fragments of half a dozen different conversations being conducted in his vicinity, and to piece them together in a comically surrealistic word-mosaic. Profoundly philosophical observations had begun to flow, on the slightest encouragement, in and out of his mind. Then in an instant he flashed from a mood that bubbled on the verge of frivolity into one of gentle sorrow, as he thought of Laura and her predicament. Sad it was that she should be impeded in the reconstruction of her life, and therefore obliged to banish herself. Inexorably the present moment, and the future, inherit the past, he thought. This he repeated out loud.

As for his own small mistakes, Beckett had seen the red light in time, and from now on he would at least contrive a superb outward masquerade of conformity. He had already promoted himself to a full-blown naturalised citizen, of which in Vedra there existed so far only three examples— Brahmins among the Anglo-Saxon expatriates, separated by a social abyss from the mere residents, as the residents in turn were from the untouchable winter visitors.

One or two foreigners, released from their sick-beds, and full of antibiotics, drifted past into the sun again. Beckett acknowledged their greetings with a slight movement of the hand. Spongers, slackers, fakes, all of them, with the exception of the few who were here on business. Their days were numbered, but they knew it not. Haskin was for the high jump, ditto Youngblood, ditto Koch. The Governor was about to descend on them like a Pharaoh and drive them into the sea. The last piece of information his cleaning woman had given him before he had sacked her was that a batch of deportation orders had been made out, and only awaited signature.

Beckett took another sip of alemana. Now he was bold and hilarious. He permitted himself to wink at a passing peasant girl, who repaid him by twisting her angelic mouth into a grimace of ugly disdain. The whore he had seen earlier in the day was coming towards him. He winked at her too, and she smiled. The passage of an hour had embellished her, and she was no longer angry with the purchasers of her body. The spasm of gratitude he felt for her smiles was so acute that his eyes watered.

Beckett wanted to sit in this beloved place and let his surroundings soak into his skin, become part of his being. He wanted to capture within himself the beautiful accidents of the port; this gathering of sea-calloused ships, the noble reticence of these buildings, the music struck out of the imprisoning bronze of bells into the wide sky. In a magnified and telescopic vision he saw the fishing balandra *Rafael Irene* made ready at the end of the port, newly dyed nets hoisted to dry like brown Tartar tents against the bleached bone and carved pearl of the ancient façades beyond. A little of the sky had been bundled up in the balandra's furled sails. To the right of the *Rafael Irene's* prow a ship chandler had hung out his goods all over his shop-front, his coiled ropes, lamps and turtle shells like votive offerings to a fulminating sun. On the left the butcher had prepared a sprightly ballet of cadavers of goats and sheep, headless but collared with rubies, all leaping heraldically heaven-wards. Beckett put out his arm, prodding at them with his finger-tips, while a puff of sweet breeze silvered him with fish-scales.

The canary man stood at his side, balancing his brash, pebble-eyed bird in its cage on the end of its pole. Out of a benevolent whim, but also out of a flickering, half-formed fear that with destinies too one got what one paid for, Beckett gave the man a starchy new twenty-five-peseta note, and waved away the twenty-three pesetas change. The canary picked him a destiny and held it out, head cocked sideways quizzically. Beckett took the tiny envelope from the bird's beak. The words *Destino y Existencia* were printed on it. He slipped it into his pocket unopened.

Existencia. But do I exist? Have I a reality? And had these been Laura's questions, or his own? The answer in his own case was a triumphantly shouted yes, yes, yes! I am not drunk. I have been released from a peculiar servitude to myself by a single droplet of alcohol in the blood. My nerves have opened into flower. Now am I risen from the dead. Now I hold the whole universe in my arms. I see the future taking shape. I read thoughts. I know that tomorrow's tumbril is a Cadillac. I know of the stars rotating at the bottom of their abyss of light-years. I hear the coverlet of singing linnets drawn over the sky. At this instant, too, Beckett found his thoughts intertwined with those of Laura. They had established a telepathic interchange. In Rome she had not done as the Romans. *But what was it the Romans did?* ' I love her,' he said loudly. Who could escape love with its petalled fingers? He would compel her to remain, and they would cleave together to protect each other from the idiocy of the world, the flesh, and the Devil.

The Devil. He had a vision of whirling grass skirts and a beaked mask. The Devil. Africa. Basilisa. He looked for her, knowing she would be there. A woman called his name twice. He saw an aged motor-car flapping and shuddering at the kerbside; a brass dragon with a kangaroo's body and bat's wings on its radiator cap. It was Basilisa's favourite taxi, in the drooping frontal contours of which he made out an irresponsible human face. Basilisa was smiling and gesturing at him through the taxi's half-open door. He jumped up and rushed forward, arm outstretched. Basilisa caught his hand and tugged at it, and he stumbled over the ridged running-board, cracked his head, and sprawled in the worn plush and broken bed-springs of the interior. He half straightened himself, pivoted, then collapsed on the seat at Basilisa's side as the driver ground into bottom gear and snatched them away from the kerb.

Recovering, Beckett was startled for a moment by a small, malevolent doll, bobbing and gesticulating on its wire over the windscreen (surely the bush-devil in miniature?) and then by a bloodshot and slightly magnified eye staring back at him from the driving mirror.

He felt the touch of Basilisa's lips on his ear. ' I've come for my picture to be finished.'

' The picture,' he said. ' But, above all, lies are insipid.'

' Augusta's sick. It was the chance of a lifetime.' She caught his head in her hands, and as their mouths joined an anaesthetist's mask of perfume closed his nostrils.

He was free again.

' You've been drinking absinthe,' she said. ' I can smell it.'

' And on an empty stomach. I've been ill, but I'm no longer ill.' He was going on to say, ' I'm better now,' but unaccountably he said instead, ' I'm free now.'

He waited in vain for Basilisa's comment. His thoughts were forming, dividing, proliferating. They were multi-coloured, subtle, profound. But speech had become a matter of a foreign tongue, with a wooden syntax and a sparse vocabulary.

' Absinthe,' he said, ' known locally as alemana, can't be

said to be like any other intoxicant in its effects, which are pleasing but insidious. But I am I, and I remain I. At the worst a foolish loquaciousness. Where are we going?'

'To your studio, of course.'

'Let us go there, then.'

'I've already been there once to look for you. The caretaker seemed very strange.'

'She's been deprived of most of life's blessings,' Beckett said. 'I can't hate her. So at last the moment, so long desired, so evasive, has arrived.'

'It's the one chance,' she said. 'Until I get rid of Augusta. Then we can be together whenever we want to.'

He ran his finger over her ear and her cheek. 'You remind me of someone,' he said. 'An historical personage.' He kissed her and encountered the tip of her tongue.

'What historical personage?'

'Nefertiti.'

'And who was Nefertiti?'

'A Nilotic woman.'

'Nilotic?' She was doubtful, her eyebrows drawing slightly together.

'On second thoughts, I've changed my mind. It's the Empress of Ethiopia. Not the present one, needless to add.'

'Should I be flattered?'

'Your manner is regal,' Beckett said, 'and your beauty arrogant. Look not upon me because I am black, because the sun hath looked upon me . . . You shun the sunshine, don't you?'

'I like to see it, but not to be in it.'

'The sea,' Beckett said. 'I won't be parted from the sea.' He picked up the speaking tube, shouted into it, and waved to the driver to turn. The driver dragged on the wheel, swinging the car round, and they bumped off in the opposite direction back along the sea front again.

'Is this safe?' Basilisa said.

Beckett put his finger to his lips. He spoke into the speaking tube again. ' Slow down. Go slower.'

' I wish to take this opportunity,' Beckett said, ' to demonstrate pleasure in its purest form. But first note the ship. Although it is at anchor, it appears to be moving. And not only the ship, but the houses in the background across the port . . . Stop the car,' Beckett called to the driver. The taxi stopped while he peered through the rigging at the sepulchral, sun-paled houses that were shivering as if made of flesh.

' Well? ' he asked her.

She smiled. He was an artist. Anything was permissible to an artist. ' That's the heat waves rising, that's all.'

' And now the fair,' Beckett said . . . ' Slow again, driver.'

They were passing the permanent funfair at the end of the sea front, and children, eyes a-goggle, the blood drawn from their faces by startled pleasure, were being whirled above them in glittering chairs.

' The only complete pleasures,' Beckett said, ' are the unsought-after pleasures of innocence. Send me to a paradise where I can watch children at play . . . The pigeons,' he said, ' look at the pigeons.'

The children in the fairground were feeding a crooning multitude of pigeons. They wore pigeon-epaulettes on their shoulders, and pigeons showered about them out of the sky like broken icicles of light. Beckett struggled with a stubborn door-handle to open it and get out, but Basilisa pulled him away.

She drew the curtains across the partition and the windows and put her arms round him. He sensed, rather than saw, that concupiscent flesh, freed of cotton and lawn, was exposed to him, invited him, opened its portals. But in it Beckett could see the oblivion of this exquisite moment of consciousness, followed even by a token surrender, in the moment of generation, to death. This was one of his life's

moments of triumph—his victory over the incarceration of
the things he had lived for. He disengaged himself from the
soft, straining coils of Basilisa's limbs, and tore aside the
curtain over his window. Fishermen who were dismembering
a shark acknowledged him, raising their vermilion hands in
a kind of Roman salute.

Earnestly Beckett turned his attention to Basilisa again.
' Have you ever grown wings and flown away from yourself? '

She shook her head, puzzled, but still dutiful and
indulgent in her laughter.

Beckett had learned a new trick of detaching himself—
of seeing himself in the third person; his life as he had led it,
at the best a piece of jaunty puppetry against an obscure
backcloth. Again he had a sensation of awareness of all the
secret things of the world: of the sea battering everywhere
on the rocks in the way that an eagle destroys sick lambs;
of the mobile wash of atmosphere through endless orange
groves cancelling out and re-forming the shapes of millions
of leaves. Above all, he wanted to paint his new vision of the
universe before it could fade. At last I'm a painter. At last
a painter. All that was necessary, after all, was to see.

By the time Beckett's infinity of revelation had emptied,
they had come to the end of the sea front and turned into the
crooked lanes of the old town. The Panhard fumbled its
way with an old man's caution, nibbling at the yards,
wriggling past up-ended blocks of stone and uncovered drains.
It stopped for a moment to take breath where flowers spurted
from the cracked, white walls, and Beckett leaned through
the window, grabbed a fistful of zinnias, and threw them in
Basilisa's lap. He kissed her again, but with wild curiosity
rather than passion.

The taxi squeaked to a standstill. They had arrived at
Beckett's house, but the courtyard gates were closed. This
was an act of aggression, Beckett knew, on the part of the

woman who was allowed, with her sick husband, to occupy
the porter's lodge in return for her grudging and perfunctory
services as caretaker. She controlled the gates and, by closing
them as soon Beckett had gone out and keeping him waiting
when he returned, she punished him for his suspected enjoyment of acts of profligacy never within her reach.

But now he and Basilisa were stranded in the naked street,
alerted to their presence. The taxi driver, saying that he
was already late for another mission, turned and departed,
and the Panhard, taken suddenly with a bout of misfiring,
cannonaded them loudly from its exhaust. Beckett rattled
the gate, then kicked it, then raised the iron-ring knocker
and brought it down twice. He realised, although splendidly
isolated from concern, that his enemy expected him, knew
that he would come back with a woman, and had arranged
his punishment. He saw her now as another Augusta, a
member of that bitter heresy against life, witch-hunters of
satisfaction, who disguised their frantic obsessions behind
gestures of piety. While Basilisa cowered close to him, the
knocker thundered again on the huge drum of the street.
A shutter opened overhead.

He heard movements in the porter's lodge, a rumbling
drawl and the gates fell open. The woman was there,
muffled in her black virtue, ready to read the guilt in faces.
Behind her, Beckett's discharged cleaning woman rusted the
sunshine with her dead-dyed locks and habitual mourning.
An acid smile that had eaten into her face was directed away
from them. In the background the porter, a consumptive
Beckett had never expected to see on his feet again, hung
between the door posts of the lodge, chest caved in, coughing
and gobbling his sputum.

Beckett, passing the porter's wife, was taken by an impulse
to reveal to her a truth in his keeping, but was unable to
find words in which to frame his vision. He caught her by
the hand, but his thought failed to take a communicable

shape. 'Dear lady,' he said. 'Remember me to all your loved ones, and never despair.' As an afterthought, he dropped Basilisa's arm just as they reached the foot of the staircase, and turned back to her. 'If only I could induce you to understand,' he said.

Following Basilisa up the stairs, he recorded with detachment the steatopygous backthrust of her buttocks. This amalgam of Africa, he thought. Visibly, the smoky, china eyes of the Niger; the temple, the brows of Senegal; the sweetly arching mouth of the pastoral Semitics of the Sudan. Concealed, the breasts of Dahomey; the remarkable haunches of a Hottentot, and—who knew—perhaps the uniquely elongated labiae of that race? Curiosity burned up with the strength of a passion. In a moment he would know. In a moment he would undress her, or she would undress herself, and he would know the truth about all he had speculated upon so pleasantly.

They reached the studio.

'This is my gaol,' Beckett said. 'And these my gaolers.' He pointed towards the six unfinished portraits. 'They have a life of their own, but I apologise for their presence.'

He went to turn the smoothly vacuous faces to the wall.

'I've been released on parole, but I've absconded; which is to say, I don't intend going back,' Beckett said. 'From now I paint as the fancy takes. Would you paint as the fancy took if you were in my place?'

'Of course I would,' she said.

'These things are of the past. They're at an end. In fact, they're finished. This too. This above all.' He took the Venetian gown on its hanger from its peg. Twisting the hanger so as to be able to subject both back and front of the gown to a grave inspection, he let it fall to the ground.

'My gown,' Basilisa said.

'It shall be changed into chair covers.'

'And you aren't going to finish my picture?'

Beckett shook his forefinger at her. 'To all these things I have said, never more. Today, we start again, from the beginning.'

'And what am I expected to wear?'

'Your beauty,' he said. 'What else? Take off your clothes.'

Above all things, realism, he thought. I'm a painter of human flesh—therefore a respect, a reverence indeed, for the flesh in all its aspects. Therefore due value and homage to all. The ingrowing toe-nail is as much my subject as the eyebrow of a young girl. Impatiently he wrenched at the buttons on Basilisa's dress, and she put away his hand, laughing with relief, her doubts at rest, and went behind the screen.

Beckett found himself closing the windows. Beyond them, a slow, unfamiliar thumping on the sounding-board of the sea below drew him out on to the balcony. Three small, brightly painted ships, steaming in line, were just about to enter the fishing port. Currents of agitation had entered the crowd gathered at the *Almirante Cervera*'s berthing place in the main harbour. It was dissolving, beginning to stream away in tentacles of ant-like movement towards the position where the first of the newcomers seemed likely to tie up. Four guards, riot guns on their backs, humped like buffaloes over their frail, power-assisted bicycles, went pitter-puttering down the hill. A rocket hissed up on its thread of smoke and popped tautly in the sky directly overhead. Seconds later Beckett heard its stick rattle on the roof-tiles across the way. 'The revolution will now take place,' he said aloud.

As if in confirmation of this prediction, there was a crash and a scream in the room behind him. A door banged on a gabble of male voices. The window had half-closed. Beckett wrenched it open and rushed back into the studio, at first startled, but then calming quickly. A man stood in front of the screen behind which Basilisa had disappeared. A nervous mannerism made him appear to be trying to swallow his lips. Beckett was coolly observant again. He was interested in the enormous height of the man's forehead, above which the articulations of the skull were lightly sketched in on a polished scalp. Black coat with numerous flecks of fluff, starched collar and cuffs, heavy gold rings trapped between the whitened knuckles of clasped hands.

'Fulgor,' the man said. 'My name is Fulgor.' He spoke English. 'Mr. Beckett, I believe? I'm the Notary Public. I trust you'll forgive an intrusion made unavoidable in my official capacity. This is my assistant, Cabra.'

A second man had bobbed from behind the screen, black and professionally melancholic like his master.

'Fulgor, you said?' Refulgence, Beckett thought. A strange name, and perhaps not altogether suitable.

'Gentlemen, please replace your hats,' he said. 'Needless to say my house is yours, and regard me as your servant to command. At any other time I would have pressed you to stay—perhaps to have joined me in a lunch, consisting for the most part, I'm sorry to admit, of tinned tomato soup. As it is—as it is—perhaps the moment's not altogether propitious . . . Señor Cabra—would that be some sort of a firearm you have there?'

Fulgor bowed. 'The law provides for my assistant to be armed in certain circumstances.'

'Of course, of course,' Beckett smiled. 'A reasonable precaution when in the presence of a furious adulterer. Although in this case—as you shall hear anon—happily superfluous. I believe I'm right in saying the gun mustn't be loaded?'

'That *is* the case, sir.'

Cabra, embarrassed by Beckett's smile, was slipping his small, plated pistol back into what looked like a tobacco pouch.

' My assistant is present in his capacity of official witness,'
Fulgor explained. He blew his lips clear of his teeth between
sentences. Beckett found that the room was slowly filling
with the odour of the paper mouldering away in ancient
ledgers.

' Have you seen all you think necessary, Cabra? ' Fulgor
said.

' I have, sir.'

' Have you been able to establish beyond any possible
doubt the identities of the parties involved? '

' Yes, sir.'

' And have you noted down the exact time? '

' Eleven-forty, sir, by the cathedral clock.'

' Well then, I think that is all . . . Mr. Beckett, then—
once again my apologies; and nothing personal, I assure
you.'

' I appreciate it,' Beckett said. ' But before you go—
if go you must—I feel I should first dispose of some mis-
apprehensions that may exist. First of all, am I to understand that an aggrieved husband enters in some way into
this? '

' That is so, sir. If you wish to make a statement, I think
perhaps Cabra should take it down.'

' Not a statement,' Beckett said. ' Merely a clarification.
Can Señora Escoba, by the way, still be behind that
screen? '

' Señora Escoba has taken refuge in an adjoining room.'

' She should hear me, but never mind. So should the
supposedly aggrieved husband, who—please accept my
assurance—has no grievance.'

' Do you wish Cabra to put a statement in writing? '
Fulgor asked.

' Why not? ' Beckett said. ' Are you ready? '

Cabra opened his notebook, fountain-pen poised.

' What was about to take place here,' Beckett said, ' was

a search for truth—a search which, most of us will agree, can never entirely be concluded.' He stopped.

Cabra waited expectantly.

' The Kaaba of Mecca,' Beckett said, ' is a solid object—a cube of stone, in fact—geographically defined, and kissed smooth, as they say, by the mouths of its adorers. But lustrous truth has no central shrine—no place of pilgrimage. Your truth, O Fulgor, is not mine, although you and I and Pontius Pilate have all limped after it, all going our several ways. My truth is not the truth of curved space and time. And again—a rose is not a rose to a rose, nor indeed is a scorpion. How shall I know? How shall I know? Let's say that what I have sought has eluded me hitherto. I have heard a cuckoo call, and perceived the shadow of a shadow. Nothing more . . . Have you put that down? '

' Not in its entirety.' Cabra said

Beckett held up both arms in salutation of an invisible audience. ' Never mind, whatever you have written will do.'

CHAPTER 15

T UR went straight from his interview with the lawyer, to Valentin's office.

' I see no reason why we shouldn't come to an arrangement,' Valentin said.

Tur had not been entirely surprised by his reception. He had learned that with Valentin it was impossible to form an advance estimate of the composition of any interview. Valentin was mild and friendly, his features composed in an introspective Mongolian tranquillity. When he spoke, Tur noticed the fluty, sacerdotal quality of his voice, favoured by the acoustics of the cell of polished stone and glass in which they sat. Tur had discovered an ingredient of sympathy in Valentin's manner, which he felt ought to have been out of place.

' My suggestion,' Valentin said, ' is that we treat this episode entirely as a family matter—that we exclude outsiders and discuss the possibility of reaching a satisfactory settlement entirely among ourselves.'

It sounded as though he were about to break into an invocation, even a chant. Suddenly Tur found that Valentin reminded him of Don Firmín. It wasn't surprising. After all, wasn't he marked with the sign of a high priest of the secular age to come?

' And what do you propose? ' Tur asked.

' I merely desire to be the master in my own house. In every way,' Valentin said. ' I'm sure we both understand what's involved.'

' Yes,' Tur said. ' We both understand that.'

Try as he might, he found it impossible to suppress a flicker of grudging admiration for his son-in-law. Tur was cornered and beaten now. Whatever happened Valentin would get the land. Wasn't there something to be said, then, for giving in with what good grace he could muster, and accepting whatever peace of accommodation this amazing man might be willing to offer? If only Valentin would show him some means of saving his face.

' Neither of us has any desire to court unpleasant publicity,' Valentin said. ' Provided that I can be conceded full control of my wife's affairs, I have no objection to a reconciliation.'

Incredible, Tur thought. ' You mean you're prepared to forgive your wife? ' he said.

The word seemed to puzzle Valentin for a moment, but he nodded.

' Of course.'

While Tur marvelled, Valentin took a quick sniff at the blossom of a flowering plant he kept on his desk—the room's only adornment. His puzzled expression relaxed.

' There are certain obvious steps to be taken,' Valentin said, ' to ensure that what has happened remains a purely family affair. I think we can rely on our legal representatives' absolute discretion, but I must confess I feel far from happy about Augusta. It might be advisable for her to be induced to leave the island.'

' It could be arranged,' Tur said. ' I must say, though, that I should have thought that precedence might be given to the problem of what's to be done about the wretched fellow who's been the cause of all the trouble.'

'That has been attended to,' Valentin said. 'We needn't expect any further difficulties from that quarter.'

Tur would have been happy to have detected an under-current of venom in this assurance, but Valentin made it sound like a casual mention that he had closed a bank account. A strange and in many ways repellent man, he thought. But there it is, I'm too old to fight him. Besides, he holds all the cards. If only my girl weren't so stubborn.

Tur wondered if Valentin understood, fully appreciated his daughter's essential innocence, her vulnerable other-worldliness. 'Some people are born with trusting natures,' he tried to explain. 'They don't sin, they're sinned against. They wouldn't believe you if you told them the Devil was a liar. In a way they're too good for the rest of us. That English monster probably managed to administer some sort of drug.'

If only Valentin would agree with him now, Tur would be ready to surrender on any terms. He'd even give the man more than he was asking for. He waited for Valentin's nod, his smile of assent for Tur's assessment of his daughter's indomitable virtue.

Valentin blundered. He blundered as he had blundered in telling Basilisa of the grocer's rejection of her as a suitable bride for his son. He was too apt to give people credit for more rational attitudes than they possessed.

'I have a further recommendation to make,' Valentin said. 'This is that your daughter be encouraged to travel more. I suggest at least a couple of continental trips a year. I understand that the Italian lakes can be very pleasant in summer. A reasonable climate and a gay atmosphere. Venice too, of course. She'd be sure to find it most stimulating.'

Foreign travel? Tur didn't see much point in it. 'In any case,' he said, 'the question arises of a suitable chaperon. It's been agreed that we get rid of Augusta—

but where do you think we're going to look for another companion?'

'That's just the point,' Valentin said. 'The trip must be unchaperoned. Your daughter must be alone.'

'I don't think I understand you,' Tur said.

'Her temperament demands an occasional outlet of a certain kind,' Valentin said. 'Which could most conveniently and prudently be found in this way.'

Temperament . . . Outlet. Tur could no longer evade the brutal reality of the suggestion—this suggestion so charged with poisonous and lying inferences. He felt a shortness of breath, a sudden tightness in the chest.

'You're quite ready, then,' Tur said, his voice reduced almost to a whisper, ' to see your wife corrupted. Have you no sense of shame or dishonour?'

Once again Valentin seemed puzzled.

'The world has changed,' Tur said. 'I don't understand human beings any more. They seem lost to natural feelings.' The tightness in his chest was increasing. It made him angry. 'Do you realise my daughter hates you?' he said.

'Hates me?' Valentin took his measurements of the word, eyes slightly upraised. 'Really—would you put it as strongly as that? Personally I should have been inclined to say that I bore her. I suppose too much boredom can produce emotional states one might be tempted to describe as hate. Personally it's a word I distrust. In any case I assure you that whatever the nature of your daughter's feelings for me may be, it needn't affect this discussion. Naturally enough, I should never allow such a thing to influence my attitude towards her in any way.'

Tur had never felt so much like striking a man in his life. He controlled himself. 'I reject your proposals,' he said, ' and with scorn.'

Valentin bowed his head slightly, like a shopkeeper resigned to the whims of an impossible customer. He was disappointed but resigned. He had always suspected that the old man would rather die than swallow his pride.

' And therefore,' Tur said, ' there's no alternative but to allow events to take their course.' He got up, then remembering something, sat down again. ' This, I imagine, is likely to be our last meeting. I wonder if you'd agree to satisfy my curiosity about a certain matter that's caused me a great deal of troublesome speculation over the past ten years? '

' If I can.'

' The wedding present of half a million pesetas. Have you any objection to telling me what you did with it? '

' None at all,' Valentin said. ' Why should I? I invested it in the harbour improvement scheme. As a matter of fact, I became the principal shareholder.'

' Fantastic,' Tur said. ' Who would have thought it? You were only twenty-seven years old, weren't you? '

Valentin nodded. ' I wanted to suggest the idea to you,' he said. ' But you gave me no reason to assume that you'd be receptive to it. It turned out to be a most fortunate speculation. The company paid forty-eighty per cent this year.'

' One last question, then,' Tur said. ' How did you know there was water under the Salina? '

' I studied for the priesthood for a year under Don Fidel . . .' Valentin said.

' I wasn't aware of that,' Tur broke in, ' but it accounts for a lot.'

' We often discussed the island's history,' Valentin said. ' Don Fidel mentioned the fact that in the old days the Salina was covered by a laurel forest. Our native laurels can't grow unless they can put down their roots to water at a depth of no more than twenty feet. Any arboriculturist will tell you that.'

For a moment it seemed to Tur that a sardonic intelligence

had occupied itself with the planning of his downfall. Nemesis? Divine retribution? . . . Certainly not. But in another age how easy it would have been to see himself the victim of some trivial-minded, freakishly malicious deity.

'Young man,' Tur said, ' you've come very close to converting me to an unforgivable superstition.'

He got up again, and Valentin, laughing good-humouredly, held out his hand, but Tur ignored it.

CHAPTER 16

Don Arturo had interrupted the interrogation to confront Tur in his dignified despair, to console and to reason with him.

'My dear friend, the law can be stretched in all directions. If absolutely necessary it can be turned inside out, but it can't be abolished altogether. A marriage contract is a contract like any other. Evidence is evidence, and witnesses are witnesses. Quite frankly we might have been able to do something if it hadn't been your son-in-law—but as it is we'd be knocking our heads against a stone wall. Regrettably enough, money talks. We may as well face it.'

Money talks, Tur sighed. He got up, shaking his head. Of course it talked. Until yesterday it had been *his* money that had talked, had spoken with an authoritative voice heard from one end of the island to the other. He'd got used to his money silencing the others. He supposed it would take a little time to accept the change.

As soon as the door closed behind him, Don Arturo went back to his inner office and sat down again at his desk. He swivelled his chair sideways to face his middle-aged corporal, his profile to Mila.

'Now let's see, where were we? Ah yes—we were

considering this man's record, which in all conscience is depressing enough. Seven years for political crime on the mainland, followed by several woundings and assaults . . . all the usual minor troubles, it goes without saying.' A natural bandit, you could see that from just one look at the man. Yet a common enough product of the terrible years. What did the record also say, that he hadn't thought fit to mention? ' Father executed. R.P.' That meant as a political reprisal, and that there had been no charge and no trial. After that the boy had spent ten years in a special orphanage—in other words being rehabilitated with regular thrashings and potato soup. To these things Destiny had condemned him, just as it took the sight from the blind. Destiny had also condemned him to the ultimate irony of punishment at men's hands in their belief in his possession of a malignant free will.

Don Arturo's interrogations were known by Don Arturo as discussions. He believed in gentleness, alternating with menace, and the victim was offered a cigarette. So far his tactic had been to discuss Mila's probable fate with his corporal as though Mila had not been there in person. But for his low opinion of his corporal's efficiency, he would much have preferred to leave the whole thing to him. His doctor's sombre warning rang in his ears: ' Boiled fish, watered wine, and excitements of any kind absolutely debarred.'

' As he perfectly well realises,' Don Arturo said, ' his release was conditional. Ask him if he realises the conditions on which he was released.'

The corporal put the question, and Mila mumbled that he did.

' Even now, my feeling is that he's showing a far from co-operative spirit, corporal. I wonder if he realises that it rests with me whether or not he goes back again when his probation comes up for review? ' He swivelled suddenly to face Mila. ' Do you realise that? '

' Yes, sir.'

' Well, so long as you do. So long as you know what to expect if you keep up your present somewhat un-co-operative attitude.'

' Excuse me, sir——'

' Well? '

' I reported to you as instructed.'

' But what you've produced is hearsay, not evidence. Shall I tell you something? I believe you've something up your sleeve. Wait a minute, corporal, how does this man get a living these days—by pimping? '

' There is a conviction for living on immoral earnings, sir '

' A pimp. That's shameful. Aren't you ashamed of yourself? '

' Yes, sir.'

' Well, I'm glad of that. Now to go over the ground again, remembering that what I expect from you is the unadorned truth. When, in the first place, did the famous meeting take place? '

' Two days ago, sir. That would be the eighteenth. At the Bar Micalitus.'

' And who was present? I want the names of all those who were present.'

A shifty-eyed silence. They were back at the end of the same blind alley as before.

' Why don't you answer? '

' Because I don't know, sir.'

The man knew all right. Don Arturo was quite certain of that, but only with the most delicate handling would they get any information of value from him. They had him in a trap, but he was a natural enemy. He would give nothing away. Don Arturo had taken the trouble to examine the numerological aspects of this case based upon the man's name and date of birth, and they showed him that he was dealing with a stubborn, irreconcilable criminal. Few people these days would have been prepared to sit in judgment on a life's tragedies made inevitable by an injury from the delivery forceps, or the germs of syphilis inherited with the blood, and Don Arturo merely went a step further. He held no man responsible for his actions. It was all written in the sky, and numerology was the most reliable system for the deciphering of Destiny's code. In this case a name, place and date had come together with fatal results, condemning a child at the moment of his issue into the world from the womb. Don Arturo felt a queasy compassion for him, as he did for all those who found themselves in the police's net.

' I don't trust you,' Don Arturo said. ' You're a liar, and sooner or later you'll suffer for it. If you don't know who was there, how many were there? '

' A good number.'

' You're being vague again, in the way you've been throughout this discussion. Were there five or more? '

' Yes, sir.'

' How do you know if you weren't there yourself? '

' Because they were all talking about it afterwards.'

' Do you know what that constitutes? ' But why five? he suddenly wondered. Why not four or six? Five was a number of no numerological distinction. Why should they have settled on five and not three, seven, twelve, or thirteen —all of which were full of significance?

' Apparently you don't. Well, it constitutes an act of rebellion. Are you quite sure you weren't there when this meeting took place? You realise I have ways of finding out.'

' I wasn't there, sir, I promise you. They stop talking whenever I come into any place nowadays.'

' Who was the ringleader? That's what I'm concerned with. You say that at the meeting it was decided that the women engaged to work in the canning factory were to be forced to withdraw their labour—or in other words to go on strike. Who was it who promised this action? That's what I want to know, and that's what I'm determined to know. Somebody must have proposed the solution.'

'I wasn't there, sir, so I can't say.'

'Very well,' Don Arturo said, 'I'll give you three days in which to find out. You've three days in which to produce the name of whoever it is that's at the bottom of all this. After that you needn't expect any mercy from me.'

Mila went back to the fishing port which had emptied in the hours he had been kept waiting at the police barracks for his ' discussion ' with Don Arturo. A day lost. *The* day lost. It was the first day of the melva season, when success—or its absence—set the pattern of luck, as the superstitious fishermen believed, for the rest of the year to come.

His eighteen-year-old brother waited bleakly by their boat. He had been waiting since dawn.

'Are we going then? '

'What do you think? '

'I suppose it's too late.'

'Of course it's too late.'

'It always happens this way. Something like this always happens.'

'You were born under an unlucky star,' Mila said.

There was a hidden barb in the remark. The brother, Jaime, was illegitimate—born five years after his father's death, after his mother had been obliged to become a domestic servant. Every one of the fishermen's women who had been forced by starvation into domestic service in that bitter period had had illegitimate children. What had taken place had been a mass rape of the women of the defeated behind a screen of outward respectability, through which no cries of despair had been allowed to penetrate. Both brothers hated and needed each other, although both the category of their hatreds and their needs were different.

' Yes,' Jaime said. ' I was born under an unlucky star.'

' But now you have your luck, you must wear it. Tomorrow we shall go fishing.'

' If the police don't want to see you again.'

Mila smiled. There was no violence in his treatment of his brother. He dominated him without threats or blows, imposing servitude and frustration. His brother was always there; a human target on which he could expend some of his bitterness in the way a peasant unnecessarily flogs his donkey to relieve his bile.

' Did any of the women show up for work at the factory after all? '

' Only two.'

' What happened? '

' Somebody saw them and told them to go away.'

' Who saw them? '

' Toniet.'

' And did the trawlers take any guards aboard when they went out? '

Jaime shook his head. He had made up his mind not to tell his brother of the latest sensational happening, but the need to share the news with someone was too strong for him. ' Last night . . .' he started.

' Last night what? '

' Last night Cosmi's son went aboard one of the ships— just to have a look round.' Jaime paused for dramatic effect.

' Well, what about it? '

' They broke his face and threw him into the sea. Tonight we're preparing a reception.' Jaime tried to look like a cowboy avenger.

' *You're* preparing a reception. If there's to be any reception it will be for you. There are more guards than rats in this town today. Give me a cigarette.'

Jaime gave his brother a thin, badly rolled cigarette made from butt-end tobacco bought from street urchins.

' Light it.'

Jaime struck a match and held it up.

" Keep your hand still.'

Mila inhaled, blew the smoke out in his brother's face, and coughed.

' Dried donkey shit.' He threw the cigarette away.

' I'm going to have a sleep,' he said. ' If anyone wants me you can call me.'

' But who ever would want you—except the police? ' Jaime called after his brother's back.

Mila made for a wedge of shade between a pile of nets and the upper quay wall. He took off his jacket, folded it to make a pillow, and lay down to sleep.

Ten minutes later he was awakened by his brother tugging at his shoulder.

' What's the matter now? '

' We've got a passenger. A tourist woman. She wants to go to La Caleta.'

CHAPTER 17

L<small>AURA</small> had picked up the phone and a voice rasped and scratched in the ear-piece. All voices were unrecognisable over Vedran phones, it being possible at the most to distinguish male from female callers, but Laura knew this must be Beckett.

'Hullo Laura—is that you? Listen, I'm terribly sorry, I can't make it after all.'

'Shouldn't you have let me know?'

'You know I'd have done so if I possibly could. Something turned up. Are you there? I say, can you hear me? I've been trying to get hold of the Cartwrights. Could you possibly try ringing them for me?'

'They'll have gone by now.'

'Yes, I suppose they will. Anyway, you'll still be going over to La Caleta, won't you? I know they're looking forward to seeing you. Could you do something for me? Could you say goodbye for me? Tell them I'm sorry I couldn't make it, and that I've been trying to contact them.'

'What on earth are you talking about?'

'I'm departing. My permit's been revoked. They're kicking me out.'

'You're joking.'

' I wish I were.'

' I think I'd better come over,' Laura said.

' No, don't do that. Better not. There's a guard here.'

' Did you say a guard? '

' That's what I said. He's here to make sure I really catch the boat tonight. Says his orders are not to let me out of his sight.'

' But Alex, what have you done? '

' I got involved in something. I can't explain now.'

' Can't you tell me anything? '

' No, and it's nothing really. It's all been a bit of a frame-up. You know what they're like when you tread on someone's toes. I'll write and explain.'

' Can't I come down to the ship and see you off? '

' I'd just as soon you didn't. I expect they'll take me straight aboard.'

' Oh Alex, that's terrible.'

' Laura, I've always had a terribly soft spot for you. I may not have succeeded in making it very obvious—but I have.'

' Darling, I know. I have too.'

' Do you think there's any chance of our being able to get together some time? '

' If you want to.'

' I don't know where you're thinking of going, but I expect I could get there somehow or other. Anyway, you'll write to me, won't you? '

' Of course I will.'

' You don't know how I'm going to miss you.'

' I'm going to miss you too. Dreadfully. I simply can't believe you're going off like this.'

' I want to say all sorts of things to you,' Beckett said, ' but now it comes to the point, I don't know how to put them into words. I'm in such a panic here I can't think straight. I've only got a few hours to clear up this terrible rubbish dump.

Haven't the foggiest what I'm going to do with half the stuff.'

'I'll come over straight away, and give you a hand.'

'No, please don't. I'd only feel upset if you turned up here when I'm in a mess like this. I can't tell you why, but I would. You just go out with the Cartwrights as arranged. I'd far sooner you did that. And, oh yes, I was nearly forgetting—I've found someone for your house.'

'That's marvellous news. Do they want it now? I mean straight away.'

'I believe so. It's a chap in the old man's firm in Tenerife. He's coming over to see it on the next boat. Man by the name of Watkinson. Cecil Watkinson. You won't show it to anyone else in the meanwhile, will you?'

'No, I won't let anyone come near it.'

'I shouldn't let him off too lightly—he's got plenty of money.'

'As long as I can get someone to take if off my hands—that's all I'm worried about.'

'Laura—there is one thing you could do for me. Perhaps you could come over here as soon as I'm out of the place tonight, and have a look round. I expect I'll have to leave an awful lot of junk behind. If you want anything you can have it. Otherwise you might get someone to store the odds and ends of furniture that belong to me. You know what they are.'

'Don't worry,' Laura said. 'Leave it all to me.'

'And you will write, won't you? I'll wire my address as soon as I have one. How often will you write to me?'

'Twice a week,' she said.

'That's wonderful. I feel better now. And you won't believe any rubbish going round about me? I can just imagine the kind of stories that will be floating round. It's all been a frame-up.'

'I know.'

' I'd better go now, darling, and get started on this mess.'

' Poor Alex, I wish I were there with you.'

' Goodbye darling, and write, won't you? '

' Of course I will, darling. Twice a week. Goodbye and do take care of yourself.'

And Laura had put down the telephone, picked up her things and hurried down to the port. A hush seemed to have fallen on the town.

Laura had never seen the port so silent and deserted before. The main harbour held only the *Almirante Cervera* and Tur's schooners. As she had feared, there wasn't a small boat to be seen. Reluctantly she walked on to the fishing port. The Cartwrights, who lived on the other side of the town, on the road to La Caleta, always insisted in the interests of regular exercise on walking to the beach. La Caleta was two miles from the Cartwrights' villa, and three miles from the port. This was a distance that no native of Vedra, or no long-standing resident like Laura would have contemplated undertaking on foot, and the taxis refused to tackle the ruinous La Caleta road.

Laura found that the fishing port, too, was strangely devoid of activity. Mechanically she registered the components of the scene around her. A line of lavender and grey flat-bottomed chalanas, tied stem to stern. Rosettes of small fish just below the water's surface, nibbling at floating scum. The dried carmine lacquer of shark's blood on the flagstones. Policemen posted at intervals, like brooding Napoleons in their old-fashioned hats, all round the horseshoe of the port.

Distantly a few aged shrimp fishermen had risen from the dead and were afloat in their blue coffins on the town's reflection in the pitted mirror of the harbour, dangling their handkerchief-nets through the cathedral's belfry, the barred windows of the prison, and the blind umber walls of the Palace of the Inquisition.

She felt flat, as she had never felt before. She seemed to herself to have lost interest in life. But over Beckett of all people. I must have liked him quite a lot more than I ever realised. Well, it's no use worrying about it now. I suppose I'll get over it. It usually doesn't take long for the mood to pass off, however much I always think at the time it's with me for good.

Laura walked on a few more paces, and a felucca tied up behind a jetty came into view. It was the only felucca in the whole port. A boy squatted on the deck fiddling with some fishing tackle.

' I want to go to La Caleta. Can you take me? '

He nodded.

She hesitated. The deck seemed a long way down.

' Jump,' he said. ' I'll catch you.'

She shook her head. ' Give me your hand.'

The boy held up his hand and she took it to steady herself and jumped down.

' Make yourself comfortable. I'll go and get the boss. Back soon.' He was gone. Laura scrambled across the deck to reach the bows, away from the petrol fumes of the engine. She sat with her legs dangling in the well where they kept the gear, her back to the port, eyes, unfocused, on the sea.

She heard the thud of a man's weight drop on the deck behind her, and felt the boat tilt. Someone was tinkering with the engine. The exhaust gulped several times as whoever it was wrenched at the starting handle. Then the engine fired, coughed, and settled to a sullen, sluggish thumping. Laura turned her head and saw Mila.

She pulled up her legs and tried to stand up on the deck but couldn't. She was on the point of screaming; of throwing herself into the water, and swimming the two, four, six, eight yards that separated them from the quayside. Then she gained control of herself. Mila seemed unconcerned with her. He fixed the throttle setting, then

scrambled to the stern to grasp the tiller. Why should I
be afraid of him? After all, there's nothing to be afraid of.
He can't hurt me in any way. He can't do anything to me.
I'm too well known, and so is he. She made up her mind to
treat him like some uncertain, only potentially dangerous
animal of the kind that only became vicious when it scented
one's fear. All I have to do is to show him I'm not afraid of
him.

Now the quayside was fifty yards away. If she ordered
him to turn back, he might refuse, and her position would be
worsened. It was better to go through with the thing as
coolly as she could. She decided to make a start by talking
to him in a perfectly normal, confident manner. So far
Mila, dark-faced and saturnine, had not looked in her
direction.

' How long does it take to get to La Caleta these days? '
Her voice sounded to her satisfactorily brisk.

Mila's head swivelled, but his eyes still looked away.
' In these days you may say it takes fifteen minutes. More
or less.' After three winter seasons as a tourist guide,
he spoke a stiff, solemn English.

' Good,' she said. ' I ask because I'm late, and friends are
waiting for me.' Friends are waiting for me. That was a
brainwave.

' In fifteen minutes' time you will be there.'

This aloofness, this unwillingness to meet her eye, was a
little disquieting. She shifted her position so as to face him.

' Why aren't there any boats in port? '

' Because the fishing has begun.'

' That's good, isn't it? '

' Good and bad. Yesterday the trawlers from Las Palmas
came. The poor are not allowed to live.' Mila was
embarrassed. He was a man increasingly beset by daydreams, and these daydreams more and more overlapped
and entangled with the situations of real life. This virtual

kidnapping of Laura had begun as part of a daydream. It was the realisation of the first part of a complete dream-adventure compressed into the few seconds that had elapsed between his awakening by his brother and his leap down into the boat. In its full extension Mila's fantasy had included carrying Laura off to an island some distance off the coast, and there forcing her to understand and capitulate to his love. But now with Laura actually in his boat and in his power, the fantasy had collapsed, and he was encumbered with a reality over which he had little control.

He left the tiller, scrambling towards her, eyes still averted. Laura's chest tightened. He dropped into the engine-well, found a wicker-covered bottle, a glass and an old newspaper. ' Country wine,' he said, holding up the bottle by its neck and shaking it at her. A kind of strained, pleading geniality had taken possession of him.

Mila tore a sheet off the newspaper and began to polish the glass. He inspected it, head cocked, one eye closed, against the sky. Then he poured wine into the glass and held it out.

Laura shook her head, and was instantly sorry that she had done so. Mila's face changed again, went dark and taut. The almost cringing expression of a moment before had been replaced by a grimace of wounded pride. He had recoiled as if she had slapped him, the glass still held out to her. For a few seconds he held the glass at arm's length, staring at it. Then he tossed the wine overboard.

' What am I to say? I am poor. I agree with you.' He seemed to be talking to himself.

' Our proverb says, " Even seaweed bread smells sweet in a rich man's house, but the poor man's honey stinks." '

He backed away to the stern and seemed to be pondering this, nodding his head, his arm over the tiller.

Shorewards, Laura recognised the heat-misted landmarks of the coast. She thanked God they were heading for

La Caleta. She risked a glance at her wrist-watch. Four
minutes of the journey had gone.

'A man of no education,' Mila said. 'You should turn
your back on me. And this I understand. Poverty is not
good.'

'Whether you're poor or rich doesn't concern me,' Laura
said. She tried to say this kindly.

'But even the poor have their pride and their ideals.
I have suffered for my ideals.' Mila's brain was invaded by
another daydream. 'I resisted,' he said challengingly,
not to Laura, but to some internal audience. But it was
not true. Resistance had been impossible. A few months
in prison were enough to break the resistance of even the
bravest, among whose ranks Mila had never stood. The
nerves made their separate coward's peace, betraying the
will-power, and a pure animal body took control, blind to
all the issues but self-preservation.

'Do you say, then, that nothing, not even ideals, are
permitted to the poor?'

Laura didn't reply, following the first rule laid down
for the guidance of all foreigners in their dealings with
Vedrans, which was never in any circumstances to allow
themselves to be drawn into a discussion that might
conceivably be labelled 'political'.

She hates me, Mila assured himself. She refuses to speak.

Five more minutes to go. The land, a shadow over the
sheen of the sea, was slipping by, measured by headland,
lighthouse and fort. A boat swung into sight, passing
between them and the shore. Laura recognised it from its
dark red sail as belonging to a man called Valls, a consumptive whom she knew slightly. Valls was a small black
silhouette, hardly bigger than a chimpanzee, hunched in the
stern. Laura, suddenly taken with the idea that it might be
a good plan to be sure that Valls saw she was in Mila's boat,
waved to him, and Valls waved back.

Mila's thoughts darkened again. She had gone to the gardens at night with Toniet, as everyone in the port knew. She was prepared to waste her friendship and perhaps her love on a wretched, dying consumptive like Valls. And yet, causelessly, she had refused his wine, and would not even reply to him when he spoke to her.

His headache started. He knew by two symptoms when an attack was to be expected. The first warning was the sudden headache, and the second was the voices. The voices he heard in crowds, insulting words separated from random conversation and argument, which pieced themselves together to slander him. Mila had learned that the only method of dealing with such an emergency was simply to go away quickly. He knew that if he stayed within range of these insinuations and slanders, a rage would come over him, and he remembered that the Judge had warned him that if this ever happened again he would be sent to the prison for incorrigibles. Terrible stories circulated about the fate of criminals who were committed to this prison, never to return.

The fatal headache that preceded the voices and the attacks was now beating in his temples. In the ordinary way he would have taken to his heels at this point, but now he was trapped at sea with the object of his hatred in a boat only eighteen feet long. Hatred had flooded into his loins; a tide of bitter concupiscence. This was a passion that satisfied itself with a man's life and a woman's honour. He squatted scheming revenge, but then another vision intervened: that of the paper sent with a man, so they all said, when it was decided he should never return, and the warders were given a free hand, coming with strait-jacket and gag. Special treatment number 3. A quart of water forced down the throat, then the penis tied up for twelve hours. Only chance to beat one's brains out against the cell wall before the bladder burst. Better, far, that they should

simply crack his legs with their clubs and then kick him
to death.

That was what they would do to him. That was the end
for him they had planned. They. The originators of the
plot against him that had started from that moment when
he had stood wetting himself as his mother, having rolled
his father's body over on to its back, scooped the earth with
her fingers out of his mouth—the earth that he had been
chewing in the agony of death. 'They'. Mila could no
longer separate the conspirators from the general mass of
humanity among which they had so craftily infiltrated. In
the first place they had been quite simply limited to the
masters of the orphanage, a compact body against which it
had been possible to defend himself. But then he had gone
to prison and the 'theys' had multiplied, seeding themselves
like weeds, until they were everywhere. Policemen of all
varieties, judges, warders, stool-pigeons, prison commis-
sioners, were the obvious self-proclaimed 'theys', but the
world's conspiracy against him had continually enlarged its
membership until it included even the greater part of the
fishermen he worked with. His brother was on the road to
becoming one of the 'theys'. Toniet was an important
'they'. A quick new fantasy rooting itself in his mind
spread its baleful foliage: her encouragement of him,
followed by a reasonless rejection, had been all part of a
scheme to involve him in a new humiliation.

Laura counted the seconds. She forced herself to count
slowly, curbed the temptation to check the passage of the
precious minutes with known landmarks. A headland came
out to meet them, then sank back into the coastline. Mila
shifted the tiller a few degrees. They were turning into the
bay of La Caleta, half encircled by low cliffs that had a
strangely compressed look, as if flattened by the weight of the
sky. A dozen pelicans, disturbed by their arrival, went
labouring away, thrashing the water with their wing-tips,

then finally, severed from their reflections, rose and turned
to pass over them.

The presence of the pelicans made it clear that there was
no one on the beach. Laura had expected to find several
English families already installed under their beach
umbrellas. La Caleta was a favourite with newcomers to
Vedra and recently promoted residents, although the old
hands and the natives were never seen there. She remembered that the Grants, and the Dempsters, and the
Laughtons would have had the same difficulty in finding a
boat to bring them as she had had. She glanced at her
watch. Ten past ten. It would be at least eleven o'clock
before the Cartwrights came on the scene, purple-faced with
exposure to the sun, led by their nine-year-old, dutifully
carrying his pail and spade as another child might have
carried a parcel of school books.

The thump of the engine's exhaust faltered to silence and
the boat slowed suddenly, its bottom hissing on sand, and
then stopped. Only a few yards of rippling water separated
them from the beach. Now another problem arose. That of
payment. Laura was determined to pay, yet sensed that
Mila would make the offer of money an excuse to show
himself offended.

' How much do I owe you? '

He shrugged his shoulders, turned his back on her rudely,
and busied himself with the anchor.

Laura felt in her handbag. She found a crumpled
collection of five-peseta notes, and a single hundred-peseta
note. She was dismayed at its condition. It was exceptionally dirty, and had been torn in half and mended—as so
many had—with stamp paper.

Mila threw the anchor into the water and turned round.
Laura held out the note. ' I hope that's enough. Don't
bother to wait for me, I'm going to walk back with my
friends.'

He took the note, opened it, uncurled the edges between his fingers, looked at the back and front of it, then folded it neatly.

' I'm sorry it's in such a mess.' She felt herself flush.

He held the note between finger and thumb, looking down at it. I'm got rid of with a tip, like a waiter, he said to himself. He looked round. They were alone between the sea and rocks. The pelicans had settled again farther up the beach.

Laura slipped her shoes off and put them in her bag, swung her legs over the side of the boat and dropped into knee-depth water. She shouted up, ' Would you please pass me my things? ' Silently, Mila pushed her bag within her reach with his foot. Laura reached up and took it. Holding her bag in one hand and her skirt above her knees with the other, she waded ashore. Mila, squatting on the deck, watched her.

Laura walked up the beach towards the nearest clump of oleanders. She stopped to pick up a strange, veined pebble, one of many of the same kind that were lying about, and examined it. The pebble reminded her of a bloodshot eye. She threw it away and walked on. A sea-bird passing overhead gave a prolonged, sobbing cry, and she couldn't help shivering. There was something sombre about La Caleta. It was a place for beach parties, for people in groups who brought their gaiety with them along with their picnic baskets and portable radios. She remembered now that the reason the Vedrans were supposed to avoid it was not because it wasn't smart, but because it was supposed to be haunted. It was one of the many places where the peasants had found the dried-up remains of Guanche aboriginals who had crept into rock-crevices at the time of the conquest, to die of weeping and starvation.

She decided to go for a swim, not because she particularly wanted to, but to use up time until the arrival of the

Cartwrights in a human and frivolous way that she felt
might diminish her sense of the inhumanity of the surroundings. She had compelled herself not to look back
until she reached the screen of oleanders behind which she
would undress. Now, from among the sheltering branches,
she watched Mila pull up his anchor, settle at the oars, and
begin to row away from the shore. Soon he was twenty or
thirty yards from the beach. She watched the gleaming
white scar left by the boat on the water's surface slowly
merge into the tin-plate grey of the sea. Pulling off her
blouse, she wondered why he didn't start his engine.

She put on the discreet, Madrid-made swimsuit, approved
by the Church and the Police, and therefore favoured by
foreign residents. Idly she wondered why Mary Cartwright
with her intense sympathy for the local mores and her
determination to conform had not yet realised that two-
piece swimsuits were not worn. The Cartwrights, a sober
and assiduous pair, were learning quickly. Nowadays the
only obvious pockets of nonconformism that remained were
their non-Vedran devotion to physical exercise, and their
resistance to the siesta's devouring of the daylight hours.
They possessed a quite patrician incapacity for astonishment.
A few Saturdays before, Toniet, back from his fishing, in
holiday white shirt, black trousers, and chewing a cigar,
had joined the party. They had received him with grave
interest, quite naturally, and without even unspoken
question, and the little boy Michael, a happy truant from
play, had engaged him, in Spanish studded with sub-
junctives and local slang, in a lively discussion on seafaring
matters.

Ready almost for the sea, her clothing hung on an
oleander branch away from the lizards, Laura saw the
whiteness of her skin under the almost vertical sun. She
found her bottle of Ambre Solaire, dabbed a yellow coating
on her arms, shoulders and thighs, put on her shoes again

for the naked sand, and went down to the water. The tide
was exhausted at the turn, swelling up with a limp impulse
to burst and throw out a lacing of foam. This the dry sand
immediately guzzled, leaving only pock-marks and a few
sticky bubbles on the surface.

Laura kicked off her shoes and waded into the water.
She threw herself down, swam a few lackadaisical strokes,
and turned over on her back. Through narrowed eyelids
screened with a soft feathering of lashes she saw an orange
sun, oscillating on the taut cords of its own rays. She
turned over, and making as vigorous splashing as she could,
swam into shore, and lay on the cool, wet beach surrounded
by the faint, intimate garglings of the sand drinking up the
water.

She wondered whether she had ever felt quite so completely
alone in her life before. Perhaps on the first day that she
had left home, but never since. Beckett had gone. She had
hardly noticed his presence when he was there, treating him
as a comfortable and familiar irritation. Now she knew how
much—without realising it—she had leaned on him. The
problem was to use up time, to ward off the demons of
solitude. She began to sing the garbled words of a fado
imported from Madeira which had suddenly become a hit
in the bars of Vedra, but the great baking silence seemed to
pounce on the sound of her voice, and she gave up the
struggle in mid-verse.

She got up, brushed the wet sand off the backs of her
thighs and started for the oleanders again. An uncomfortable
thought had entered her mind. Mila's boat had disappeared.
It had been nowhere to be seen when she had gone down to
swim, and yet she had not heard the engine start up, and
it would not have been possible to row out of the bay in so
short a time. There were a few small islands off shore, and
the only likely explanation for his sudden disappearance

was that for some reasons of his own, Mila was lurking with his boat behind one of these.

Laura tried to cure herself of the small, nagging disquiet that had lodged at the back of her mind by a contemptuous dismissal of Mila's power to harm her in any way. He had probably had one or two successes with the empty-headed little adventuresses who sometimes found their way to Vedra in the winter season, and it had gone to his head. He was despicable but not dangerous.

In the heat of the sun she had felt a slight sensation of light-headedness, and she was grateful for the shade of the bushes. She picked up her watch, glanced at it and put it on. Still at least a quarter of an hour to go before she could expect the Cartwrights to arrive. She undid the shoulder straps of her costume and pulled down the top. When she reached down for her bag to get out her towel a huge lizard suddenly shot from underneath it, stopped, head erect, tongue quivering, then poured the black quicksilver of its body into a crevice. She almost screamed. Her heart was bumping against her ribs. I really must try to do something about my nerves she thought. She rolled her costume down over her hips. It dropped on the sand, and she picked it up, shook off the sand and spread it on a rock to dry.

Having watched Laura go towards the oleanders, and knowing that it could only be to undress, Mila rowed quickly to the nearest island. He anchored the boat out of sight of shore, slipped off his trousers and, wearing his underpants only, dropped into the water and began to swim shorewards. He made for the cover of some massive rocks that had broken away from the cliff and that barricaded the beach about a quarter of a mile from where Laura was undressing. The sudden upsurge of wild hatred Mila had felt towards Laura had calmed, and his temples had ceased to throb. The present manoeuvre had no connection with the past fury. Mila would have played the same trick on any other girl. Practically all the foreign girls who visited La Caleta made a point of taking a dip in the sea before returning, and the nonchalant way in which they changed into and out of their swimsuits on this and other beaches, had turned a high proportion of the boatmen or tourist guides who brought them into Peeping Toms. The thing had become a popular sport. Every beach had a spot which was obviously the most suitable for undressing, and in one or two cases such as this, resourceful young men had constructed a sort of hide, which allowed them to keep their prey under comfortable observation, like ornithologists studying the habits of a rare bird.

It took Mila fifteen minutes to reach the rocks, and raising himself cautiously to take stock of the situation, he saw that Laura was already in the water. He clambered quickly up through the great blocks of sandstone and reached the top of the low cliff. Here, he plunged into a jungle of cactus and underbrush, through which the pioneers of this kind of adventure had hacked out a pathway. This was the fourth opportunity of the kind that had come Mila's way, and he was already the prisoner of a deadly appetite. Soon he came to the edge of a ravine. It was through this ravine that the track passed from the road above down to the beach, and the end of it was almost closed off by oleanders, which put down their roots there to what was left of the water that filled the ravine for a few days in spring.

Mila, crouching down, treading softly as a hunter, crossed the ravine's bed. He climbed the farther bank, hauling on protruding roots, worming his body soundlessly into a position where, in the cover of thick bushes, he could afford to stand upright again. Then watching the ground before every step he took and tenderly unlacing the branches in his path, he went delicately, step by step, towards the place invariably chosen by foreigners for its promise of privacy. Immediately above this floor of clean sand, screened from the beach by the hedge of oleanders, was a natural hollow in the sandstone, a kind of dug-out, across the front of which —as a further protection for the illicit viewer—a parapet had been built up and cunningly disguised with trailing undergrowth.

Here Mila ensconced himself, and having waited a few moments for his breathing to quieten, he climbed into position to peer over the top. Laura was already there, back from her swim, but to his intense disappointment he now found that since he had last enjoyed an experience of this kind the oleanders had put on a new growth, and all he could see of her was a quick flashing tantalus of white skin through a dense screen of leaves and branches. Laura's body had been pieced into a jigsaw, hardly any part of which was identifiable. He saw a calf, a forearm, and once through a clear polygon among the leaves, what might have been a nipple appeared, but was instantly withdrawn.

Mila, staring-eyed, teeth clenched, his blood pounding again now in the cavities of his head, struggled to interpret these abstract shapes and these flashing purposeless movements. Hatred had returned with lust. Once Laura's head surfaced momentarily from among the leaves, her nose and mouth raggedly haloed in wet hair. He was startled when she spoke—not understanding that it was to herself, until the meaningless murmur of her voice trailed away and merged into a humming of the tune of the Madeiran fado. Then an undulating arm reached through the foliage, and as Mila watched it, his lust gripping him like an attack of cramp, the hand closed on white clothing folded over a branch. Mila saw the last seconds of his opportunity running out; throwing away his caution, furiously, recklessly, he climbed higher so that his head and shoulders appeared above the parapet. A small stone, dislodged, fell, then trickled, then stopped. Laura, startled by the slight noise, quite naked, but her underclothing held in front of her, came through the branches. She looked up and saw Mila. Her jaw dropped, and Mila saw her eyes swivel away. The vest and knickers fell from her open hands and Laura, moving with a last dazed effort against the centrifugal tug of a gyrating landscape, groped for them before falling over backwards. Mila heard the thick, hollow sound of bone striking rock.

He jumped down from his hiding place and leaped on her, raging, widely separating her legs, and pressing his body against hers. She lay, head to one side, the whites of her eyes showing, slapping feebly at the sand with the palms of her hands. Mila crushed his mouth against hers, and she coughed a little vomit into his lips. He was on the point of forcing himself into her when, a few inches from his eyes, he saw the dark stain spreading through the sand from her head, and instantly came the vision of the garrotte, the slow turning of the screw that would drive his tongue out of his mouth and his eyes out of his head, and the blood ebbed out of his loins. He had done nothing, but now they would garrotte him for rape. He crouched watching her for a moment, as she lay slowly colouring the sand round her head, breath snoring through her open mouth, and Mila knew that the last link in the conspiracy against him had been forged. Now they would kill him, triumphantly justified. The only possible hope was to make sure of her, to make quite certain that if she recovered she would never give him away. He snatched up a small boulder with the intention of beating in her skull. He had bitten into his lips in a dozen places and was drooling gore and saliva. Then he remembered Valls, Valls had seen Laura with him, and Valls was one of the worst of them. Panic suddenly cut off Mila's capacity for thought. He threw down the boulder and rushed away across the beach down to the sea, where he fell into the water, blinded and choking and flailing his arms. He was half-drowned before he reached the boat.

Twelve minutes later the Cartwrights passed within half a dozen yards of where Laura lay on their way to the beach, and twenty-three minutes later she was discovered by their small boy, who had slipped away from his parents to be alone with his imagination in the woods. By the time Mary Cartwright rushed to the scene she found Laura sitting up. She was dazed but her memory had returned, and horror had come upon her.

CHAPTER 18

Toniet's boat had left two hours before dawn. He was fishing with Cosmi who owned the boat's engine, and with four boys in chalanas they were taking in tow to the fishing ground. They had only five miles to go to the headland known as the Charraca where they were to fish. Toniet had drawn the Charraca in the lottery no longer recognised as valid by the authorities represented by the Port Commandant.

The deck was piled with the folded melvera net, two hundred and fifty metres in length and six in depth; a valuable piece of property, owned by a widow, who would receive one third of the catch as her recompense for its use. It had been folded scientifically in a way that allowed it to be fed smoothly and swiftly into the waves. The men squatted separately on the deck, peering into the darkness. The sea curved past them like black oil, a few blurred stars on its surface. They did not speak. Cosmi was a melancholic, so silent by nature that strangers assumed him to be dumb.

The boys in the chalanas astern were silent too, mute with excitement. This was the moment when the ocean had come to life again, after the dearth, the emptiness, and the silence of summer. The vertical and horizontal pastures of the sea were restocked with uncountable herds of fish. Fish with their fear, their speed, their intuitions, their cool financial eyes, were spawning everywhere in their trillions. There were a trillion times more fish in the sea than all the other living things of the earth put together, and now they were erupting from the depths in their annual autumnal ferment. Everywhere off the Canaries and the Atlantic coast of North Africa the fishermen were about to cast their nets among the countless shoals of fish. They would net the melvas, the tuna and the bonitos of the local seas, and with them the straggling migrations of marlins and sailfish from the south, and the mackerel and sardines from the north. Prayer, or the invocation of the name of God, or of Mary, would be taboo, out of fear of the dolphins, those servants and avengers of the fish god who came to tear the nets of fishermen who went to Mass. The line fishermen, plagued continually by the useless, bait-stealing anchoas they would punish with knife-thrusts before throwing back, would be out for the rock-fish, the sheepsheads, and the groupers, now repopulating the underwater caverns. Specialists of another kind would troll for yellowtails and dentexes, and giant rays, thirty feet across, would take their spoons and drag them all over the sea. Others would stalk the sleeping bass at night with torch and double trident; while the piratically-minded would make secret raids with dynamite on lonely reefs, destroying a hundred fish for every one they recovered. At this season the old women would be kept busy night and day mending the nets, and the grandfathers who were too feeble for strenuous fishing would spend their time hooking octopus out of their rock-lairs for use as bait. Now, after undramatic summer, autumn brought excitement and windfalls, cruel losses and casualties, and sometimes death.

Cosmi's engine slugged heavily with an occasional cough,

and a gargle of big ends. Shorewards a dark silhouette of cliffs crouched and leaped beyond the phosphorescence ribboning from the felucca's bows. Toniet watched Cosmi's shape, a steeper projection from among the nets against the sky. Unlucky as ever, he was thinking. If anyone had to have his face smashed in it was certain to be Cosmi, or— in this case—his son. Cosmi was so notoriously unlucky that although he was a splendid fisherman, most of the other men were afraid to have him in a boat. Bad luck sometimes went to extraordinary lengths to disguise itself when it plagued him, as when that spring he had caught a monstrous fish which, once in the boat, had thrown up one of the two hooks it had swallowed, and flailing and thrashing with this, had torn half the calf out of his right leg.

Toniet tried to draw him out about the violence done to his son.

' How did it come to happen, then? What made him take the chance? '

' Eh? '

' I said what ever made him take the chance? '

' The chance? Curiosity, I suppose. Natural enough.'

' They'll be able to put him right. They can do anything these days. Fit him up with a few new teeth. You won't know any difference.'

Cosmi didn't reply. He had lived among them for twenty years, but nobody knew where he came from. They could tell by the way he spoke that he hadn't been born a fisherman. Whatever his secret was, the men respected it. They supposed that once he had been someone, but now he was a fisherman, and generally speaking, an unlucky one.

' Three or four teeth in front. There's nothing in it these days. Sometimes turns out to be an improvement,' Toniet said.

Just before dawn they reached the Charraca, a huge limestone mass that looked like dark, newly-baked peasant bread bulging over the sea. Cosmi cut the engine—to avoid disturbing the fish, and the two men began to row. When they were within a hundred yards of the cliff, Toniet let go the anchor, and they awaited sunrise. Here, as a slight swell reached them from some remote storm, smooth grey muscles of water tensed and relaxed under the boat. The sky was full of cavorting sea-birds which splashed and stained the lacquered sea all round them with their droppings. About half a mile away gulls and pelicans were ripping into the water's surface as if tearing the flesh off a living body. The men sat wordlessly while a frontier of pale sunshine crept over the water towards them. Then, as the first sunrays from the clifftops reached them, shafting into the sea, Toniet took the glass-bottomed box known as ' the mirror ', signalled to Cosmi to hold his legs and leaned down over the gunwale of the boat until he could press the glass into the water's surface and look through it.

Half expecting to see what he saw, he still felt a shock of surprise and excitement. Wherever he looked the fish were there, slow-moving and docile; pacified by some immense biological need, the nearest of them only a few feet away. Beyond, an endless repetition of bland-eyed, unwink-ing, toy-like metal shapes, had been packed into the spaces of the water, those close to him seen with an almost magnified clarity, coldly crisp in every metallic detail, and then sketched in ever more lightly in the smoky, receding planes of water. Seen from one angle, they shuttered the sea so closely as to overlap one another like the scales of a single huge marine monster. These were the melvas—big fish weighing up to thirty pounds—in honour of which the nets were named. Occasionally Toniet saw a racing pene-tration of their orderly formations by tuna and bonitos, shot like projectiles up and down whatever empty corridors of water they could find. The bottom was of dim coral, a bony, eroded world of miniature peaks and ranges, valleys,

and forests of sea-grasses, from which a resident population
of parrot-fish and wrasses spiralled in and out uneasily.

Toniet signalled up to Cosmi to haul him back into the
boat. The chalanas were called up and, going upon Toniet's
observations of the movement of the current, the tactics
were worked out by which the manœuvrable net called the
cortina and operated by the two chalanas would be dragged
in from the direction of the open sea to sweep the fish into
the jaws of the static melvera opened to receive them.

The two men in the felucca prepared themselves. Cosmi
had braced himself against his internal weeping. For an
hour or two he would be freed from an enmiring futility,
rescued from a battering inner self by the need for precise,
intelligent action. Toniet, foreseeing a remarkable catch,
felt himself threatened by the duplicity of fortune. Whichever way the problems of the next few days were resolved,
he was bound to lose. If they succeeded in defending their
livelihood against the trawlers it would be a year of
abundance, of the general settling of debts; and the prize
the sea would award him would be the virginity of Luisa,
now waddling towards the threshold of middle age. Should
they be crushed in their struggle with the fishing fleet,
there would be no marriages that year—but also there would
be near-starvation.

The chalanas were rowing away.

' Do you know who it was who did it? ' Toniet asked.

' The boat,' Cosmi said, ' I know the boat.'

This act of violence threatened the ruin of a peace of
compromise that was in the making. Toniet saw that in
forbidding the women to work for the canning factory, they
were preparing their own ruin. The trawlers would be
certain to retaliate by unloading their fish, at any price,
on the Vedran market. The fish merchants, in fact, who
were possessors of an almost supernatural sensitivity to
market conditions, had already dropped their prices.

Toniet's last action on the previous night had been to sound out the factory manager on the possibility of a compromise: the women to start work as arranged provided that the trawlers undertook to see that none of their fish was sold in Vedra.

The two chalanas, the cortina net stretched between them, awaited their signal a quarter of a mile away. Toniet had judged from his inspection with the ' mirror ' that the drift of the current was carrying the melvas with it in towards the nose of the Charraca, and where the current itself was deflected to sweep down the northern flank of the headland, he foresaw that the fish would be crowded into a sort of submarine bottleneck. It was decided then—Cosmi merely nodding his agreement—that the melvera should be placed across this bottleneck, with one horn of the net anchored as closely as possible to the rocks. They rowed back to the chosen position, and Cosmi, whose expertness in such matters was acknowledged by the others, anchored and buoyed the end of the melvera. Here the cliff leaned over them, its caverns sucking at the sea. The nearest cavern's black mouth opened on them, a single fang of water in its upper jaw. Even on calm days such as this, the sea at the Charraca possessed a leaping vivacity of a kind only seen in dangerous places. The current was squeezing the felucca into the rocks. Cosmi, rowing, had to pull with all his strength to overcome the thrust of the water.

It took two men to handle a melvera in comfort, while one man rowed, and Toniet heaved and strained under the net's immense weight as he paid it out, metre by metre, into the water. Cosmi had rolled up his trousers to show the wound on his leg, still pus-charged. He rowed on, grimacing under the strain. For a hundred yards he rowed back towards the shore, then began to turn with the bobbing line of floats curving behind, then once again out to sea, parallel with the cliff.

At last only a small pile of netting with its lead weights and floats remained on the deck. The chalanas had been waved away, the line of net stretched between them shifted from left to right by hand-signals and shouts, and now they awaited the final call that would bring them closing in. What could go wrong now? Toniet asked himself. Was there anything that could conceivably go amiss? There was a chance in a hundred that that scourge of fishermen, a school of dolphins, would suddenly come charging up out of the deep sea, hurtling straight through the fragile, precious melvera, abolishing in a matter of seconds months of labour, and materials that had been bought with the savings of years. There was a one in a thousand chance that the thistledown of clouds puffed up out of the east would be followed by a squall which would drive the vulnerable chalanas scuttling for shelter. In what other way could Cosmi infect them with his misfortunes? If Toniet had been a peasant he would have crossed himself and mumbled a propitiatory prayer, but as a fisherman at sea this comfort was denied him. The winged seeds of cloud separated themselves from the horizon as Toniet watched, leaving a sky pressed cleanly on the sea in all directions. The last metre of net and the last buoy went into the water. Toniet waved to the chalanas, giving the signal to move in.

With the sun rising, shadowy movements of the fish through the water could be seen from the boat. The chalanas were still between two and three hundred yards off, moving in; the one nearer to them caught in a current, coming in faster than the other.

Toniet stripped to his underpants, took the glass-bottomed box, and lowered himself over the boat's side. Holding on to a rope, he peered down into the sea again through the box's bottom. The melvas were going past beneath him in a drifting multitude. He could see the curtain of the net, partially visible among the fish for about twenty feet, then gradually dissolving in the soft green murk of the water. The net, attached to the end buoy and by a line to the boat's stern, divided the movement of the fish. Those that were barely trapped by the net with only inches to spare were immediately deflected by its gentle curve, and turned jostling into the ranks of their companions. This caused something of the confusion and excitement that Toniet had seen in cows being herded down a narrow lane. These beautiful, shining, streamlined cattle dived and ducked, and leapt each other's backs. He saw an unpleasant sight. Two fish, one after the other, appeared to go right through the net. The widow's melvera, he knew, was aged and rotten and much patched, and the fish had found a hole opened by the weight of the leads. Toniet wondered how many more weak places there were in the net.

Glinting lights swirled suddenly in the space below; a fused comet's tail of metallic colours blurred in darting movement, a thousand bright fillings snatched out of sight by a magnet. Now the box showed him an empty green cube of sea. Sharks, he thought, with a tickle of fear in his spine. He scanned round anxiously, tilting his box from side to side, for onrushing grey shapes. A shout from above brought his head out of the water, but before Cosmi could make him understand the reason for his excitement, Toniet heard the hollow drumming of a diesel engine on the water, and knew what was happening.

He threw the viewing box back into the boat, and hauled himself up over the gunwale. He balanced himself, crouching like a sprinter on the rocking deck, staring, unaware that his mouth had fallen open, at the trawler that had just come into sight round the headland, and was making straight for them. The farther chalana had closed to within thirty yards of the anchored end of the net, and the trawler was on the point of passing through this gap. Toniet

squatted, paralysed, watching the full-bellied gentle roll of
the trawler as it bore down on them, a lip of water curving
away on each side of the bows, trailing a wake of tangling
seagulls and foam. He heard the engine speed up, picked
up an iron bar as if to defend himself and threw it down
again. The nearer of the two chalanas, carried on by a
racing current, was closing swiftly and was only fifteen
yards away. Frantically Toniet waved it back. He screamed
to Cosmi to row and the two men grabbed for the oars and
began to pull with all their strength on their port oar so that
the felucca swung round sharply away from the trawler,
towards the shore.

Ros, the trawler's skipper, found himself faced with one of
the primeval emergencies of the sea, in which none of the
electronic equipment surrounding him, the radar, the
course-plotter, the navigator, the dials, gauges, scribbling
contour tracers, or winking lights, was of the slightest avail.
He had seen the floats marking the nearer end of the melvera,
and the net stretched between the two chalanas; but
knowing nothing of the local fishing methods, which were
different from those of Gran Canaria, let alone from those
of the Galician coast where he came from, he did not at
first understand the manœuvre the fishermen were engaged
in. He realised this in the instant that the trawler was level
with the first chalana, and at that moment Ros's only
reasonable course would have been to ring down 'full
speed astern '—thereby coming quickly to a standstill—
and then reverse out. This he was prevented from doing by
a natural stubbornness of character, and the need, as he saw
it, to impress a covertly hostile crew with his determination
to stick to any decision he might take. He rang down to
increase speed from half to full-speed ahead, in the hope of
getting safely through the further gap, which by this time

was only a matter of a few yards wider than the width of the trawler.

With its engine speed nearly doubled the trawler thumped ahead. A boiling wake fanned out from its stern, which caught and nearly upset the first chalana. Ros heard the screams and curses from the two boys in the chalana— neither of whom could swim—and looked away. Ros was a northerner from La Coruña, the youngest man on the boat, and the second youngest in the fleet, and defended himself from the older men under his orders by an unconvincing tuft of blond beard and this cultivated inflexibility. This was rapidly turning into the worst moment of his life. By taking this risk rather than climb down, Ros realised that he was staking his future. He knew also that in reversing his order and thereby admitting defeat he would be finished with these people. His contract had another year to run, after which he would return joyfully to the celebrated mists and rainfall of his own country. After that he would be free of the dirty, boastful, violent men with whom he was at present forced to associate.

Now the men in the two boats ahead began to scream and rave. The gap was still closing. Ros threw open the door of the bridge, took off his beret, and tried to wave the chalana back with it, not realising that the boys in it were fighting to hold it against the tide. As their oaths reached his ears, he changed colour. The Galicians he had been born among were intellectuals. He himself wrote simple nautical poems and played several musical instruments. Here the people ate filthy contemptible food, lived like animals for the bodily pleasures only, and murdered each other on the slightest excuse.

They murdered each other, and that was just what would happen if this insanely reckless piece of seamanship failed to come off. There would be murder. Ros forgot his pride. He rang down 'full speed astern', and caught the wheel with both hands. The gap between the felucca and chalana was now impossibly small. He had a moment in which to choose between throwing the helm hard over to starboard or to port, in the first instance cutting through the cortina between the two chalanas, and in the second, the melvera. In a calculation occupying a second, Ros realised that in steering his ship through the cortina he would almost certainly carry it along and collapse the chalana. Just as he was about to swing the wheel over to port, the felucca with the two men struggling at the oars swung away and the gap opened slightly. Ros held his breath and aimed the bows at the centre of it. The trawler, slowed suddenly by the back thrust of its engine, passed easily through. What was outside Ros's calculation was that in turning away, the felucca left in his path a loop of net. This the trawler's bows fouled and tore through, and then as the trawler passed over the ruined net, the propellers ripped out a dozen yards and cut them to shreds.

The trawler had stopped, propellers racing, in a flurry of churned-up water. Ros rang down 'slow' and swung the wheel. The ship pulled round. The felucca came into sight, dipping and rolling in the foam. Ros glimpsed one of the men on the felucca in the act of pointing up at the trawler, and at the same instant the bridge window exploded, pricking Ros's face and arms with flying fragments. The felucca rocked away out of sight. Ros saw two of the deckhands run across the deck away from a third man who was sitting down. We're being fired on, he thought. He rang down 'full speed', then called the mate on the inter-com. The mate, who seemed to have been waiting out of sight behind the back door of the bridge, came up blue-lipped and panting. Ros told him to take the wheel, then ran down to the deck. The deckhand sat there perfectly still, a thread of blood at his lips and both hands pressed together over his chest. He was an aged version of the man he had been when

Ros had last seen him. Ros tried to take the hands away, but the man resisted and shook his head. Ros slipped his arm behind the man's back and felt the stickiness where he was afraid he would find it, on his shirt between the shoulder-blades. The touch of warm blood made him feel faint.

' You're all right,' Ros said, in a pleading voice.

The man whispered, smearing the clean line of blood on his lips, but Ros could not understand what he was trying to say.

I'm finished, Ros thought. Finished at twenty-five. Done for. All the certificates and diplomas in the world won't do me any good now.

A depressed, silent semi-circle of crew, the second fisherman with them, had backed away under the trawl. Ros called the second fisherman. ' The first-aid kit. Quick.'

Two men carried out the medical chest of many drawers, straining under its weight. A third man presented him with the bound index and manual of instructions, and the separate anatomical chart with key. Ros took the chart in jointless fingers. The cover showed an heroic figure, a hairless Apollo whose organs were to be displayed by raising a series of paper flaps. Successively Ros stared appalled at the tender pinks, the magentas, the corals, and the greys of heart, lungs, pancreas, liver, spleen, stomach, and intestinal coils; all of them layered and compressed so miraculously among the bold red tubes of arteries, the blue veins, and the white threads of nerves. There was no wasteland of the body. Every cubic millimetre was counted in its economy. Ros's eye went from chart to man—now turning into a waxen effigy of himself—and back to chart. He opened drawer after drawer of the cabinet. This thesaurus of medicines and appliances offered him the means of dealing with a limitless variety of physical emergencies. Its assemblers had been prepared for cuts, burns, bruises, fractures, for foreign

bodies in the eye or ear, for snakebite, tetanus, sunburn and
electric shock. There were injections, antidotes, febrifuges,
sedatives, antiseptics, analgesics, and purgatives, and more
categories and more. But they had made no provision that
Ros could find, with the seconds and minutes ticking by and
a life leaking away, for a man with a bullet hole clean through
his chest, clean through all that immutable order and those
crowded indispensables of the body which the chart had
allowed him to glimpse.

The first engineer, who had come on the scene to squat
by his side, had discovered with a small, encouraged cry a
pair of bullet forceps, tied to a probe tipped with unglazed
porcelain ' for locating musket balls ', according to its faded
label. But there was no musket ball. All that was needed
was some contrivance to plug in the life, now oozing not only
out of the two small holes but through the lips of a man no
longer able to speak, with his mouth trembling in and out of
a puzzled semi-smile.

The engineer seemed to have taken over. Ros found a
roll of wide but perished adhesive plaster and another of
absorbent gauze, and pushed them into his hands. Somehow
or other they must succeed in holding back the life until they
reached port.

' Strap him up,' Ros said. ' Stop the bleeding somehow.
Try giving him some brandy and water.'

He went back to the bridge to plot their positions and
to work out the time required to get to port. Twenty-two
minutes. I'm finished, Ros said to himself. Finished at
twenty-five. No catch, and a dead man on my hands. Ros
thought of himself as a scientific Catholic, a man who
struggled to construct a harmony of religion and career,
and who felt a natural devotion to clarity, precision and the
exactitudes. But now he had been lured by expediency into
a moral labyrinth in which every signpost seemed to have
been turned round to point in a false direction. He longed

to be able to recognise justice and thereafter to lead the just life—a life in which truth was to be established with the finality of an electronic computation.

Before leaving Las Palmas on this trip he had been asked to report to the General Manager, who showed signs of doubt about his capacity or his willingness to carry through the present task.

' Ros, I believe you're a man of scruples, aren't you? '

' I hope so.'

' Do you know what gauge you're fishing with these days? '

' It's my business to know.'

' Well, what is it? '

' Forty-two.'

' Is that legal? '

' It depends.'

' But you don't fish for tuna with a forty-two. You didn't in my day anyway. Shouldn't it be ninety-eight? '

' In theory.'

' The real fact of the matter is that every ship in port is using forty-two. Isn't that true? '

Ros didn't reply.

' Well, aren't they? '

' Yes,' Ros said. ' They are.'

' Of course they are. They all do, so you have to. Isn't that the way it is? Because if you didn't, it wouldn't be long before the firm would be out of business, and you'd be out of a job. In other words, if we're going to make the grade as fishermen, we have to string along.'

After that the General Manager had come round to the question of fishing inside the limit, because they all did it, didn't they? Just the same way as they used a cod-end with a mesh so fine that it wouldn't let a shrimp get away. Ros knew that perfectly well, too. He was the skipper of one of the three best-equipped ships in port. The owners had spent

a fortune, the General Manager pointed out, in safety devices
and in looking after the men's comfort. The company looked
after its employees, and expected its employees to look after
the company's interests in return. He was obliged, at this point,
to make it clear that the company expected a satisfactory
return for its outlay, and if Ros—with all his qualifications—
couldn't assure them of this, they would have no option in
the circumstances, etcetera, etcetera.

' The Lord deliver us from evil,' Ros murmured to himself.

' I don't say that it *is* your attitude, but I must tell you
that that's what it's rumoured to be. A lot of people in this
town would be going without food if many skippers felt that
way.'

There came a time when, as Ros saw it, conscience ceased
to be an exact instrument for the assessment of right or
wrong. There was no better Catholic to Ros's knowledge
than the manager who had been sent to the Vedra canning
factory. But he had had to conform to the practice of treating
tuna with a colouring agent, and canning and labelling it
as salmon—in the knowledge, too, that described as salmon,
a fifty-per-cent higher charge would be made than for the
same fish, in the same cans, but minus the colour, and
labelled tuna.

They lived in a world of snares set by the heathen; of
lies, casually fabricated, accepted and passed on. Men ate
fraud with their daily bread. Ros's crew depended not upon
their miserable wages, but upon their bonus paid on the
catch, to keep their families in food, and on the journey out
Ros had betrayed them by his rectitude. They had fished
on a sandy bottom outside the three-mile limit, and their
catch hadn't paid for the fuel-oil burnt by the engines. Had
Ros any right, he had asked himself, to penalise them for
his own scruples—to drive them to hate him? His answer
had been to come close inshore as the other two ships had
done from the first, and he had been ready to shoot the gear

over the fissured volcanic rock where the fish were spawning in infinite numbers, when the tragedy had happened.

The pointed African silhouette of Vedra town was rising out of the sea ahead. Ros called the second fisherman. This man was a battered ex-wrestler forced on him by the company. It was he who had found the local youth on board on the previous night, knocked him silly, and thrown him into the water.

' How is he? Still bleeding? '

' The same.'

' Didn't anybody see how it happened? Nobody get a look at the fellow who did it? '

The man shook his head. Ros didn't quite return the man's hate, but his antipathy for him was intense.

' They'll be waiting to pick you up for assault when we get in.'

The man stuck his jaw out at him. He didn't believe it, and Ros knew he was right. The company would see to it that no harm came to him.

What am I doing here? Ros suddenly asked himself. I'm a deserter, a coward. My place is below with the others, fighting to keep the blood pumping through a man's veins and the breath through his lungs, death out of his cells and tissues until we get him to port and into the doctor's hands.

He went down the companion-way to the crew's quarters, the awful, shivering tenderness and vulnerability of his own flesh increasing with every step. They had the man on the mess table; one boot off, his shirt pulled up under the armpits. One of the crew had his arms round his shoulders and another had just given up his attempts to pour brandy and water into his mouth. The rest had drawn away, grouped round the first engineer still clutching his useless gauze and strapping. The man's eyes were half open, his chin and neck were wet and there was a small puddle on the table. The heaviness in Ros's chest rose to his throat when he saw that the man no longer held his hands over his chest, and that his arms, which had turned to yellow wax, had fallen to his side. The hole in the centre of his chest, now uncovered, was like the mouth painted on a celluloid doll. There were hardly any signs of blood. Nobody moved or said anything. In the church-silence Ros's ears were ringing. He knew that he was in the presence of violent death.

CHAPTER 19

With the dawn paling through the grey panel of the window, the Governor sat at his desk, which he had reached many hours before by way of a track through the stacked-up files and documents. He was fumbling through a report, once again, on the statistics of the island's crimes of violence, produced by one of Don Arturo's junior police officers. The Governor ran his finger slowly along the report as he read, as if in attempt to assist a drowsy brain by absorbing the meaning through his finger-tip. He forced his way to the end, put the papers aside and took up the decoded telegram again. After his brief glimpse of victory, the telegram from Madrid had come to threaten him with defeat. He re-read the curt questions, adding for himself at the end of the message, ' You have lost our confidence.'

In the few weeks that he had filled his office, the Governor would have been inclined to claim for himself that he had been a quick learner in the tactics of the Vedran situation. He had taken it for granted that he was engaged in a battle fought behind bows, smiles, and compliments, and he believed that he had soon mastered the art of handling the local weapons. He had discovered how to defend himself with procrastination, half-promises, and a cultivated

amnesia, before delivering his counter-attack prepared
behind a screen of false complaisance. The Governor
listened blandly to all points of view, kept his counsel, and
laid his plans.

His greatest achievement in the short time he thought,
had been to familiarise himself with the art of playing off
one interest against the other. For example, he had benefited
from a concealed antagonism, by encouraging Colonel
Rocamoro's protests when Don Firmín wanted to appoint
himself the island's film censor. The same temporary alliance
had served to reduce Don Firmín's list of undesirable
foreigners to a single one, when it came to action. Cautiously,
the Governor was beginning to congratulate himself on
having set the long-standing feuds of Vedra to work for his
own ends—which were the creation of a small island
Utopia of regular work, prompt justice, and freedom from
fanaticism, made viable economically by such enterprises
as the new canning factory, and La Palomita's prosperous
transformation of Tur's latifundia at Sagral.

And then the Governor had discovered from Don Felix
what the cost of the canning factory had been. Don Felix,
bubbling with amiable cynicism, had described to him the
circumstances in which the Port Commandant had come by
his new Volkswagen. Since then, it appeared, the car had
simply vanished. No such vehicle had even been registered.
But Don Felix insisted. He had seen the car himself, and
could describe it; and all the Governor could do was to
order the Volkswagen's seizure for investigation if ever it
appeared on the streets.

The Governor's misgivings about the canning factory
increased when he stumbled across a secret file which had
escaped the fire in which his predecessor had burned his
private papers before leaving. This discovery, which marked,
perhaps, the turning point of the Governor's brief career
in Vedra, showed the man who had preceded him in his

high office as involved in a tangled complicity with Valentin, and not only in the matter of the granting of the licence to build the canning factory. The previous governor had, for example, been in the habit of keeping Valentin informed in advance of all public works projects, and it was to be assumed by certain allusions in the letters that he had had some share in the profits made in the successful land speculations that were the outcome of the co-operation between the two men.

The Governor was obliged to fall back on Don Felix's aid once more in the unravelling of these murky transactions, but half-way through the investigation he had regretted this decision and got rid of his assistant. The kind of man who would sell his sister to a brothel, was the Governor's final verdict on Don Felix. He started to copy all the incriminating documents himself, with the intention of sending the whole file to Madrid, but before he could complete this task, the blow fell.

The illegal strike had been followed by violent incidents in the port, and then—as quickly as if the Minister himself had been there, looking over his shoulder—had arrived the telegram. The Governor found himself without allies. He had alienated Don Arturo by a reprimand for his lack of energy in prosecuting the case of the rape of a foreign woman. Colonel Rocamoro had taken offence, he suspected, when he had suggested that the enormous garrison be relieved of some of their ceremonial duties and set to work on road building. He could no longer hope for support from Don Firmín, and Tur's constant reproaches on the subject of his vanishing peasantry had only subsided since his family tragedy had overtaken him. The Governor remembered his Minister's pessimistic warning when he had gone to say goodbye. ' A den of wild beasts, my boy. Whatever you do, keep your wits about you. They got together and tore the last fellow to pieces.' Only the Alcalde, the man with no

tongue in his head, as they called him—and with no influence
worth talking about that the Governor could discover
—had still appeared respectfully sympathetic when he had
been called in for a purely formal consultation on the crisis.
Someone was sending unfavourable reports on him, as well
as grossly distorted accounts of what was happening in
Vedra. This was clear from the telegram.

The Governor read through the sharply worded questions
on the Vedran situation, fumbling with his sleep-numbed
brain after underlying inferences and charges. Presently he
fell asleep, his head on the desk. It was nearly ten when the
telephone awakened him to the terrible news. The Governor
held the receiver, stunned, watching the papers on his desk-
top sliding away on the surge of morning air through the
window. It was the junior officer who had prepared the
statistical report on crimes of violence.

'Your commanding officer's not there? Well, find him
and instruct him to report to me . . . wait a minute. Have
the crew of every boat arrested as they come in, and hold
them pending my instructions.'

Ten minutes later Don Arturo, who had been found in
The Cultural Peak, presented himself. He had stopped the
victoria at the pharmacist's on the way, for a calming
injection. 'Make it a double dose,' he said to the pharmacist.
The effect of the overdose was already marked. But in
addition to this Don Arturo was soothed by his opinion that
the Governor's days were numbered. Don Felix, for example,
had withdrawn his originally enthusiastic support, conveying
to Don Arturo a hint of his coming defection in the character-
istic remark, 'When my neighbour's beard's on fire, the
time has come to sprinkle water on my own.'

'Well,' the Governor said. 'So now we've an armed
revolt on our hands.'

'Hardly that. A few shots don't make an armed revolt.'

' But a man assassinated! Please tell me something—
what purpose are you supposed to serve? '

' Do you mean what purpose am I supposed to serve in
person? ' Don Arturo asked.

' I mean the police.'

Don Arturo thought about this, his brain tranquillised
and lucid.

' The police exist to rectify the errors produced by defective
government.'

' Am I to take it that that remark carries any reflection
on the régime? ' The question, the Governor realised, was an
unfair one that had slipped out in his anger before he could
stop it.

' Not at all,' Don Arturo said. ' All governments make
mistakes. Some make more mistakes than others. The more
mistakes you make, the more policemen you need. And after
all, we may as well remember that we're both part of the
system.'

The Governor dismissed him. Don Arturo's words
rankled. Yes, I suppose I am part of the system. The
Governor had hoped in some way that was not even clear
to himself to remain outside the system—which, on the
whole, he disapproved of so strongly—while manipulating
it for his own ends. He had used the corruptions of others
as a weapon, and had tried to advance the cause of justice
by the employment of such champions as Don Felix. After
two short months he himself sensed the danger of becoming
like some oriental pasha at the mercy of mind-poisoning
eunuchs. Was it possible to listen to the vile secrets the
walls whispered to him, yet remain untainted? He recalled
the tragic life-history of Judge Peñaflor as outlined in a
secret file he had stumbled across only a few days before.
The record contained a verbatim report of Peñaflor's speech
to the court at his trial for subversive activities, in the days
before His Excellency came on the scene. ' We shall never

surrender. Even if you amputate our arms we shall not give up the fight. Even if, in the days to come, we appear to have joined your ranks—beware of us. We shall be preparing our attack on you.' Thirty years had passed, and the pages of the record, reporting annually on Peñaflor's progress, like that of a promising pupil, had shown the transition from non-compromise to a show of conformity, to real conformity, to partisanship, and finally to the pitiable, self-disgusted thraldom to the interests of such as Valentin. The system had skinned Peñaflor and stuffed him with sawdust.

From now on, the Governor resolved, I'll be alone. Whatever happens, I'll go my own way.

The inquiry was held in the Governor's council chamber, but the frowns and smirks of his sixty-nine gorgeously uniformed predecessors seemed to have cowed the forty-eight men the police brought in into an impenetrable obtuseness. Men with all the signs of natural intelligence in their faces seemed to have been stricken with an almost animal incomprehension, unable to understand—let alone give an intelligible reply to—the simplest question. The Governor did all the questioning himself. He had washed his hands for ever of the *New Manual of Police Procedure*, and of all that it stood for; but he soon saw that in the face of this mass witlessness, he was getting nowhere.

An incomplete picture had been furnished by the trawler's crew of the man seen with a pistol in his hand. He was between thirty-five and forty-five, medium height, dark hair, sun-tanned face. The Governor estimated that this description more or less fitted half the men present. An attempt by Ros and his crew to pick out their assailant or assailants in an identity parade proved equally unsatisfactory, and there was a damaging moment when the mate singled out a man who was instantly able to prove that he had been prevented that morning by engine-failure from reaching the fishing ground.

The Governor fought on, single-handed against this invulnerable mixture of malice—as he was beginning to see it—and crass, bovine stupidity. He was becoming angry. These people did not appear to realise that they were being handled fairly, that he was on their side, that he had protected them from the bullying and the trickery of the policemen. He could not make them understand that it was their duty to come to his aid.

Six men had been involved in a shooting affray resulting in a death. In ordinary circumstances the charge would have been banditry, and the case sent for trial by the Judge. But as a strike was in progress it could be classified as armed rebellion, to be dealt with by court-martial presided over by Colonel Rocamoro (who, as the Governor remembered, was notoriously lenient whenever given the chance). In either event, the Governor believed that a successful trial would have rehabilitated him, and have given the lie to the senders of the telegram. Ros produced a map to show the trawler's exact position at the time of the attack, but each felucca crew in turn were ready with evidence and the solemn corroboration of witnesses that they had been nowhere near the fatal spot. The police archives showed that every man had a clean record. The Governor even paid a visit to the harbour with Ros and his men in the hope that someone might be able to identify the felucca involved, but all such boats were identical in shape and painted in the same regulation colours.

At this point, frustration drove the Governor further than he had intended to go. A message awaited him at the Palace that the two other trawlers had returned to port with their catches, but that the women engaged by the manager of the canning factory had not yet put in an appearance. The Governor sent for the women, and embittered by the way his investigations had gone, told them they would be set to work, whether they liked it or not, under an armed guard. Their menfolk went back to gaol.

In the meanwhile Don Arturo had been conducting an investigation into another circumstance, and with more success. This time his discussion was with Cartwright, whom Don Arturo visited in his office directly after his dismissal from the Governor's presence.

' Your friend let us down, or rather, let you down,' Don Arturo said. ' I wonder if you'd mind repeating once again just what she said as soon as she came to? '

' Word for word, I can't—as I think I told you,' Cartwright said. ' When a distressing thing like that happens, one's apt to be a little vague about what actually is said.'

' Naturally enough. That's understandable—but would you try? '

' The gist was that she'd been attacked.'

' Did your wife hear her say that? '

' I suppose so. Yes, of course she did.'

' And yet for some reason the young lady now chooses to deny it. She absolutely denies having been attacked, or that she told you she had been.'

' I must say it's all very strange,' Cartwright said.

' What's your personal view of what took place? ' Don Arturo said. ' I'm speaking as a friend, of course. Whatever you care to say needn't go any further.'

' I can't say I really have a personal view. I recall her saying something to the effect that she'd been attacked or hurt. Of course she may have been rambling. A knock on the head, after all——'

A face incapable of lies, Don Arturo was thinking, but it's no use trying to put the words into his mouth. He admired both Cartwright and the girl enormously. He knew he would never persuade Laura to tell him the facts, or

Cartwright to commit himself to something definite that he could have used as a lever with her.

' She said, " I've been attacked "—or words to that effect,' Don Arturo said. ' We know that she had been in the company of an individual who was quite capable of attacking her, or anybody else, and we've also other information I can't divulge, which strengthens the theory of an attack.' The other information was a doctor's report that Laura had sounded him out about the possibility of terminating an eventual pregnancy—but it couldn't be treated as more than a remarkable coincidence.

' I'm sorry I can't do anything more to help,' Cartwright said as they shook hands.

Conforming to standard practice in such matters, Don Arturo put his real question as a casual afterthought.

' This man—Mila. Was there any previous acquaintance that you know of ? '

He trapped the tell-tale hesitation and felt a trace of disappointment at his misplaced assessment of the man.

' No,' Cartwright said. ' No—at least, I wouldn't imagine so. Not for a moment.'

Back at the barracks, Don Arturo had Mila brought up from his cell.

He tapped the file on his desk. Bluff was the only hope, but the chemicals injected into his blood only a few hours before helped him to bluff with a confidence he had rarely possessed.

' The miracles of modern science,' Don Arturo said. ' A tiny particle of human skin embedded in a garment's fabric so that even immersion in sea-water doesn't wash it out. A microscopic comparison, and there you are.'

He picked up the file and shook it at Mila. ' Rape, committed under the most brutal circumstances imaginable. It's all here. The testimony of the unfortunate victim. The doctor's evidence. The laboratory tests. My poor young man, you're finished! You've had every chance, but now I'm going to be obliged to send you to the prison for incorrigibles.'

The prison for incorrigibles. A terrified child's voice squeaked out of Mila's throat. ' No, sir, please—no! '

' Unless,' Don Arturo said, ' unless———'

He got up, smoothed down his uniform, and made for the door. With a hand on the latch he stopped to turn back, smiling, waiting for news of victory.

Half an hour later he laid a paper on the Governor's desk. ' The name of the man you want.'

' The assassin? '

' The strike organiser. He may be the assassin too, but that would be stretching the arm of coincidence. I was under the impression that you wanted to conduct the investigation in person in this particular case.'

CHAPTER 20

T HE small, sizzling firework display in the electric plant of the canning factory's refrigeration room started at midnight. By one o'clock a cautious emigration of flames had reached the paint shop, and spread itself ecstatically through numerous cans containing combustible liquids left open by deplorable negligence, through half a mile of wooden shelving, through a million labels in their cartons and clean through a partition wall to a store in which a thousand packing-cases were piled to the ceiling. By one-thirty the windows were cracking and falling out, releasing rushes of fire that fitfully illuminated the factory's ugly façade; and the pigeons that had so promptly colonised the eaves had been startled out of their sleep to dash distractedly in all directions, many of them crashing into adjacent buildings.

At about that time one of the municipal night-watchmen woke up, and was amazed to see signs of the moonrise in the wrong quarter of the sky when no moon was expected. After he had decided on the cause of this portent, it took him ten minutes of shuffling, broken-winded running to reach the tower recently re-named after Columbus, in which the

tocsin bell was housed. Here several more minutes were
used up while he tried to telephone the fire brigade, but
found that he could not even get through to the exchange.
Then he gave up and began to haul on the rope of the tocsin
bell.

When Tur heard the tocsin ring in the Columbus Tower,
he got up and went to his bedroom window. His room
overlooked the harbour, on the dark waters of which the
Almirante Cervera floated, brilliantly and wastefully
illuminated as ever, and at the same time—to Tur—
indescribably ghostly and deserted. Tur had decided that
Basilisa must leave the island, and on its next visit the ship
would carry her away. The sense of melancholy and loneli-
ness that had returned immediately he had awakened was
for some reason increased by this sight, but a moment
later relieved by his excitement when he realised where the
fire was. The canning factory's brutal interruption of the
skyline across the harbour was haloed by pink, pulsating
light, and its long row of windows were a-sparkle. Beneath
him the street had come noisily to life.

Fires in Vedra had been transformed into social events,
ranking in popularity only slightly below the excitements of
the Feast of the Epiphany, with its processions, firework
displays and dog shows. It was a rare year when one of
the old, wooden-framed houses was not burned to the ground
from lack of water to put out the fire, and when this
happened at night, most of the town turned out to look on
and admire. These occasional night entertainments were
marked by a conventional informality, originating in the
days when the sounding of the tocsin usually announced the
arrival of Algerian raiders—an emergency held to justify
some relaxation of the social code. Men arrived on the scene
in dressing-gowns and slippers, accompanied by their
children in their night-clothes clutching oranges and rattles.
Only the womenfolk were expected to struggle hastily into

their normal street attire. The frankly carnival atmosphere permitted total strangers to chat amicably, remaining firm friends for the duration of the fire and ignoring each other in the street the next day. If the cafés had closed, many of them would re-open to serve coffee, snacks of marinated liver on toast, and water-ices, to people who wanted to sit about and discuss the spectacle.

Tur put on his dressing-gown and elastic-sided boots and went down into the street, thankful that Smith's poor hearing had prevented him from being wakened by the tocsin. He was in no mood to endure Smith. People were rushing about flashing torches in each other's faces and hailing their friends. The fire engine thundered by, cascading the street with light from half a dozen headlamps, and the jangling of its bells. Behind it, rattling and bouncing at the end of its tow-bar, went the water-tank, which looked like a colossal bath-tub on wheels. The fire engine was followed by guards, zigzagging and klaxoning on their two-stroke motor-cycles, and a squad of engineers in an army lorry, whose enthusiastic task it would be to stop the fire from spreading by dynamiting neighbouring buildings if the necessity arose.

Like all Vedrans, Tur was a connoisseur of fires, and this one struck him when he reached the scene as being of unusual quality. Chemicals flared up behind the windows in stridently brilliant greens, oranges and mauves, calling forth cries and gasps of admiration from the crowd. Tur could hear the sullen regurgitations of boiling liquids trapped in pipes and tanks followed by low-pitched, flatulent explosions as these containers blew up. It was a fire that continually presented new facets of interest. At one moment it was the sight, through a window, of a sudden eruption of sparks, dancing like fireflies in June round a ruined machine. At another it was the appearance of a huge scarlet blossom of flame on the roof itself—a blossom

which reminded Tur in its spiky and regular brilliance of the
flower on one of his cactuses. The firemen had unlimbered
their water-tank, fixed the hose, and started the pump. For
a few minutes, to the clapping and cheering of the crowd,
water had spurted from the nozzle in a magnificently
aggressive jet, but this, as the tank began to empty, had
soon slackened to a meek piddle. Now the firemen had given
up the battle, taken off their helmets, and handed them
over to the children to play with. They stood by, enjoying
themselves and exchanging jokes in loud voices. Tur was
reminded of one of Don Felix's proverbs: ' The house is
burning. Let us warm ourselves.'

Tur remembered the information that had reached him
circuitously, although almost certainly originating in Don
Felix's investigations, that Valentin had been able to
acquire several million pesetas' worth of shares in this
enterprise—payment having been guaranteed by La Palomita on the strength of the land deal about to be completed
with its parent company, Rio Santo. The shares wouldn't
be looking so bright tomorrow, Tur thought. He hardly
dared allow himself the satisfaction that would have been
natural. The Devil looks after his own, he thought. They'll
lose a season's fishing, but the building's probably insured
for two or three times its real value.

The ice had melted out of ten thousand melva fillets
awaiting processing the next day, and as the water boiled
and then boiled away, Tur smelt a succession of delicious and
then acrid odours. He realised that the trawlers' catch
was being converted into ashes. Cheap fish from now on,
after all, Tur thought. Nobody would know real hunger for
another year. Capitalism had suffered a setback on one
front, at least. This was the system that took your stockfish
away, canned it and called it salmon, and charged you ten
times its original price. Tur saw the export fallacy as

another of the delusions of progress. The poor were only allowed to fill their stomachs when a glut made food unsaleable, and it had to be eaten by those who produced it. This had been proved when the Civil War had cut Vedra off from the world and imposed its own brutal socialism, based on the reality that even a rich man had only one stomach. This was going to be the best fishing season for years, but as things had gone it would be the islanders who would benefit from it, and not the shareholders of Conservas Vedreras, including Valentin. That was to say they would benefit if only that fool of a Governor would order the fishermen's release, and let them get on with their job. And apropos of this, Tur recalled a remarkable rumour reported to him by Smith. It was all round the town, so Smith said. The Alcalde had actually taken it upon himself to go to the Governor and tell him that he was breaking the law by keeping the men locked up without bringing any charge.

' The law? ' The Governor had shown mild surprise at this unexpected explosion from ' the tongueless wonder '— as he had heard the Alcalde called. ' Perhaps you'd be so good as to tell me what law? '

' The law that even you are called upon to serve—the law of common humanity ', the Alcalde was supposed to have said, emphasizing his protest with a dramatic thump on his chest.

It was a good story, and Tur would have liked to believe that it was true, but he couldn't. It was too out of character with what he knew of a man whose forerunners, in the days of the Moors, had united in their single function the supreme military, civil and religious authority under the caliph. In any case, as it happened, it was a good thing that at that moment half the men in the port were under lock and key, because it would be no use trying to put the blame on them for what was probably a short in the electric wiring,

or a cigarette-end thrown by someone into a waste-paper
bin.

Tur turned his back on the flames and the raucous, exhila-
rated crowd, and began a slow, thoughtful stroll towards the
bright ship, afloat below him in the silence of the port.
He found the quayside stacked with huge packing cases,
stencilled with the information that they contained agricultural equipment. He was able to read their labels by the
light from the ship. *Sociedad Anónima La Palomita. Sagral.*
So they had moved with the speed of stooping falcons once
their prey was secured. And how could these massive
engines be transported along what was hardly better than
a goat track to arrive at the region they were about to
masticate and digest? An answer was clearly provided by
a pair of bulldozers squatting nearby. The company would
simply make a road.

A night-watchman, cloaked like an admiral, appeared
suddenly from among the stacks of unloaded cargo,
recognised Tur, and saluted. On an impulse Tur gestured
in the direction of the gang-plank, and the man nodded his
agreement. Treading softly, Tur went up the shallow
wooden steps to the promenade deck.

He began to walk along the deck. There were wet patches
where it had been scrubbed that evening, and had not yet
dried. Flies and mosquitoes were buzzing in clouds round the
bright, yellow lamps. Tur breathed in a briny, nautical
perfume of new paint, sun-blistered varnish, caulked planks,
and the pungent grease used on windlasses. He peered
through brass-rimmed portholes into dimly lit salons and
staterooms. White flowers wilted in vases everywhere. This
was the first time he had been aboard the ship. He had taken
it by surprise, off its guard, and found that it was soft,
luxurious, and passive. Could this be the enemy that had

beaten him, inflicting on him a slow but decisive defeat spread in instalments over the ten years—the enemy that had dispersed his family, and begun the final phase of his ruin?

Tur was beginning to question whether, in the end, there was any enemy but oneself. Defeat now seemed to him to come through error—through a fatal rigidity of tactic, a blind determination to fight present battles with the weapons of the past; perhaps through a soul hopelessly clinkered with dead pride. I've been like a mastodon, he thought. I couldn't change with the climate, and now it's too late.

He found an open door, crossed a carpeted floor, and sat in a chair facing a platform with a grand piano half-covered by a sheet. Soon the ship would carry his daughter away from him. She would come to this room, and sit, perhaps, in this very chair. In his imagination Tur peopled the room with passengers, encircled smoothly by stewards on their cat feet. The shaded lights were switched on at every table, a girl in an evening frock settled herself at the piano, smiled down, bowed her head, and began to play; his daughter came in, pale, sad and distracted, and every head was raised. The ship would soon take her from him, and although their pact was that she should be away only for a year, Tur was afraid he would never set eyes on her again.

Presented with Valentin's *fait accompli*, Tur had conceded the victory, told Valentin to do what he liked with the land. In a transaction occupying fifteen minutes he had sold one of his houses—the one lately vacated by Beckett—and had put the cheque in his daughter's hand. ' In a year you'll feel better. In a year we'll all feel quite different. Things will seem different in a year.'

A year.

'And how long would you give me, in fact?' Tur had asked his doctor.

'You've had syphilis, haven't you?'

'More than once. In the twenties.'

'It could be bad in those days. Do you really want me to be frank?'

'Of course I do.'

'Look after yourself. That's' my advice. Many a man of your age is living on borrowed time.'

Basilisa would stay with her old school-friends in London for a year. But where would *he* be in twelve months' time?

I'm at the end of my tether, Tur thought, and really not too soon. The life he had wanted to live had escaped him, ebbed away and vanished. The spectacle he had stood and watched tonight signified not the reversal of a process, but only its delay. Next year, or the year after, the ship would bring plant for a factory twice or three times the size of the one that had burned down. The three defeated trawlers would be replaced by an invincible score. Tur's peasants, enticed away by La Palomita and leaving his lands deserted, would discover a new kind of servitude, disguised as freedom. Their bondage would not be to a master of flesh and blood, who could be to some extent manipulated, or even moved by compassion, but to a brass-gutted Moloch known as the shareholder; voracious, pitiless and—above all—stone deaf. Capitalism had arrived, and the only way to survive was to join forces with it as Valentin had done. It couldn't be fought . . . But in any case, it was too late.

A china clock tinkled its trivial chimes at him. Bed, Tur thought. I really must go to bed. The next day would face him with one of his life's greatest ordeals, and he would want all the energy he could muster to meet it. Next day he must bring himself to go to Colonel Rocamoro as a supplicant. The meeting would be his last chance to save the small unexpired fragment of his life from the intolerable darkness that menaced it. A tragedy that Toniet should be held not at the disposition of the harsh but venal Judge, but at that of the mild but incorruptible Colonel. How best to present his appeal? ' I've served His Excellency well from the first hour of the first day. Haven't I the right to expect that the scales be tipped in my favour? ' ... No, that would never do with Rocamoro. ' They're crying out for their pound of flesh. Let's admit there's no real substance to the charge! '. . . That wouldn't do either. ' We're both fathers, as well as old friends. My son's in trouble. For God's sake come to my help!' ... Better. That was better. In fact, it was the only possible line of approach.

Tur stood on the quayside again now, his face to the town's dark silhouette, pricked all over with lights and set against an indigo sky. Behind him, the fire at the canning factory had almost burned itself out, and had subsided to a passive orange glow. Soon these streets would fill up to overbrimming with sad memories. Every stone would mock him with his losses. Tur had shaken off the other ghosts of his past, but he knew that while life lasted, whichever way he turned, he could never cease to come face to face with the phantoms of his children in this town.

Walking on, he was taken with a sharp pain under the ribs and forced to stop for breath. His body was failing him, seized with the cramps of old age. Why should it be, he asked himself, that love and nostalgia failed to weaken with the body and release their hold, but instead plagued him with a crueller vigour than ever? I'm in a limbo between two worlds. The peasant's sons will carry their father to his grave. For a year they will mourn, and then forget. My world has failed. Strangers will bury me.

Suddenly a cowardly, treasonable thought tempted him. Am I being punished? Could there be a Divine retribution after all, which had seized this moment to strike? And in revenge for what? For the sins I have committed, which have not seemed sins to me? For that which I have done, which seemed right in my own eyes. Would the Church have withheld its blessing, when like the others I took part in a crusade? No, he thought, to be a crusader you must believe you are one. Ah, conscience! Conscience! . . . And yet there had been a chance. They departed in hope. They might have lived.

Recovering, scandalized, he dismissed the cowardly intrusion. Really, it's amazing the ideas that can occur to one in old age. He straightened up, and forced himself to walk more briskly.

Tur caught Smith just as he was going out.

' Never mind about the fire. The fire's all over. Find me the key to my museum cupboard.'

Smith, grumbling loudly, brought the key, then hurried out of the room. He had a horror of Tur's collection.

Tur unlocked the cupboard and took out the best-preserved of his Guanche mummies. Experts said that it was a man of about forty-five, but this small, brown, foetal shape, clenched in its own arms and legs and weighing less than eight pounds, seemed more like the pathetic remains of a starved child. In recent years a little of Tur's parental feeling had attached itself even to this tiny, shrivelled corpse. He held it in his arms, stroking its monkey's head. The men who in ten years had exterminated these pacific aborigines had merely put aside their armour and changed their century. Nowadays they fought under the banner of La Palomita, instead of that of the king.

There's no justice, Tur assured himself earnestly. Therefore there's no retribution. Where was God when the King of Spain sent his men to this island? These were the meek. When will they inherit the earth?

CHAPTER 21

Don arturo marked the occasion with a symbolic act. He called the steward, took off his stiff, beribboned tunic, and told him to bring the pyjama jacket he kept at the club. Pyjama jackets had become a kind of uniform worn by members, with the exception of Don Firmín, when things were going well.

' I don't want to be disturbed,' he told the steward. ' If there are any telephone calls, just say I'm in court today.'

He put on the pyjama jacket, then went back to his chair on the verandah. He was humming the only tune, with the national anthem's exception, he could ever remember: a melancholy fado that poorly interpreted the sense of gaiety he felt. He had not felt so cheerful since before his illness.

Rocamoro, stiff in his best uniform, sat in one corner of the verandah where he could watch his men in the distance being put through their repertoire of ceremonial drill. Don Firmín, half-obscured by a palm in the other corner, breviary in hand, was among the centaurs and angels of the city of St. John the Divine, searching for a sign, a key.

Never had the sea front of Vedra seemed a more genial place to Don Arturo. The ship's funnel had just sunk from

sight below the outer harbour wall, leaving a small, plum-
coloured bruise low in the sky, to mark the spot where it had
last been seen. The line of peasants standing, saddened, all
along the quayside was turning away, and the men who had
removed their hats out of respect for the solemn moment of
the ship's departure were putting them on again. Already
a few citizens who spent most of their time fishing for pleasure
were back in position in their wicker armchairs, casting their
lines into the murky, churned-up water where the ship had
been, and to which fish were always attracted. The
Governor's Hispano-Suiza, which had broken down
promptly after carrying him to the ship, had been abandoned
in the sun. The band, scampering through its familiar
tune for the fifth and last time, marched dejectedly back
from the water's edge, and the bandsmen fell out and began
hurriedly to pack away their instruments.

' It's very peaceful here today. Quite like old times.
What's that thing they always play? ' Colonel Rocamoro
asked.

Don Arturo shifted his chair closer to the Colonel and
to the edge of the verandah, where he could see better.

' I don't know. I wish I had an ear for music.'

A playful, shifting breeze, snatched suddenly at the
palm fronds on the verandah, and brought with it a sharp
odour of fish curing in the sun. By special and extraordinary
permission of the Port Commandant, who had decided to
resume diplomatic relations with the fishermen, half a mile
of sea front had been given over to this purpose. From where
Don Arturo sat he could see the road surface thickly covered
by melvas that had escaped the chemical processes which
were to have transformed them into salmon, and were now
being converted in the traditional manner to stockfish, by the
sun, salt and the repeated visitations of leg-lifting dogs.
Don Arturo wrinkled his nose and turned away. The other
end of the sea front was full of soldiers going through a

kind of military square dance; hitching and unhitching
imaginary teams of mules hauling imaginary mountain guns
to the assault of an imaginary enemy in an imaginary war
that might have been fought in the latter half of the
eighteenth century. The spectacle bored Don Arturo. He
peered down over the balcony, and was delighted to observe
that the first swallow of the winter's tourists had arrived.
A blonde girl wearing a huge straw hat, and dressed with
delicious illegality in an off-the-shoulder dress, was snapping
her fingers without avail at the Mirasol's slovenly and
inattentive waiter. Don Arturo, remembering that the last
Mexican hat had come on the scene at an inopportune time,
began to plan a little comedy in which he would arrange for
the girl to be reprimanded by one of his policemen, and then
come to her rescue himself.

Don Firmín, too, had been distracted for a moment by
the pungent odour he approved of. The staple food of rich
and poor alike, the bounty of the sea, was being prepared
by God's beneficent sun, plus certain additions he preferred
not to notice. Providence had shown its hand in the matter
of the canning factory. In this direction things looked like
remaining satisfactorily as they had been for the last few
hundred years. Moreover, he hoped that the Port Commandant's concession, by which the sea front would be
made available for the curing of the fish, would have its
effect in producing a more co-operative spirit on the fishermen's part when they were called upon to play their part
in the coming celebrations of the Feast of the Epiphany.
Only in the matter of the imminent transformation of Tur's
latifundia into a model farm project had God's cause
suffered a setback. Man does not live by bread alone.

'So he went after all,' Rocamoro said. 'And so
unexpectedly. I must say, I was beginning to wonder if we
hadn't got him for good. Didn't even last as long as the last
man. I must admit I was beginning to have rather a soft

spot for the fellow—if only he could have kept himself from interfering.'

Don Arturo was taken by surprise by the Colonel's expression. He had produced the nearest thing to a smirk possible in a face endowed with such patrician regularity.

'I wonder what the next one they send us will be like?' Don Arturo said. He hissed down angrily at the waiter, and gestured towards the girl. She looked up and smiled. Don Arturo was delighted. I must be looking myself again. There's no doubt about it, I'm completely cured.

'Did you see our old friend Don Flavio?' the Colonel asked.

'I did; although I don't mind saying I took good care that he shouldn't see me. It was an unhappy occasion—all the more so because I had a personal reason for feeling some despondency. A friend happened to be leaving at the same time. A young lady I've been thrown into contact with in the course of my duties. I was in love with her—but to tell you the truth, it would have been ridiculous. After all, I've not been a well man. My recent illness involved me in the most unfortunate inconveniences—an imposed celibacy, for example. To put it frankly, one half of me was ready and willing, but the other half let me down.'

'Extraordinary,' Rocamoro said, only half-listening, still watching his soldiers manhandle invisible guns to numbers in a way that would have impressed Napoleon himself. A splendid job of training. Where His Excellency had gone wrong had been in not allowing himself to be persuaded to reinstate the five years' military service of old—three of them to be served overseas. That would have been the way to build real greatness.

Unable to get any sympathy for his broken dream, Don Arturo came back to Tur. 'It's going to be awkward next time he puts in an appearance here. I hardly know what I'm going to say to him.'

'That won't be for some time if I know our friend Tur,' Rocamoro said. 'His pride won't heal up overnight. I may say that I was even more anxious than you to avoid him after our recent painful discussion. Can you imagine such a thing —he's under the extraordinary delusion that Toniet Urbieda's his son.'

'The poor old fellow's in his dotage.'

'He accepted my ruling with great dignity.'

'Which was?'

'That the Army does its duty.'

'Very impressive in its way, no doubt,' Don Arturo said, 'but cold comfort for an old friend.'

'The important thing,' Rocamoro said, 'is that we shall be handling the case and not you people.'

'And what am I supposed to read into that remark?'

'Perhaps it would be kinder to let it pass,' Rocamoro said. 'At least I was able to offer a grain of consolation— it didn't seem necessary to press the more serious charge after Cosmi had the good grace to commit suicide.'

'A man who had no thought for anything but his family,' Don Arturo said. 'In its way it's a tragedy.'

'The really amazing thing,' Rocamoro said, 'is that Urbieda's the living image of his father that was. I remember him well. Poor old Tur simply won't allow himself to see it.'

'The daughter isn't his either, of course.'

Rocamoro looked up, startled, then laughed. 'You're quite wrong there. The mother was a little schoolteacher from Madrid—or something like that. I knew her.'

'So did I,' Don Arturo said, with an emphasis that made Rocamoro stare hard at him. The Colonel shook his head. 'Well, I'd have never suspected it. A colourless little creature like that.'

'She presented him with a splendid pair of antlers.

Grown over the years. He hadn't any idea what was going on.'

'It could happen to the best of us, I suppose,' Rocamoro said. He felt in his pocket for his lucky charm—the gall-stone of a murdered gipsy, sewn up in a tiny leather bag.

There was a silence. Rocamoro's lips moved as he counted time with his soldiers. One, two, three, four. One, two, three, four.

'An extraordinary car just went past,' Don Arturo said. 'I've never seen one like it before. It was shaped like one of those strange, green armoured beetles one sees at this time of the year.'

'Ah . . . who was in it?'

'I didn't get the chance to see. It was gone in a flash.'

Rocamoro twisted round in his chair. 'You know, the real tragedy of all this business is that Urbieda absolutely refuses to leave the old man to his paternal dream. It isn't even that he's merely indifferent, he simply detests the old fellow. When he heard that Tur was trying to tell us that he was his father, he got into such a fury that he had to be restrained.'

'And what did Tur say to that?'

'He said, " My son's mind's been poisoned against me. I'm being punished for a crime I never committed "—or words to that effect.'

'Referring no doubt to the famous episode of the missing boat.'

'Did he do it, by the way?' Rocamoro asked.

'Plant a time-bomb in the boat? I doubt it. I doubt it. It wouldn't have been necessary; the vessel was so unseaworthy it's a wonder it didn't sink in the harbour.'

'At all events,' Rocamoro said, 'he's bound to be thoroughly demoralised at the moment. I expect you've heard the latest rumour—that he's getting rid of his land?'

'Yes,' Don Arturo said. 'Giving it away to his peasants.

And my reply is that the suggestion's so totally absurd that it doesn't merit our consideration. Idiotic rumours are one of the specialities of island life. They're the product of idle minds. One's exposed to them whichever way one turns.'

' Is it even legally a possibility? ' Rocamoro said.

' Legally? I suppose so. But the legality doesn't come into it. Where the thing's so senseless, so completely lacking in probability——' He stopped as the door behind them opened and closed, turned in the direction of the sound, and felt his face stiffen.

' Good evening, gentlemen.' Tur came through the palms.

Rocamoro found his amulet again and caressed it with his fingertips. He moistened his lips. Don Firmín closed his breviary, put it down, and went to Tur, his hand outstretched. Don Arturo got up too, felt a sinister flutter of agitation in his chest, and sat down again.

Tur hung up his hat, then drew his chair to the front of the verandah. He tinkered with the electric fan on his low table, adjusting its angle, tightening a milled screw between thumb and finger so that the fan began its slow, sideways oscillation that would last at the most a few minutes. He dragged his footstool within reach, and sat down, his feet up. The old steward came in on the balls of his feet, stood pawing with one foot for a moment, like an aged, nervous horse, and was backing out when Tur crooked his finger at him without turning his head. The steward came forward, bending a little lower with every step.

' The calendar's a month out of date again,' Tur said.

Don Arturo had been conducting an agonized internal struggle. How, if at all, was one to insert the thin edge of the wedge of comfort? He was afraid of the silence that threatened them. He stared for inspiration at the sky and at the charcoal smear left by the ship, now so faint as to be hardly noticeable. 'No wind whatever. At least the sea's remarkably calm,' he said absurdly into the vacuum.

Tur held out his hand for the last month's leaf of the calendar, examined it, shook his head with a slight smile, screwed the paper up into a ball and dropped it. 'I've been having thoughts about our club,' he said.

Nobody could find anything to say.

'I repeat, I've been having thoughts about the club.'

For some reason, Don Arturo was not reassured to note that Tur's voice was firm, even cheerful.

'What sort of thoughts, Don Flavio?' Rocamoro asked.

'I see it as symbolical in a way of a general situation,' Tur said. 'Let's put ourselves in the position of a new member or some ambitious visitor. Have you ever thought of that?'

'Frankly, I haven't.'

'You come in off the street; out of the crowd,' Tur said. 'You see a staircase, a good carpet, and on the landing facing you, a brass spittoon on its stand—usually, I must admit, kept well polished. This encourages you to go up. What's that remarkable potted flower on the second landing?'

'An amaryllis.'

'An amaryllis of course. No scent, but a wonderful splash of colour. The club door's at the top of the next flight. Blue and gold mouldings and a cut-glass door knob. I believe it's supposed to have come out of a palace.'

'The Palace of the Viceroy, to be exact,' Rocamoro said.

'Whether it did or it didn't,' Tur said, 'the fact remains that people who haven't had the chance—and are never likely to have the chance—of seeing for themselves, are bound to imagine there's something wonderful on the other side of that door. It's harder than heaven to get into—it must be like heaven, they think. Wouldn't you say so?'

'There may be something in what you say,' Rocamoro said.

'But turn the knob, open the door, and what do you find?'
Tur looked from face to face.

' You find,' Tur said, ' worn linoleum, hatstands, a wash-
basin with a dirty towel, an out of date calendar, leaving out
Don Firmín, a collection of tired old men, and——' he
looked up and was on the point of saying ' a picture of His
Excellency,' but stopped.

' My dear friend,' Don Arturo said, ' I can't help agreeing
with you. The fact is, what we're used to we're inclined
to put up with. But after all, things—let's say with one
unfortunate exception in this case—can always be rectified.'

' Rectified? ' Tur said. ' But how? '

' Very simply indeed. By bringing your objection to the
secretary's notice. After all, that's what the secretary's for.
A thorough clean-up wouldn't do the place any harm.
I'm sure we'd all agree that.'

' But is there a secretary? ' Tur murmured. ' Is there
really a secretary? ' He looked round apologetically. ' I'm
sorry. I'm afraid I was thinking along another tack.'

He shifted the position of his chair. There was a certain
angle when he could see the bronze dolphins leaping along
the top of the balustrade, and beyond that, nothing but the
sea, darkening under the evening sky. The vision of the sea
soothed him. But would the phantoms of those who had
gone from him come to walk upon the water, just as they
filled the streets with their presence?

Deserted, he whispered to himself. Why, why, had time
annihilated all recollections of pleasure and desire, yet left
miraculously intact in every detail the structure of remembered humiliation and grief? Broken friendships, betrayed
loves, continued to live on their shadow existences; mocking
with calm, ageless faces, his grief, his hopelessness, his old
age. This is the moment I should have prepared for. This
is the moment I should have spent my whole life arming
myself against. The great fear that had possessed him had

been that his name and race might die, but the far more terrible reality was that he himself had been sentenced to live on purposely.

Suddenly he remembered a practical consideration.

'Don Arturo, please refresh my memory. What are the qualifications of membership?'

Don Arturo jumped gratefully into the breached silence. 'The qualifications for membership? I don't know whether I can remember off-hand. Really, it's so long since I read the rules. Well, in the first place, membership is open, as we all know, to what some persons are pleased to describe as distinguished servants of the Church and State.'

'And in addition to that?'

'In addition to that, leaders of the legal and medical professions. Outside the Judge, we don't have any, of course. And then property owners like yourself.'

'Property owners,' Tur said. 'Wasn't there some sort of minimum qualification?'

'I believe there was. But *what*, I really can't say. It's all rather archaic.'

'Yes, I believe there was too,' Tur said. He was thinking, Ah well, I can't expect to have it both ways. At least I've put paid to La Palomita, and their scheming. I've clipped the wings of *that* dove. Whatever it's cost me, it's a satisfaction that can't be taken away. I'd like to see what success they have in trying to wheedle my peasants away to work for them, now that they'll have their own land.

But what will they want to do about me here? he wondered again. Get rid of me? They'd be within their rights . . . And if they do—where else is there to go?

He comforted himself. Probably they won't bother. After all, I'm really part of all this ramshackle furniture that nobody seems to notice. In all likelihood they'll hardly notice I'm here, for the short time I'm likely to last.